JESTER
No Prisoners MC Book 2

by Lilly Atlas

For my youngest *sister*. Thank you for all your support and excitement.
We're getting your room ready for when you move in…

Thrust into a world of danger and fear, first grade teacher, Emily, is forced to comply with a terrifying MC president's demands in order to save her brother's life. Her only port in the storm is Jester, a member of a rival MC she's supposed to use and betray. Jester proves to be the opposite of everything Emily expects, and before long she's in his bed, and he's in her heart.

Jester would give life and limb for the No Prisoners Motorcycle Club. His sole focus needs to be on the impending attack against their enemies, the Grimm Brothers. Meeting sweet and innocent Emily wasn't part of his plan, and falling for her is out of the question.

Can Emily save her brother's life without destroying the man who opens her eyes and heart to an amazing world of pleasure? She'll do anything in her power to help her brother while protecting Jester, but when Jester finds out she was sent by his enemy, she may lose everything she's trying to preserve.

JESTER
No Prisoners MC Book 1

Chapter One

Bile burned its way up Emily's esophagus, then straight back down when she refused to give in to her body's need to revolt. She was in trouble. Serious trouble. The kind of trouble that could result in her being wheeled from her house in a body bag.

"Johnny," she whispered. Her heart broke a little as the reality set in of how low he'd sunk.

Across the living room, her brother was bound to one of their kitchen chairs. Purple bruising mottled his face, which was swollen like a balloon, displaying the evidence of what must have been an awful beating. Each time Johnny inhaled, a pain-filled wheeze hit her ears. Rivers of sweat ran down his face and despite his limp posture, he quivered, no doubt craving the heroin that ran his life.

Her lower lip stung and she forced her jaw to relax and end the punishment her teeth inflicted. Whenever she was nervous, she bit her bottom lip, and right now she could have bitten straight through.

Four gun-toting, tattooed bikers took up residence in her living room. The house she'd spent her hard earned time and money turning into a home had been violated. She racked her brain, trying to think of a solution, a way out of this terrifying situation, but fear clogged her mind and nothing came to her.

"Well, Emily, what's it gonna be? We ain't got all fuckin' day." Snake's voice was dark and threatening. He towered over her, all six-foot-three of him. A single muscle in his jaw twitched and his eyes narrowed. But it was the way he stared at her that sent chills down her spine, like he took pleasure in her fear, got off on it even.

"I—" The words stuck in her arid throat, and she coughed. "I'll do whatever you need me to do. Just don't hurt Johnny anymore."

"There you go, boys. At least one of the Carver siblings ain't a complete fuckin' moron. She's pretty too." Snake winked at her. His tongue darted out and flicked back and forth before disappearing into his mouth.

Her breath stilled. The end of his tongue was forked and each half wiggled independently.

"Emily, shut up. Don't—" Johnny's slurred protest was cut short by a quick blow to his already battered face.

She winced as the short, wiry man, whose pale bald head resembled an egg, connected his fist with Johnny's face. Johnny's head snapped back, and blood sprayed from his mouth across the beige carpet like a geyser, seeping into the fibers. The crimson splatter would stay there, deep inside the wool, no matter how much she scrubbed. She'd never forget this moment—one more thing ruined by the trauma of the day.

"Stop," she cried out. "Please, don't hurt him anymore. I said I'd help you." Her voice cracked with the effort to hold back a sob.

Twenty minutes ago, Emily had bounced into the house she shared with Johnny, elated that school was out for the

2

summer. Teaching first grade was her true passion, but by the end of May she was beyond ready for the decompression time the summer months afforded.

Instead of beginning her much anticipated vacation, she'd been cast as a character in Johnny's nightmare.

Two steps into her home and a man grabbed her arm. She'd fought against his hold, but was no match for his strength. Snake then *invited* her to sit on her own couch while he presented her options. Comply with his demands, or watch Johnny die. Not much of a choice for someone who was more a mother to Johnny than a sister.

A firm hand took hold of her chin with a vice grip. Snake's eyes bore into hers, like two windows to nothingness. Black, soulless orbs that didn't reveal a hint of what was brewing behind them. He made a sound she swore was a hiss, and she prayed she wouldn't see fangs when he smiled.

"This is all very touching." Snake laughed and drew away, waving his hand back and forth between Emily and her brother.

He turned his head, the motion making the snake tattoo on his neck look like it was slithering. The inked reptile rose from his shirt and climbed up his neck. Johnny had talked about a man nicknamed Snake—before Emily knew Johnny was part of an outlaw biker gang—saying the man had a tattoo of a three-foot-long rattlesnake from his neck to his groin. The serpent's head moved as its master did, its mouth open wide, revealing two fangs that dripped with venom, ready to strike at any time. Even the way Snake moved resembled a reptile studying its prey, looking for weaknesses and an opportunity to attack.

"Perhaps, Johnny, you should've given more of a shit about your sister when you were stealing from me." He shook his head and tsked, much as Emily would when one of her first graders broke a classroom rule, except the consequences here were far worse. "If you'd done your job, and sold the merchandise instead of snorting it, we wouldn't have ever known you had a sister. But, lucky for you, she seems willing to step in and clean up your mess."

Story of her life. She'd been cleaning up after Johnny since he was a kid, years before their parents died.

Johnny was thirteen when their parents were killed in a devastating motor vehicle accident, just three miles from their L.A. home. Even as a young teen, he'd set a precedent for trouble. Small time offenses mostly; petty theft, smoking, hanging with a rough crowd. Life took a turn for the worse when, at seventeen, he was initiated into a gang. The Killing Machines, or KMs to Los Angeles natives.

Hours after she found out, Emily had them packed and heading east, finally stopping in the tiny, off-the-grid town of Sandy Springs, Arizona. They resided here for the past four years. Emily thought she'd been successful in removing Johnny from the temptation of drugs and gangs. For a while, he even held down a steady job busing tables at a local restaurant. But, at twenty-six, she was apparently still very naïve.

A few months prior, she discovered a wad of cash in his dresser drawer. After snooping around, she learned he'd quit his job, and was now a prospect for the Grimm Brothers MC. Dealing drugs, no less.

The mistakes he made didn't matter. She'd do anything in her power to help him. He was her only family, and she loved him.

"Okay, kids. Here's how this is gonna go." Snake rubbed his hands together and slid his split tongue across his bottom lip as he paced the distance between Emily and Johnny.

The small, quiet man who'd beaten Johnny—Snake called

him Casper—smiled so big each tooth was on display.

Emily swallowed a groan. Whatever they were about to make her do was not going to be pleasant.

"I know a broad who lives over in Crystal Rock. She's gonna get you into a No Prisoners party tomorrow night. You, pretty Emily, are going to make friends, rub elbows, hell, rub cocks. I don't give a fuck."

Emily's head spun. What the hell was he talking about? A No Prisoners party? Was he insane? "Wh-what?"

"Emily!" Snake clapped his hands in front of her face and laughed when her muscles jolted. "Focus. I need you to cozy up to the No Prisoners. I know they're planning to fuck with me and I want to know how. You're gonna find out. In two weeks we've got a very expensive deal going down. The No Prisoners would love to see it crash and burn, and I need to know if they are planning something to interfere."

Emily shook her head, her mind racing with all the reasons this was a horrible idea. "I can't do that." This plan would never work. "Why can't your friend just do it?"

"Two reasons, Emily."

She hated the sound of her own name coming from his lips. Probably why he said it so frequently.

"She ain't the type of girl they share secrets with. She's the kind of girl they fuck. But you're so sugary sweet they'll be tripping over their dicks to get close to you. Besides, Trixie doesn't have the strong motivation you do." He grabbed Johnny by the hair and yanked his head back so Emily had a full view of his beaten face. "This is not a discussion. You need to concentrate on getting me what I need, so Johnny doesn't end up as buzzard food in the desert."

Why on earth would Johnny get involved with these men? One look at his dilated pupils, sweaty brow, and subtle tremors and the answer was obvious.

Addiction.

If only she'd been paying closer attention, maybe she would have noticed he was using again. Then she could have…what? He'd refused countless offers of rehab or counseling. His joining a gang had been the last straw after years on a never-ending merry-go-round of begging and pleading with him to get help. She'd thought moving was the answer, but his demons just followed them. She was clueless as to what else to do to help him.

"Two weeks, Emily." Snake wiggled two fingers in her direction.

Emily shook her head and her stomach somersaulted.

"Maybe I haven't made myself clear. You need a little more convincing?" Snake pulled a gun from the small of his back and pointed it at Johnny's head.

Her heart nearly pounded out of her chest, but her brother didn't react in any way. Had his self-worth decreased to the point where he no longer cared if he lived or died?

All background sounds blended together. Emily heard nothing but the rushing of blood in her ears. "No, no, no!" She leaped from the couch, hands out in front of her as though she could somehow prevent Snake from killing her only family. "I'll do it. Just let him go and I'll do it."

Snake laughed again. "I like you, Emily." He came to a stop in front of her and leaned down so his mouth was against her ear. His stale breath wafted across her skin and she shuddered in revulsion. The hand holding his gun wrapped around her waist, securing her in place. She froze as though she were standing on a landmine. "I'll let him go *when* you get me what I want," he whispered.

Tears flooded her eyes. She soaked in Johnny's image, memorizing how he looked: vulnerable, damaged, and lifeless. That image would need to be burned in her brain to drive her over the upcoming days.

Snake straightened and paced the room, waving the gun as if he were a conductor in a symphony instead of a murderous sociopath. Emily swallowed, her attention glued to the movement of the weapon.

"Johnny will remain our guest for the next two weeks. If you get me what I need, he will be returned to you. Take your time. Don't rush. Don't think you're gonna feed me some bullshit tomorrow, get your junkie brother back, and live happily ever after. He stays with me the entire time."

Damnit. Her first instinct had been to fabricate a believable story and disappear with Johnny.

Snake halted in front of her and stroked the muzzle of his pistol down her cheek. A bead of sweat rolled down her spine, leaving an itchy path in its wake. Frozen in fear, she ignored the minor irritation.

He tapped the gun against her cheek twice, before turning to his henchmen. "We're done here, boys. Load him in the van and let's roll. Emily, Trixie will meet you at the No Prisoners' clubhouse tomorrow night at ten. She'll know who you are."

Casper sliced at the zip ties that bound Johnny's limbs to the chair, while two men she'd forgotten were in the room came from behind her and gathered him up. They ignored his grunts of pain as they dragged him by the arms toward the door.

Emily prayed he wouldn't be stupid enough to try and fight them, but it wasn't necessary. His knees buckled and his head lolled, not an ounce of rebellion left in him.

Snake nodded at her and started for the door. "You'll be hearing from me," he called out before following his goons out of her house.

The instant her door clicked closed, Emily bolted to the

bathroom and emptied the contents of her stomach into the toilet. After many minutes, the violent heaving subsided, leaving her weakened and exhausted. Sweat ran down her face, mixing with her tears and stinging her eyes.

How would she ever survive the next few weeks? How would Johnny?

Chapter Two

Jester held his breath while the vote went around the table. The room spun a bit as too little oxygen permeated his brain. For weeks now he'd been playing it cool, telling his brothers he wasn't worried about the vote, hadn't even been thinking about it. But it was all bullshit.

"I vote yea. No one better for the job." Acer nodded at him.

"It's a hell yeah for me." Gumby slapped his long-fingered palm against the table.

"Yea." Striker had a huge grin on his face as he rounded out the vote.

Jester's breath rushed out, and he refilled his lungs with much needed fresh air. He'd been a damned loyal warrior for the No Prisoners over the past decade, and at thirty-five he was satisfied with his high standing and reputation within the club. This club, his bike, and his brothers were all that mattered to him. Now it was officially his job to maintain the safety and security of his family.

"Well, that makes it unanimous. Jester is now our Sergeant at Arms. Come take your new seat, brother." Shiv, the club's president, named for his luck in surviving an assassination attempt in prison, rose as he spoke. He pointed at the empty chair to his right.

Jester stood from the table and strode toward Shiv. He pulled out the chair, raking it across the cement floor, before he dropped into the seat, claiming his new position. The men whistled and pounded their boots on the floor, the mood much lighter now that the formal voting was complete.

Pride bloomed in Jester's chest as he took in the looks of respect and admiration on his brother's faces.

"Congrats, man." Striker, the club's VP, and one of Jester's closest friends, reached across the table and handed Jester the Sergeant at Arms patch he'd now wear on his cut.

"Thanks, bro. All in a day's work." Jester was replacing a man who was well loved by the entire club. But cancer was eating away at his lungs, and he couldn't fill the role any longer.

Shiv held up a hand and the uproar quieted. "Okay, one more order of business then we can get out of here and start the celebration. I hear there will be some prime pussy here tonight, boys."

Even though the official vote hadn't been until two minutes ago, no one besides Jester had had any doubt how it would turn out. The guys had been planning a blowout for weeks. Booze, strippers, and his brothers would guarantee a night of unforgettable fun.

Striker commandeered the meeting, and reminded everyone of the ongoing conflict with a motorcycle club just one town over. "Grimm Brothers are back to running drugs through our town. As you all know, after all the shit went down with Lila, Snake had his hands full getting his guys back under his thumb. Now he's back to pissing in our pool. The asshole can't seem to stay away."

Around the table the men nodded. Anger simmered under

the surface as Jester recalled the role the Grimm Brothers played in terrorizing Lila, Striker's fiancé.

"A prospect spotted three Grimms in our territory again. They ain't even trying to hide the fact that they're running their shit through our turf. We tried to play nice, and it didn't work. Time to toss their asses out of our sandbox."

Jester reached behind Shiv's chair and snagged a large, rolled up, laminated map of the area. He spread it out on the table, and placed a beer bottle on each corner to keep it flat. While Striker continued to speak, Jester used a black marker, circling locations on the map as Striker mentioned them.

"We have intel, from a source in Mexico, that the Grimms are purchasing a fuck ton of product from the Fuentes Cartel. In two weeks they'll be meeting with the cartel to exchange the cash for the goods. The transfer is set to take place here in our territory, down near the mountain pass. We need to hit that. Rumor has it near a million dead presidents will be handed over to travel down to Mexico that day. It's a double win for us. Shows the Grimms what happens if they play on our side of the line, plus we get quite a nice chunk of change."

A low whistle sounded, and Jester looked up. Gumby had risen and leaned his lanky body forward, getting a closer view of the map.

"We gonna hit them before or during the exchange?" Gumby asked, as he stretched an extra-long, gangly arm out and tapped a spot on the map that would be an ideal location to hit before the deal happened.

"Before," Jester answered. "We don't give a shit about getting our hands on the drugs, but a million large? That is more than enough to have Snake shedding his skin."

Shiv nodded as the men snickered. "That gives us less than two weeks to come up with a solid grab plan. I want it swift and I want it fierce. A few humiliated Grimms along with the missing money will really drive home the fact that we won't be bending over for them. They need to conduct their business in their own town."

"We'll need to be prepared for retaliation as well," Striker added. "Knowing Snake, there will be blowback for sure."

Striker's gun had a bullet in the chamber with Snake's name on it. Lila had been taken prisoner after she and Striker were ambushed by the Grimms. Striker nearly went out of his mind with worry for her. Jester took in the satisfaction on his VP's face. This payback was overdue.

Snake had taken control of the Grimm Brothers MC in a coup last year. The man he replaced vanished, although Jester was sure he was buried out in the desert somewhere.

"We'll work on how to handle whatever shit they throw our way when we finalize the details of the hit. Next week I want to discuss it further and come up with a solid plan to fuck over these assholes." He looked around the room. Each man gave a short nod, bloodlust on their faces. "All right, then. Meeting adjourned." Shiv banged his gavel on the table and the room erupted in excited chatter. The men were eager to get drinking and get some action.

"Hell yeah." Jester rubbed his hands together in anticipation of a wild night. "Bring on the pussy."

"You trying to tell us you haven't already been laid today?" Hook ambled over. Topping out at just under six-foot and with a deadly left hook, he'd been one of the first friends Jester made when he prospected fifteen years ago. He slapped Jester on the back. "Congrats, bro."

"Thanks, Hook, and I'll have you know my dick hasn't been serviced in two days."

Striker snorted. "Two whole days, brother? You must be losing your charm."

"Fuck you all. Just because I haven't been stupid enough to go and shackle myself to a buck ten lead weight—even if she is hot as hell—you think you can make fun of me? Not my fault married sex sucks balls…or doesn't." Jester smirked at his own play on words.

"Hey, man I ain't got no complaints. My fiancé is insatiable." Striker smiled, the kind of goofy smile men got when they were totally whipped. He wore that smile most days since Lila agreed to marry him.

"Yeah," Hook added, bouncing on the balls of his feet. He constantly looked like he was in the ring, ready to box. "You oughta know, Jester. You've walked in on them enough times."

Jester shuddered dramatically. "Don't remind me. I still have nightmares about Striker's pasty white ass."

As they bantered, the three men made their way out of the meeting room into the open area of the clubhouse that was rapidly filling with club members, their ol' ladies, and plenty of unattached broads looking to bag a biker for the night. Ol' ladies weren't always permitted at club parties, but since tonight was a celebration for Jester, everyone was invited.

Off to the right, the heavy wooden bar was bustling. Three prospects scrambled to keep up with the demands for alcohol. Tables and chairs that normally littered the open area lined the edges of the room allowing space for dancing.

When the partying crowd noticed Jester, the room erupted with cheers and whistles. Gumby dragged a chair over and shoved him down. He thrust a shot into each of Jester's hands.

After he tossed the fiery tequila back, a tall, leggy blonde with a teeny tiny hot pink skirt and nothing more than a black lacy bra that barely contained her stacked chest, straddled his lap and began to gyrate to the music.

13

"Congrats, brother," Gumby called out with a wink, pointing to the chick. "This one's on me."

Jester linked his hands behind his head, and leaned back to enjoy the show. There were definitely some perks to this life.

Chapter Three

Emily stood on the sidewalk outside the gates to the No Prisoner's clubhouse, reminding herself to breathe in an attempt to calm her frazzled nerves. Ever since she had peeled herself off the bathroom floor, more than twenty-four hours ago, she'd been a wreck. She had to make this work. A queasy stomach and trembling knees didn't matter. The danger to Johnny's life topped her fears. Unfortunately, the pep talk did nothing to settle her.

While she waited for someone named Trixie to find her, Emily observed the various women flooding into the clubhouse for this party. Her eyes bugged a bit further each time a stick figure with giant boobs and a lingerie looking outfit tottered by on six-inch heels. Didn't these girls have any self-respect? They looked like strippers and whores. Hell, for all she knew, they *were* strippers and whores.

"You Emily?"

She whipped around at the sound of a heavy New York accent calling her name. "Yes. You must be Trixie." She held her hand out.

Trixie ignored Emily's outstretched palm and waved her own up and down looking like she drank sour milk. "Jesus,

Snake told me I might need to bring ya something to wear, and now I'm glad I did. This ain't no church function, honey. Come. You need to change so I don't gotta be seen with you like that."

Emily glanced down. She'd worn a plain black tank top and dark skinny jeans with black heels. She looked good. Didn't she? "What's wrong with my outfit?"

"What ain't wrong with it? Girlfriend, it's boring as shit. Follow me."

Trixie wrapped a hand—long, acrylic nails and all—around Emily's wrist, and towed her clear across the parking lot, to a darkened spot behind a row of motorcycles.

"Here, put this on, and be quick about it." She pulled a small pile of clothes out of her bag and shoved them into Emily's hands then crossed her arms and tapped her toe in an impatient rhythm.

"You want me to change *here*?" She examined the two scraps of fabric Trixie handed her. "Um, where's the rest of it?"

"Honey, do you want me to leave you out here?" Trixie snapped her gum, giving Emily a frown that said she'd gladly ditch her.

Trixie leaving was the last thing Emily wanted. Without Trixie, she'd never get into that party, and Johnny's life depended on it. "No, no! I'll just be a second."

Emily stepped into a skirt that barely covered her ass before wiggling her jeans down her legs. With a quick peek around to make sure no one was watching, she whipped off her tank top, and stuffed herself into the low cut shimmery red halter Trixie supplied. She'd always been well-endowed, and right now her breasts were barely contained by the material.

"Hmmm." Trixie tapped her plump electric pink lips with

an equally shocking pink nail. "Snake didn't tell me you had that rack." She shrugged. "Whatevs, it's good enough. They'll like it in there for sure."

She pulled a compact out of her clutch, and used the glow from a street lamp to fluff her shoulder length frizzy blonde hair, and shimmy her own breasts up higher in her sparkly tube top.

Seeing Trixie's skirt, Emily no longer worried that the one she was wearing would be the shortest or tightest at the party. It didn't matter. If skimpy clothes got her closer to saving Johnny, then she'd wear nothing but a headband and heels.

"Here's the apartment key. You know the address?"

Unease crawled up Emily's spine. "I'm sorry, what?"

Trixie rolled her eyes. "Snake didn't tell you? Jesus, I gotta do everything," she muttered the last part under her breath. "You can't stay at your place. No Prisoners ain't welcome in Grimm territory and you live in Grimm country. So if you want to make friends here you need to live in town. I got a friend who's away for a month. This is her key." She handed it over and rattled off the address.

Emily shook her head and recited the address in her head, over and over. With a shaking hand, she took the key from Trixie and dropped it in her clutch, trying not to think about how much she didn't want to sleep in some random person's apartment for two weeks.

Save Johnny. It was her new mantra.

Trixie started to walk away.

"Wait," Emily called.

With a huff the other woman turned back around.

"If these clubs are such enemies, how is it that you are friends with both?" She needed to be certain Trixie wasn't going to stab her in the back.

One corner of Trixie's mouth raised. "Honey, you ever

been fucked by one of these guys?"

Heat rushed to Emily's face. "Um, no I haven't."

"You should think about it. You sure could use it." She shrugged before turning her back on Emily once again. "I don't give a shit what the guys think about each other. I'm here for one thing," she called as she resumed walking, the seductive sway of her hips validating her words.

Ok then. Emily forced herself to forget about the apartment situation for the time being and focus on getting information.

One crisis at a time.

"Let's go." Trixie stomped back to Emily, grabbed her wrist again, and dragged her toward the entrance where an overweight man with curly blond hair and a bushy beard was guarding the door.

"Hey, Tank," Trixie said running a finger down his chest. "Save a dance for me and my girl, will ya?"

He nodded, his eyes glued to Trixie's breasts. Emily turned her body slightly, so her own cleavage wasn't visible to him. She did not want him to notice her and focus his creepy attention on her body. "You got it, Trix."

Trixie towed Emily through the door, and turned to her. "Okay, girl, I got you in, but I ain't gonna stick with you all night. I gotta get mine."

Emily scanned the clubhouse, eyes wide with shock. She turned to ask Trixie to stay with her for a few more minutes, until she got her bearings, but the other woman was already gone, lost in the throng of dancing bodies. Sucking in a deep breath, Emily held it for two seconds then blew out slowly, hoping her heart rate would normalize.

Despite feeling naked in the clothing Trixie provided her, Emily was actually one of the most clothed women in the room. More than half the women looked to be wearing nothing more than lingerie as they undulated against various men everywhere Emily turned. As she continued her perusal of the party, she noticed multiple men smoking weed, a number receiving lap dances, and—wait, was that… Yes, up against a wall in the darkened, yet still blatantly public, corner of the room, a woman writhed as a man sucked with enthusiasm on her nipple.

Holy crap, Emily was so far out of her depth. The urge to run was almost unbearably strong. She closed her eyes and conjured up the image of her brother she'd branded onto her brain yesterday. Remembering his bloodied face and glazed stare was the only thing that stopped her from bolting for the exit.

When she opened her eyes, the exhibitionist couple against the wall was still in her direct line of sight. The man had switched his attention to the woman's other breast, and she appeared to be enjoying his devotion to the task very much. Her head was thrown back, eyes closed, mouth open. Emily assumed she was moaning, but was too far away to hear much of anything over the pulsing beat of heavy metal music.

As Emily watched the woman grind her pelvis against her lover's thigh, a tingle started to develop between her own legs. She was mortified to realize the scene before her was turning her on. The look on the woman's face was one of ecstasy, and the effect wasn't lost on Emily.

Oh God! What was wrong with her? She shouldn't be watching them at all, let alone enjoying it. She rolled her eyes. What was wrong was probably the fact that no man had ever put that look on her own face.

She gave herself a mental shake as she shifted her gaze away from the show, only to land on a different performance. A giant of a man sat sprawled in a chair, leaning back, his fully tattooed arms sticking out to the sides, bent at the elbows with his fingers interlocked behind his head. A woman wearing a silver G-string and shimmery triangle bra with tall fuck me heels was giving him one hell of a lap dance.

Emily couldn't make out much of his face, his arms blocked the view, but he certainly appeared to appreciate the blonde as her assets swayed at eye level. She observed him through the smoky haze of the room for a few seconds before it dawned on her that she'd been standing in the same spot like an idiot for five minutes.

Although not much of a drinker, if there was ever a time for liquid courage, this was it. She turned toward the bar and forced her feet to step and her knees to keep from knocking together. Today's fear wasn't quite as consuming as yesterday's, but it stayed at the forefront of her mind.

"Hey there, darlin', I'm Kenny. What can I get ya?" the man working the bar asked her.

Oops, Emily hadn't thought far enough ahead to plan what she wanted to order. With a quick glance to her left, she noticed a tough looking lady toss back a shot like it was water. That's what she needed, little liquid, big impact. "I'll have what she had." She motioned toward the girl next to her.

"One shot of tequila coming up."

Tequila? She'd make a complete fool out of herself for sure.

Kenny returned quickly and placed the shot on the bar in front of her. Emily eyed it like it was a cockroach, and the handsome young bartender laughed as he ran a hand over his buzzed blond hair, ending with a scratch to the back of his neck. "You sure you want that, honey?"

"Absolutely."

20

He laughed again, and a wide smile broke out across his face, which was covered with the same blond stubble his head was. "In that case I'll join you. A girl as pretty as you should never drink alone."

She smiled at him. Could she befriend him? Would he spill club secrets she could pass on to Snake? The thought made her feel dirty.

"Bottoms up, darlin'."

Emily picked up the shot glass, stared at it for a split second, tilted her head back, and slammed it down in one gulp. Her eyes flooded as fire burned a path down to her stomach. When she brought her head back down and returned the glass to the bar top she wanted to pat herself on the back. By some miracle she'd managed not to cough and sputter.

"Well, there ya go, honey." Kenny laughed. "Nice job. Want another?"

Emily shook her head. "Just a beer, please." Two of those and she'd be dancing on the tables with the rest of the women here.

Kenny shot her a knowing grin before he reached under the bar and snagged a beer. With a quick flip of his hand he popped the metallic cap off and held the frosty bottle out to her.

"Thanks." She smiled at him. It was now or never. "So, um, save me a dance?" Trixie's line worked on the big guy at the door, so why not now?

"Sorry, honey. I'm a prospect." He pointed to a patch over his heart that read *Prospect*. "That means no club who—uh, girls, for me."

Emily blinked away tears. It was unrealistic to expect that the first person she talked to would spill their guts so she could save Johnny, but it's what she'd hoped.

"Have fun tonight," he said with a wink as he moved on down the bar.

Emily grabbed the beer and spun around, leaning her back against the bar while she surveyed the room and tried to decide her next move. How the hell was she supposed to pull this off? She stuck out like a frightened cat at the dog park.

After taking a sip of her beer, she lowered the bottle, and her eyes locked on the bronze colored ones of the guy who she'd witnessed getting a lap dance. The man was enormous, he had to be close to six and a half feet tall. Even his muscles had muscles. She couldn't tell exactly how long his dark hair was, but it had to be fairly long because it was tied back at the nape of his neck.

He looked intense, tough, and more than a little scary, but man, was he gorgeous. The tingling she'd experienced earlier came back full force as the intimidating goliath walked in her direction.

Her insides shook, and Emily took a subtle glimpse right and left to see if he was walking toward someone on either side of her, but his attention remained trained on her as he advanced with purpose.

Showtime.

She swallowed her nerves. As soon as she was done here, Johnny was safe. No matter what it took—she'd get this man to talk to her. Problem was, she had no game and no clue how to entice a man like this.

~ ~ ~ ~

Jester enjoyed the bounce and sway of artificially enhanced tits moving in front of his face while the stripper—Amber maybe—raised her arms above her head, thrusting them out even farther. He winked at her before she turned her back to him, and bent down, her ass replacing her tits in his line of sight.

Despite the sexy dancer, Jester's mind drifted to the Grimm Brothers. The money grab was his project; he was fully in charge. The challenge was one he welcomed, but he wanted it to be more than just swiping Snake's money. He wanted the bastard humiliated and well aware of who was responsible.

Acer was supposed to find him so they could toss around some ideas. He scanned the room for his brother, but all thoughts of money and enemies fled his mind when his gaze landed on a raven-haired beauty standing at the bar, giving the impression that she'd rather be anywhere else on earth.

She stood rigid, back to the bar, and even from twenty-five feet away, Jester could detect waves of tension radiating from her. Damn, was she a looker. Long, shapely legs extending from a short black leather skirt and ending in black, strappy heel encased feet caught his eye. That is until he trailed upward and zeroed in on her breasts.

Goddamn, the woman was blessed.

From where he sat, her hair shone black and glossy, cascading down and ending just at the top of those mouthwatering mounds. He couldn't make out all her facial features from this distance, but he could clearly see she had a body made for sin.

Beautiful women were certainly not a novelty around the clubhouse. At some point, someone must have sent out a memo letting the unattractive ones know not to bother coming around. The difference was, however, that the chicks looking to bang a biker typically knew they had it going on. They oozed overconfidence and were aggressive in the use of their physical features as a way to get what they wanted, whereas this nervous creature didn't even seem to notice she had tits, let alone understand how to use them to her advantage. She chewed on her bottom lip and scratched at the label on her bottle.

Intrigued, Jester gave his entertainment a light pat on her hip. "Thanks, darlin'. I gotta check on something for a bit."

Amber turned and straddled his lap, plopping her tight ass down on his thighs with a pout of her painted lips. "You sure, big guy? I was just getting warmed up." Her voice was whiny, and he ground his teeth together to keep from telling her off.

"I said up," Jester reiterated, a bit more forcefully this time, rising as he spoke, which caused Amber to stumble when her spiked heels met the ground. He didn't like having to repeat himself.

Pissed off, she flounced away only to be snagged up by one of his brothers, and begin dancing all over again.

Easy come, easy go.

Jester turned his attention back to the curious little number at the bar. His focus remained trained on her as he lengthened his stride, moving in her direction. He chuckled inwardly the moment she noticed him, at the wide-eyed deer-in-the-headlights expression that crossed her pretty face.

When he reached the bar, Jester wedged himself in sideways next to her, facing her. "Excuse me, darlin'," he said, smiling as her eyes grew even wider. Eyes that he now saw were a spellbinding shade of very fair, almost baby blue. "Did you wash that skirt with Windex?"

Her eyebrows drew down and she shook her head slightly, as though trying to solve a puzzle. She glanced down at her skirt then turned to face him. "I'm sorry? What are you asking me?" She seemed completely baffled by both his attention and his question.

With his height advantage, Jester had an excellent view of her two mounds of creamy flesh as they swelled above a shirt that appeared to be a size or two too small. Not that he was complaining. "I asked if you washed your skirt with Windex?"

"Um, no I didn't. Why would you ever think I washed my skirt with Windex?"

"Well, I can see myself in it." Jester paused and waited for the corny line to sink in.

She blinked and she stared at him for a heartbeat, obviously letting his odd statement rattle around in her brain. Then, she took him completely by surprise when she threw back her head and let out a genuine laugh. The husky sound combined with the view of the milky skin of her exposed throat had Jester's blood pooling in parts south, and he had to shift his hips to avoid brushing his stiffening cock against her. That would send her running for the hills for sure. She had an air of purity about her, so opposite every other woman at the party.

"Well, that's better," he told her. Unable to stop himself, he reached out and brushed a lock of silken hair from her shoulder.

"What's better?"

"You laughing. You were standing so straight and stiff over here I thought you might snap in half if someone bumped you. Figured I could use my smooth way with words and my irresistible charm to get you to loosen up."

She chuckled again. "So you decided to go with the most awful pickup line ever?"

He clutched a hand to his chest in a dramatic fashion. Despite her uncomfortable appearance, she had some sass to her, a fact he found alluring. "Girl, you wound me. I'll have you know that line has earned me a blowjob or two in the past."

She faltered for a second, seeming surprised by his blatant language before she snickered. "You're kidding, right?"

Each time the woman laughed her breasts jiggled, and Jester was helpless to do anything but stare at them. He was a tit man through and through. The bigger the better, and this woman had a rack on her that had him salivating to taste. As opposed to Amber's, whose were obviously full of silicone, this woman's were natural, and would mold perfectly in his hands. "Okay, maybe it was just once." He winked at her. "You got a name, darlin'?"

"Emily."

"Well, Em, it's nice to meet you. I'm Jester." He held out a hand and waited. She stared at it for a few seconds like it might be a trap. She must have decided he was safe enough, which was a bit of a joke, because she reached out and placed her small feminine hand in his massive one.

He lifted it to his lips, and nipped the pad of her thumb, enjoying the soft gasp that escaped her sexy mouth.

He didn't release her, though he lowered their joined hands. Her skin was smooth and had a fresh clean laundry smell. He wanted to enjoy it for a moment. "So, Em, what the fuck is someone as sexy as you doing over here all by yourself, abusing that poor bottle?"

Emily peered down at the bottle in her hand, seeming to have been unaware that she'd peeled more than half the label off. "Oh…um…this is not my typical scene. I'm new in town. I came with a…sort of friend. You know Trixie? She, um, she lives in my complex."

She came with Trixie? Jester almost laughed out loud. The two women couldn't be more opposite. "Everyone *knows* Trixie."

Emily needed to be rescued from her solo drinking. He gave her a gentle tug, and slung his hefty arm around her shoulders. Even though she tensed under his touch her soft curves molded to him. Damn that felt nice. "A sort of friend,

26

huh? Well, hon, let me introduce you to a few people. Make you feel more comfortable."

He propelled her toward the opposite side of the room where Hook and Striker sat at a table drinking with their ol' ladies. Marcie and Lila seemed more Emily's speed, and maybe she'd loosen up a bit.

"Hey, it's the guest of honor!" Hook yelled as Jester approached.

Emily looked up at him from under his arm with a quizzical expression.

"I'll fill you in later, darlin'."

"Hey, assholes," Jester said as they reached the table. "Guys, this here is Emily. Emily, that's Hook." He pointed to his brother on the left side of the table. "And that's his ol' lady, Marcie. Next to Hook is Striker, and sitting on his lap because she's a horny wench, is his fiancé, Dr. Lila Emerson."

Lila cracked up. "Or just Lila because I'm a little drunk, and I'm horny, as he said, so no need for any formalities. Nice to meet you, Emily."

Everyone laughed at Lila's tipsy monologue, including Emily, whose wide eyes gave her a bit of a shell shocked appearance. Jester was completely charmed by her intriguing combination of innocence, an outrageously sexy body, and a voice made for bedroom talk.

"Hmmm." Striker spoke up, "I may need to take the good doctor upstairs for a house call pretty soon." He leaned in and nuzzled the side of Lila's neck as she giggled.

Jester pulled out a chair for Emily and she sat, ramrod straight, but her face no longer held the terrified look it had when he'd first noticed her at the bar. He plopped down next to her and caught sight of Acer waving to him from across the room. He'd nearly forgotten about their plans to discuss the money grab.

Never in his life had he delayed club business for a woman, but the one next to him had his full attention. He held up two hands and mouthed, "Ten minutes," to a frowning Acer.

Chapter Four

Emily sipped her beer and smiled politely as Jester bantered back and forth with the other two men. Nobody seemed to mind that she didn't join the conversation, and for that she was grateful. In the span of twenty-four hours, her entire world had tilted on its axis and she could barely process it, let alone be expected to keep up a witty conversation.

While her brain appeared to have shut down, her body was fully alert and zinging with sensations Emily hadn't felt in a very long time. Awareness of the huge, sexually potent man sitting just a breath away from her danced across her nerve endings, and every few seconds when his body brushed hers in some way, she gritted her teeth to keep from shivering in delight. A muscled thigh would press against her leg or his intricately tattooed arm would graze the side of her breast, causing her nipples to tighten and ache.

Emily's panties had dampened the moment Jester's teeth made contact with her thumb, and she now sat with wet panties and hardened nipples at a table full of strangers. What was happening to her? The stress of the situation must be wearing on her, causing her body to go haywire.

It wasn't long before Jester's friends left. Hook and Marcie made their way to the bar, while Striker and Lila headed upstairs. Apparently, since he was the VP, he had a room here at the clubhouse.

Alone at the table with Jester, Emily turned toward him only to find his gaze locked on her chest. She resisted the urge to look down and check if her nipples were showing through the thin halter she wore. If the hungry look on his face was any indication, they were.

Jester's lustful stare only served to intensify the ache, and made her wish she were at home alone so she could solve the problem herself. That was the only way this particular predicament had been taken care of for quite some time.

He moved his focus to her face, a smirk on his enticing mouth, but he didn't comment on her obvious state of arousal.

Time to take her mind off her awakening libido and get it back on her mission. "So, you're the guest of honor."

He nodded, pride evident on his face. "I was voted in as Sergeant at Arms today. Guys decided it warranted a celebration."

"What's a Sergeant at Arms?"

"Means I'm in charge of security and order in the club, discipline and maintenance of our rules and bylaws." He reached across the table and plucked the empty beer bottle out of her hand, sliding it aside so he could play with her fingers.

She nodded, not trusting herself to speak. Jesus, the man's hands were masculine; big and strong with just the right amount of roughness as they rubbed over her softer skin. They would feel unbelievable running over her belly, her breasts, and dipping into her—

Shit!

Where were these thoughts coming from? Jester was the

one hundred percent polar opposite of every man she'd ever dated, not that there had been a long list. She'd never even been attracted to a man like him before. For crying out loud, he was dangerous and most likely a criminal. She needed to get her head on straight and think about her brother instead of her long neglected urges.

"You ever been on a bike, gorgeous?"

"A motorcycle?" She tried to ignore the flare of delight when he called her gorgeous.

He nodded, dark eyes dancing with mischief. "I'm not much for a ten-speed."

Emily snorted at the image of this hulk of a man pedaling a ten-speed bicycle. "No. I've never been on a motorcycle."

"Want to? You free tomorrow? We can go midmorning, before it gets too hot."

Refusal was on the tip of Emily's tongue. She needed to distance herself from this entire situation, but then she remembered Johnny's battered face and Snake's threats. This could be her in. A chance to get in close to someone in the club, and get enough information to prevent Snake from murdering her brother. "Okay, that sounds like fun."

"It's more than fun, darlin'. There's nothing like soaring through the wide-open desert on a bike. Closest to heaven I've ever been, well, at least with my clothes on."

Emily gasped, and shook her head at his outrageous comment. He was funny, handsome, and charismatic, not at all what she'd expected to encounter here. She assumed she'd meet clones of Snake, just in a different club. She thought she'd be afraid for her personal safety the entire time. While she was uncomfortable in the unfamiliar situation, and afraid for her brother, she didn't feel that Jester or the men he introduced her to were of any threat to her. At least not while they were ignorant to her true purpose for being there.

"You free all day? Don't have to work or anything?"

"Nope, I'm a first grade teacher. I'm free for two months. Oh, and well, I'm new in town, so I haven't started working in this area yet."

Damn. She sucked at espionage. Might as well wear a flashing *bullshit* sign.

Jester threw back his head and let out a great bellowing laugh. "First grade teacher. Fuck, I should have been able to guess that one."

With a frown Emily stared down at the table. Was he making fun of her?

"Hey."

She felt a tug on the back of her head as Jester gently pulled at her hair, tilting her face to look up at him.

"No offense intended, gorgeous. You just ooze sweetness, like I imagine a first grade teacher would have to."

Emily smiled, charmed by this gigantic tattooed biker who looked like he could kill half the men in this room without breaking a sweat. Time to get out of here. Mission accomplished for the night. Time to quit while she was still ahead.

Jester must have read her thoughts because he stood, and tugged her up toward him. He slung a heavy arm across her shoulders and started for the door. "This party is only going to get crazier as the night goes on. Judging by how uncomfortable you still look, you may want to call it a night, hon."

He was right, and his thoughtfulness touched something in her she refused to dwell on.

"I'll walk you out."

"Thanks."

Bodies were everywhere, so walking side-by-side was impossible. The loss of his heated skin against hers made her

32

feel vulnerable, unprotected.

Emily followed behind him, awed by how the crowd parted as he made his way toward the exit. It was more than apparent that he was well respected among the other men in the room. When they were halfway there, a man fell in step with her, and slipped an arm around her waist. He pulled her flush against his side, none too gently, and halted her forward progression.

He wasn't overly tall for a man, she guessed about five-foot-eight, with short, spongy curls on the top of his head. He wore a leather vest similar to Jester's. Must be a member of the MC.

"You ain't leaving so soon are you, pretty girl? Party's just getting good." The words were slightly slurred, betraying the man's intoxication.

Emily stiffened, unnerved by the stranger's hands on her. Between the music and the loud chatter, it was nearly impossible to hear anything over the noise, but somehow Jester must have sensed she'd stopped moving behind him.

He turned, and a thunderous expression crossed his face. "Hey, dickhead, hands off her."

The drunk man had to tip his head back to see Jester's face where he now hovered over them, hands on his hips and jaw clenched. The man's arm was still latched around Emily's waist, and she stood frozen, unsure if she should try to remove herself from the escalating situation.

"I ain't a prospect no more, Jester. You can't just order me away from a woman." He had an arrogant grin on his face, and he rubbed his hand over Emily's hip as though taunting Jester.

"You've had that patch for five minutes, Colt. I *can* order you the fuck away from her and I *am*."

Emily swallowed around the lump in her throat as Jester

reached around her and grabbed the man he called Colt's wrist. Colt's face paled and his pupils dilated with pain. To look at Jester, she wouldn't think anything was amiss. It simply looked like he was removing the man's hand from her waist, but obviously he was punishing the guy somehow.

Jester released Colt's wrist, and Colt held up his other hand in surrender, his face chalky. "Do I make myself clear?"

"Crystal, man. My bad." He took a step back from Emily.

"Get the fuck out of here."

Emily relaxed the second Colt's hands were off her body. She stared at Jester with gratitude and a bit of wonder. "You are clearly not someone to piss off."

Jester's eyes darkened, the joking light from moments ago nowhere to be found. "You have no idea, darlin'. Come on, let's get you out of here."

Unease filled her as she took in his serious expression. She couldn't imagine what would happen to her if he ever found out the truth behind their meeting.

The pair continued outside, and Emily pointed to her little car within sight across the parking lot. "That's me, I'm good. You can go back and enjoy your party."

He studied her for a second, and she felt her face heating under his intense scrutiny.

"What's your address?"

Emily panicked for a breath before she recalled the address Trixie had provided. "Oh right, that would be helpful." She rattled it off. Hopefully she hadn't messed it up.

"I know exactly where that is. I'll see you at ten, gorgeous."

With a nod, she scurried away, suddenly very anxious to leave. She fumbled with the key fob and dropped it to the ground outside her car door. With a frustrated groan she retrieved the keys and collapsed in the seat emitting a heavy sigh when she finally won the battle with the door.

Well, she'd survived day one, and made it further than she'd expected, so she should have been elated. Instead, she just felt dirty, guilty, scared, and unfortunately still aroused. She didn't have a clue how Johnny was doing, and to make matters worse, she couldn't even go home to her own bed and cry herself to sleep.

~ ~ ~ ~

Jester drew out a cigarette and lit it, watching as Emily muddled her way into her car. He smiled to himself, imagining her releasing a huge breath of relief once she was safely ensconced in her sedate vehicle, and away from the madness. After she maneuvered out of the parking lot, he turned, tossed the cigarette butt to the asphalt, and made his way back inside.

He wasn't sure why he'd offered to take Emily out on his bike tomorrow. On first impression, she certainly didn't fit in with the club. Yes, she was gorgeous, but it didn't take more than a fleeting glance to realize she'd be better served at a book club than a biker party. But he'd been intrigued by her unsullied vibe, so in contrast to the women he typically associated with, and he had a feeling he'd be surprised by what he'd find if he could get her to relax and let down her guard.

The moment Jester entered the clubhouse, the tall, stacked blonde who'd been giving him a lap dance when he first noticed Emily, sidled up to him and plastered herself against his chest.

"You done with whatever it is you had to take care of, baby?" she purred, the sound one that promised he could have a satisfying night. Her hands slid up his chest and circled around his neck. When her fingers started to release the band that secured his hair, he stepped back and away from her touch.

"I am."

She frowned at him, her eyebrows drawn down in displeasure, clearly unaccustomed to hearing a dismissive tone from a man. Amber may not have appreciated his reaction, but she wasn't deterred. With a renewed smile, she stepped into him, and placed her hands on his chest once again, this time heading south. "You seem tense, big boy. Want me to take care of that for you?"

Jester gripped both of her wrists, and with a firm motion, plucked them off his body. "Sorry, not tonight."

"You're kidding, right?" The pout was back.

"No, Amber, I'm not kidding. Go find another dick to play with."

Anger transformed her heavily made up face from sexy to contemptuous. "I saw you talking to that little mouse. What the fuck is wrong with you? Can't handle a real woman anymore? Maybe you're going soft?" Acid dripped from her voice.

Jester laughed out loud at her comment as he recalled how he could have pounded nails with his cock just a short while ago while listening to Emily laugh at his tacky pickup line.

"No, honey," he said. "I'm just sick of playing with fake tits and looking at faces slathered in gallons of war paint. Not much real woman about you." It was true, there wasn't much authentic about this woman, up to and including her name. Whereas Emily's hair was real, her nails were real, her makeup was minimal, and, though very large, he'd bet his bike her tits were real.

The zinger had the desired effect. Amber turned with a huff, and stomped toward the bathroom, her undeniably delectable ass twitching with annoyance.

Jester approached the bar, and nodded to Kenny when a double of Jack was placed in front of him without him having to ask. Kenny had been prospecting for just over a year, and was due to be voted in within the next month. He'd been a good prospect, took the shit and didn't bitch about it like most. He'd also taken a knife to the gut for the club last year and remained loyal. Devotion like that wasn't overlooked.

He stared at the liquid in the glass. This was his night. He should have been more excited to be at the party. He should have left with Amber. Hell, he'd slept with a hundred Ambers. What was one more?

It had to be the problem with the Grimm Brothers. It weighed heavily on his mind. The monumental task of planning the attack on the Grimms was never far from his thoughts. He had plenty of ideas, but needed to flesh them out.

As the pleasant burn of whisky warmed his stomach, a pair of wary powder blue eyes flashed through his mind. Emily reeked of innocence, and Jester did not do innocent. It was obvious she was lacking the sexual confidence, and probably the experience, that most women he bedded had. When it came to sex, he had basically tried it all; threesomes, foursomes, public sex, you name it he'd done it at least once. Well, everything except for an innocent.

Why then, did the thought of being the man to introduce Emily to all the pleasures her body was capable of have him growing painfully hard? Why was he sitting there, alone, thinking of the satisfaction he could find in her untried body, and the ecstasy he knew, without arrogance, he could offer her? And why was he thinking about a woman who was doing the very thing he didn't want—distracting him from the more important mission of obliterating the Grimms?

He tossed back the last of his drink and stood. Time to find Acer and get this night back on track.

Chapter Five

At exactly ten o'clock the next morning, Jester pulled up to the drab apartment building just in time to see Emily emerge from a weathered door on the second floor and descend the outdoor steps. He'd been here once before, for what he couldn't remember, but he wasn't crazy about the thought of her living in this complex. It wasn't the worst part of town, but it wasn't desirable, and Emily seemed so harmless and vulnerable.

Christ, he just met the girl last night. Who cared where she lived? It wasn't any of his damn business. He had enough on his plate, what with planning the seizure of a million dollars. Saving naïve girls from themselves was not on his to do list.

He watched from astride his bike as she approached, looking far too sexy in ass-tight jeans and an unzipped, black leather jacket. On her feet were black boots. They weren't riding boots, but he was impressed that she'd had the foresight to wear some kind of boot. As last night, an air of anxiety swirled around her.

"Damn, woman," he called out when she was about fifteen feet away. "You look smokin'. You sure you want to go for a ride? I could throw you down on the pavement, and ravish you until you scream my name, instead."

Her gait faltered, but she laughed and shook her head at him, while a charming blush rose on her cheeks. "I didn't have a clue what to wear. Is the jacket dumb? I figured if I did something stupid and fell off, I'd fare better with this on, even if it's way too hot for a jacket." She sent him a half smile, rolling her bottom lip in and working it between her teeth.

Jester reached forward, and ran his thumb over her lips. She gasped, the action causing her mouth to gap far enough, her lip popped back out. He soothed the spot she'd been abusing. "Don't do that. I had fantasies about that mouth all night long. It won't be any good to me if you make yourself bleed."

Her eyes widened, and he smiled. He loved how easy it was to fluster her. "And you look amazing, the jacket and the boots were a smart thought. Around here sand blows across the road all the time. It can hurt like a son of a bitch if your arms aren't protected."

"What about your arms?" She asked, pointing out the obvious fact that he wore a short sleeved T-shirt under his cut.

"Excuse me, woman? Did you just question my manhood? I'll have you know I'm one bad motherfucker. Sand is nothing to me."

Emily chuckled again. When she relaxed enough to let out a real laugh, the sound was fantastic, full bodied and arousing. "I believe you completely."

"Damn straight."

A phone chimed and Emily reached into the pocket of her jacket. "Excuse me," she said. She drew out the phone and glanced at the screen.

She transformed before his eyes, intense fear burning

bright in her eyes. She gasped and shook her head, a soft, "No," leaving her lips.

"Jesus, Emily, what's wrong? You look terrified."

She blinked at him, and a neutral mask replaced the fear. "What? Sorry. It's nothing. It's…uh…just a problem with a shipment. Something I ordered for the apartment. Took me by surprise."

She pasted a smile on her face, but he didn't buy it, or her flimsy explanation. Something had scared her, and he didn't like it one bit. But he didn't even know this girl, so he respected her privacy and took her lead, smiling back at her.

"Okay, here's a helmet for you. It should fit pretty well." He placed a shiny black helmet over her head and secured it under her chin. "Perfect. Climb on behind me. The only thing you have to worry about, Em, is holdin' on and enjoying the ride. I'll do all the work." He winked at her as she followed his instructions and mounted the bike behind him.

When her full breasts nestled against his back and her delicate arms encircled his waist, he had to clench his back teeth to suppress a groan. Feminine hands rested low on his stomach, mere inches away from his stiffening cock. The urge to push them lower nearly consumed him. Damn, this was going to be a torturous ride.

~ ~ ~ ~

Emily had to stretch her arms to reach all the way around Jester's broad torso. Maybe in the future she'd feel comfortable holding his sides, but she was terrified she'd fall off if she didn't have a firm hold on him.

The future?

She needed to nip that thinking. The only future here was one of hatred and blame. And hopefully not death.

Damn Snake, sending her a picture of Johnny and his

41

message, *Hope you enjoyed the party.* She needed to be more careful. She almost blew it. Deception was never something she excelled at.

She scooted as close to Jester as she could get, pressing fully against him, which gave her arms an extra inch or two. She used that length and interlocked her fingers around his waist. "Is this okay?" she called over his shoulder.

"Is it okay that you're plastered so tight against me I can practically feel your nipples on my back?" He snorted. "Yeah, baby, it's more than okay."

Emily buried her face in his back, embarrassed by the blatantly sexual talk. She'd never been around anyone who spoke like he did as far as the dirty talk and the profanity. It didn't offend her; it fit him, and she couldn't imagine him speaking in any other manner. It was just foreign to her. If she was honest with herself, it was a bit of a turn on, and added to his bad boy persona. Johnny could swear with the best of them, but typically tried to curb it around her. Jester just let it all fly.

Johnny...

She needed to keep him foremost in her mind. This wasn't meant to be a fun day out. It was a job, a mission. Worming her way in with people she'd never normally associate with, the end goal being to keep her brother, and probably herself, alive.

"Here we go, Em." Jester kicked the bike in gear and rolled out onto the road. He kept a slow pace as he navigated through town, until he reached the highway, where he finally let the full power of the man and the machine soar.

At first, Emily wanted to freak out, and she held on with a crushing grip that would have damaged a man who wasn't built like Jester. After about five minutes, when she caught on to the fact that the bike wouldn't tip over every time he made a turn, she began to relax. By the time Jester let the bike fly on the open highway, Emily realized they were heading toward the lake and her excitement grew.

The town of Crystal Rock bordered a gorgeous lake, an oasis in the middle of the dry, dusty desert. Most of the towns surrounding the lake thrived with tourism. Crystal Rock, however, didn't seem to draw many outside visitors. Might have something to do with the reputation of a certain motorcycle club.

As they neared the lake, cruising at top speed, Emily's blood hummed with anticipation. The scenery was breathtaking. Miles of sand and emptiness surrounded them, and, despite the wide-open space, the warmth of the sun and the intimacy of their position had Emily feeling like they were cocooned in a tiny world all their own.

Jester was huge and rock solid beneath her arms, and he made her feel extremely safe and protected. The thought nearly had her laughing because in truth she was anything *but* safe and protected. Snake wouldn't hesitate to harm her, and most likely when Jester found out her true purpose, he'd share the sentiment. But for these few moments Emily felt wonderful, invincible and elated.

Jester cruised around, circling the lake for about half an hour before he began to slow down, and pulled the bike off the road close to the lake. Emily had a perfect view of the shimmering water as their speed decreased and they rolled to a stop.

She yanked off the helmet and hopped down from the bike. "Oh my God, Jester, that was unbelievable. I had no idea it would be so much fun. I completely understand why you love it. Thank you for this."

With a hum of pleasure, Emily stretched her arms out wide and spun around, soaking in the warmth of the sun.

When she finished her three-sixty, her gaze locked with Jester's. Desire shone in his eyes, hotter than the sun overhead. She acted on impulse and launched herself at him. He caught her with ease, and she wrapped her arms around his bulky shoulders, pressing her mouth to his. It was a chaste kiss of gratitude, only lasting a second or two, but the feel of his lips on hers was electric.

Emily jerked back. She'd never been so forward in her life. Her heated face had nothing to do with the temperature of the day. "I'm sorry...I shouldn't have... I mean, I just got caught up in the moment."

Before Emily had the opportunity to step away, Jester fisted his hand in the thick strands of hair at the back of her head, holding her immobile as he tipped her chin up. "Fuck that," he ground out, and fused his mouth to hers. This time there was nothing chaste about the kiss as he ran his tongue over the seam of her mouth, demanding entry.

Without any thoughts of self-preservation, Emily opened to him and welcomed the invasion. All worry for Johnny, and fear of Snake and the danger she was in fled her mind at the feel of Jester's warm tongue gliding against hers.

She moaned and greedily tried to get closer to him, winding her arms around his neck, but he still sat astride the bike, and she couldn't get as close as her body demanded. Without breaking the kiss, Jester released his grip on her hair and hooked one hand under each of her thighs. With minimal effort, he lifted and swung her over the bike so she straddled his lap.

Legs spread wide to accommodate his width, Emily's sex made contact with the sizable bulge in Jester's jeans. He slid his hands from under her thighs, back to cup her ass, holding her even more firmly against his hard length. With thoughts of nothing but having more of the delicious friction between her legs, Emily rocked her pelvis against him, and moaned at the sensation.

If only fewer layers of clothing separated them.

Jester devoured her mouth with deep drugging kisses. Powerless to do anything but cling to him, Emily rode out the storm. He trailed his lips to the side of her neck. She sucked in much needed gulps of air, and tilted her head back to give him better access.

None of her limited experience with men had come close to this kind of passion, and both of them were still fully dressed. Emily was wet and needy, and Jester gave her more pleasure with one kiss than her only previous lover had, the three whole times she'd slept with him.

Jester loosened his hold on her bottom and trailed one hand up under her shirt. Just when he neared her breasts, which throbbed and swelled, the sharp sound of a car horn shattered the spell.

He twisted, shielding her with his body until it became apparent the noise came from a car full of teenage boys driving by, honking at them and yelling catcalls out their windows. "Fucking pricks," he muttered under his breath.

Still with her legs spread around his hips, Emily tried to come up with something intelligent to say. Another few seconds, and Jester would have had his hands full of her breasts in public and out in broad daylight. This was probably laughable as far as sexual encounters went for him, but Emily's head spun with a combination of lust, embarrassment, and a heavy dose of guilt for finding selfish pleasure in this screwed up situation. With each second that ticked by, her panic rose. She'd obviously lost her mind.

She shifted, needing to put a little space between them so she could think.

"Stop."

Her head snapped up at Jester's harsh command. She glowered up at him. "What?"

"Stop moving, Emily. You're fuckin' killing me."

"What do you...oh." Every movement caused her to rub against his still full erection.

"Yeah, *oh.*"

Emily giggled despite her reeling mind, delighted by the idea that Jester was as affected by their kiss as she was.

He leaned forward and rested his forehead against hers, as he blew out a long breath. "You hungry, Em?"

Well, that wasn't at all what she expected him to say next, but once the question was out there, her stomach growled. Saved by the hunger. This couldn't happen again. Sex with Jester—sex with anyone—wasn't part of the plan. "I'm starved."

Jester groaned again. "Fuck, babe, don't say it like that."

"Like what?"

He thrust his hips forward and ground his cock against her core. "Like you're hungry for way more than food."

"Um," she whispered on a pant as he set off shocks of pleasure all over again. "We don't even know anything about each other."

"What's your point?"

"That is my point. I don't know you, yet here I am. This is not something I usually do," she said as she motioned with her hand to indicate their intimate position. "I don't want you to think I'm a slut or anything." She worried her bottom lip between her teeth, her focus on the still water, unable to make eye contact with him.

"Believe me, Emily, that is the last thing I think about you. Ninety-nine percent of the women I know are sluts. You stand out like a diamond in a pile of shit."

She wasn't quite sure what to make of that equally

uncouth and sweet declaration.

"What did I tell you about that lip?" he asked.

Releasing her lip from the confinement of her teeth, she ran her tongue over the imprint left by the bite.

Jester groaned, lifted her, and set her back on the ground. "Get on behind me," he rumbled. "Before I really give the next car something to honk at."

Emily scrambled back on the bike, and shoved the helmet down over her mussed hair, her pussy clenching at his tempting words. Tears pricked her eyes as shame swamped her. Johnny's life was on the line, and all she could think about was how much she wanted to throw caution to the wind and have wild sex with an outlaw biker she barely knew on the side of the road.

Chapter Six

Jester killed the engine after coasting to a stop in Striker's driveway. Striker and Lila lived in a one-story Spanish style home with a breathtaking backyard setup that opened to the lake. Sunsets were killer, and since Lila moved in, the pair had been entertaining on their deck almost every week.

He wasn't sure why he hadn't clued Emily in to the fact he was taking her to his friends' house. Maybe it was because he really didn't know why he brought her there. He didn't take women anywhere. He didn't really date, just got laid, frequently. So why was he bringing a woman who wasn't his type, and who he didn't even know, to brunch with two other couples?

Because her hypnotic combination of sweet and sexy peeked his interest. And because she'd been like fire in his arms. When was the last time he had spent the day with a woman he could call sweet, besides his buddy's wives? Probably never. Her mouth had intoxicated him, with its honeyed flavor uniquely her, and he'd nearly ripped her clothes off so he could taste all of her.

She didn't want him to view her as easy. Jesus, if she had any idea the type of women he typically slept with she'd laugh her head off at the notion he could think she was anything but pure.

"Where are we?" Emily's soft voice floated over his shoulder with the gentle breeze.

"This is Striker and Lila's place. Remember them from last night?" He stepped off the bike and helped her down as well.

Emily nodded as she looked around at the sight of Striker's beautiful spread. "Why are we here?"

"Brunch." He smiled. It was fun to keep her off kilter.

"Brunch? Seriously?" She raised one eyebrow, and looked at him like he'd told her they were about to meet the queen.

"What's wrong with brunch?"

"Nothing's *wrong* with brunch. It's just so...normal."

Jester grabbed her hand and let out a booming laugh, as he led her up the driveway. "And I'm not normal?"

She stopped, and he halted his motion when he felt the pull of her hand. A frown marred her pretty face when he turned. "I didn't mean to offend you. But no you're not normal, at least not normal for me. You're big, and powerful, and this really sexy badass biker." Emily's face turned bright red as she closed her mouth. "I'll shut up now."

"Sexy, huh?" He winked at her.

She rolled her eyes. "Like you don't know it."

He resumed walking, keeping a firm hold of her hand. It felt tiny nestled in his, feminine and delicate, with buttery soft skin. Jesus, what the hell was wrong with him? He'd lose that badass card if he kept thinking along those lines. Thank God none of his brothers could read his mind or he'd be tortured endlessly. "Lila grew up in a wealthy, politically connected family, so brunch was the norm. She's started a Sunday brunch tradition. Since I like to eat, and I hate to cook, I'm a regular customer."

"Sounds more like they're your family than your friends."

"They are for sure," he said, pleased that she was insightful enough to pick up on their importance to him. "They are my club family, my only family. It's that way for many of us. We love like a family, fight like a family, and think of ourselves as one. If anyone fucks with a member of my family, they might as well start digging a grave."

Emily didn't respond and Jester looked down at her, noticing her face had paled and she had that look again, the one that said she wanted to bolt.

"Hey, you all right?"

She flinched a bit. "Yes, of course. Sorry, I got lost in my head for a second. You sure it won't be a problem that I'm here?"

"A problem?" He chuckled as they reached the door. "Just wait and see, babe."

Jester rang the doorbell and waited. For years he'd treated Striker's house like his own, coming and going as he pleased, but after walking in on Striker and Lila going at it more than once, he started ringing the bell. He didn't really give two shits, but Striker was a possessive beast and had threatened to unman Jester if he saw any part of Lila that wasn't sanctioned.

The door flew open and Lila stood just inside, practically bouncing with excitement. "Hi! Emily, right? Welcome! Come on in." She pulled Emily away from Jester and guided her into the house. With a glance over her shoulder, Lila shot Jester a look that said she'd be cornering him later.

He tried not to laugh. Lila's reaction was just as expected. She'd been harping on him to find a woman who didn't, "Wear panties full of dollars." He had a feeling she and Emily would hit it off. He shot Lila a playful smile.

Of course, what did it matter if the girls got along? He just met Emily, and he didn't date. Even if he did date, it wouldn't be an innocent woman who looked like she belonged in a room surrounded by children, rather than a biker's den. But he sure had enjoyed the time he spent with her so far.

"Hook and Striker are outside, Jester. I made mimosas, but Striker told me he wouldn't drink my pussy drink so I think there's beer out there." She made air quotes and rolled her eyes at Striker's apparent drink prejudice.

"Glad I'm not the one who has to tell you." He grinned and reached for Emily's hand again. "Come on out back with me, Em."

"Oh, no you don't. Emily can come into the kitchen with me. Marcie and I are just finishing up with the food. We'll bring it, and her, out in a minute."

Jester gave Emily a questioning look, trying to ask if she was okay with the plan. She sent him a tremulous half smile and nodded. He shifted his gaze back to Lila, who wore a gleeful grin similar to a child on Christmas morning. He attempted to give Lila a stern glare that would warn her to go easy on Emily, but she just kept grinning at him, so he turned and stepped through the sliding door out onto the sprawling deck. The girls would make Emily feel welcome, after they grilled her of course.

"Hey, brother," Striker called and tossed him a beer. "You get my message?"

Jester snatched a bottle opener from the table and popped the top off his beer. The frosty brew was always welcome as the year went on and the desert grew steadily hotter. "Yeah, I got it."

Striker had left him a voice mail letting him know Shiv wanted a workable plan for their attack on the Grimm Brothers within a week. "I have some ideas." He tapped his beer bottle against the side of his head. "But I want a few days to let them marinate before I talk to Shiv. I'm gonna pick Acer's freakish brain for ideas as well. A week's time should be more than enough."

Striker nodded and his eyes lit with a murderous gleam. "I'll let him know."

Striker would take more pleasure than anyone in ridding the Grimm Brothers of a million dollars. He and Lila had gone through some traumatic shit just a few months ago and Jester was eager to give his vice president this opportunity for payback. "They'll never see us coming, VP."

"I know that, brother. I'm not worried about what you're gonna come up with." Striker rolled his head back and forth between his shoulders, and Jester winced at the sound of his neck cracking. "I've just been waiting at a shot at the bastards for a long time now."

"You gonna tell Lila?" Hook asked. He tossed his empty beer bottle into a trash can a few feet away, and bent to retrieve a second from the cooler.

Striker shook his head. "Nah. She'll get wind of it I'm sure, but she already knows too much. Makes me twitchy. By the way, what the hell is going on in there?" He jerked a thumb toward the house. "We heard you pull up then we heard all sorts of squealing from Lila and Marcie. Hook said it was probably safer to stay out here."

Jester shrugged and took a long drink. "Nothing's going on. I brought Emily with me."

Hook choked, spewing beer onto the deck. "Holy shit. Aliens sneak in your room last night? Maybe there is something to all the UFO sightings out here in the desert. They probe you, brother?"

Jester flipped him the bird as he drank from his beer.

Striker laughed, and moved to take a seat at the large

eight-person table that lived on the deck, propping his feet on the chair next to him. "Seriously, Jest. You, bringing a woman anywhere is a news worthy event. And who the fuck is Emily?"

"I introduced you to her last night, asshole. You two girls need to mind your own fuckin' business."

"Hey, you bring it into my house, it's my business."

"The pretty one with the nervous eyes?" Hook whistled. "I gotta say, she looked way too sweet for you. Not your usual type at all, brother. Must have been some lay if you're willing to keep her around for a second day."

Anger bloomed, hot and swift inside Jester. The words barely left Hook's mouth before Jester grabbed him by the shirt and slammed him against the railing of the deck.

Striker rose from his seat, poised to jump in if necessary, but he kept his distance. Striker may be an excellent fighter, but Jester was just plain huge, and most people tended to avoid a physical altercation with him if they could.

Hook raised his hands in surrender, and a slow smile crept across his face as Jester let him go with a shove. Damnit, he'd been played.

"So who is she?" Hook asked.

Jester shrugged. "Just some chick who tagged along with Trixie. Met her last night. She'd never been on a bike so I took her around the lake today."

"And brought her to brunch."

"And brought her to brunch. You want to keep making a big fuckin' deal about it?" Jester asked Hook through clenched teeth.

"Nope. Just checking the facts. I'm done."

Hook and Striker exchanged an amused look that wormed its way right under Jester's skin. Being the butt of their jokes wasn't how he'd planned to spend his day. True, bringing

Emily was very out of character for him, but so what? He could do whatever the fuck he wanted with whoever the fuck he chose.

He glanced toward the house. Was Emily holding her own in there with Lila and Marcie? The fact that he'd rather be inside with her than shooting the shit with his brothers was new, and not necessarily welcome.

~ ~ ~ ~

As Emily followed Lila into the kitchen, she wiped her sweaty palms on the front of her jeans and chewed her bottom lip. The action caused her to remember Jester's declaration about his plans for her mouth, and suddenly her sweaty palms were the furthest thing from her mind. When she entered the kitchen, Marcie and Lila stood next to each other with identical grins on their faces.

Not uncomfortable at all.

"Sooo…" said Marcie.

Lila elbowed her, not subtly, and jumped in. "It's great to see you again, Emily."

"Thank you. I'm sorry if Jester didn't tell you he was bringing me." She had to work to keep the quiver out of her voice.

Lila waved her concern away. "We have an open door policy." Marcie let out an unladylike snort and Lila's face turned the color of the strawberries sitting on the counter. "Okay, har har. Jester walked in on Striker and me having sex, I get it. The open door should be closed sometimes."

Emily giggled at their byplay. These women seemed so down to earth compared to the majority of the girls at the party last night. "Well, thanks just the same. I'm sure he's here with a different girl every week anyway." Oh Lord, did she really say that out loud? Way to sound like a jealous girlfriend fishing for info. Of course, that's exactly what she was doing, but it was the last thing she should be doing, and she didn't want to be so obvious.

Both Lila and Marcie laughed. Emily's entire body grew hot with embarrassment. "What?"

"Girl, I've known Jester for, let's see, about six years now, and I haven't seen him take a date anywhere, to anything, at any time." Marcie turned to flip pancakes sizzling on a griddle over the stove.

Emily's brows drew down. "I don't understand."

Lila moved to the refrigerator, and pulled out a chilled bottle of champagne. "What she means to say is that Jester doesn't see his women outside of the bedroom, if you catch my drift."

Emily blushed as the meaning sunk in. "Ahh."

"Which is why we are so excited that he brought you here. You must be special to him." Lila poured the champagne into three glasses and topped them off with orange juice.

With a sharp laugh, Emily took the offered glass. "I literally just met him last night."

"Hmmm." Lila tapped her finger against her lips like she was contemplating the mysteries of the universe. "That's interesting. Well, look, I'm not going to pretend to understand what goes on in any of these guy's minds, but I will say that Jester would not bring you around his family if he didn't think you were special."

Under normal circumstances news like that would have melted Emily's heart. Now she just felt conflicted. She could use this information to her advantage, cozy up to Jester in hopes of him spilling some information. On the other hand, it gave her the power to hurt him, and for some reason that didn't sit well with her.

Emily pondered that as she watched Marcie pile pancakes on a large platter, then add bacon and sausage to each end.

The smells wafting around the kitchen reminded her of a much simpler time, when her parents were still alive and Johnny was too young to be in serious trouble. Weekend breakfast was always a big deal during her childhood.

Lila handed a bowl of vibrantly colored fresh fruit to Emily, and she followed the two out to the deck.

The backyard was gorgeous. Jester hadn't been exaggerating when he said Striker's house had a stunning view. The deep blue lake glittered in the midday sun, and at least five boats cruised around on the water. The deck was large and spanned much of the yard making a wonderful outdoor haven for entertaining.

Food was set out on the table and everyone took a seat. As she dug into the pancakes that turned out to be delicious, Emily glanced around the table. How the hell was she supposed to do this? *Um, hey, everyone. Thanks for having me in your home. Would you mind telling me if you have something planned to mess up a business deal for the Grimm Brothers? You see my brother stole from them and now they want to kill him. But they'll let him go if I find out what you guys are planning so that Snake can be ready for you. I'm sure Snake will just use the info to protect himself, and not to hurt you guys in any way.*

Emily swallowed the hysterical laughter that wanted to bubble out. With a deep breath she reminded herself that she had two weeks to find the information. Getting it today wouldn't make a difference. Snake planned to keep Johnny until her information proved useful. She needed to chill out, and use this time to forge bonds that would get someone to open up to her.

"Yo, Em! You alive in there?"

She jumped. Everyone at the table was focused on her, and Jester gazed at her with concern on his face. "Oh, I'm so sorry. I zoned out there for a second. Did someone ask me a question?"

Striker chuckled and swatted at Lila's hand when she tried to grab a piece of bacon off his plate. "I asked what you did for a living?"

She swallowed a tart and sugary strawberry. "I teach first grade. But, um, I just moved here so I'm not working yet."

"Oh, that's great!" Lila exclaimed.

The three men shared a look between them.

"What?" Lila asked.

"We all saw that. Why are you guys making strange eyes at each other?" Marcie asked.

"It's the voice, right?" Jester looked to Hook and Striker.

Confused, Emily switched her gaze between the three men as she tried to figure out what they were referring to. Lila and Marcie wore identical looks of perplexity, which Emily imagined matched her own.

Hook nodded. "Yep, the voice."

Marcie huffed out an impatient breath. "What the hell are you talking about?"

Jester turned to Emily with an unrepentant grin. "You have a voice that makes men think phone sex operator, not educator of America's youth."

Heat suffused Emily's face and her mouth fell open. "You can't be serious!"

Jester gestured to Striker who nodded his agreement. "Sorry, hon, but he's right. You have that whole sexy sultry thing going on in your voice."

"I actually agree with these three for once," added Marcie. "Your voice is super sexy."

Both embarrassed and amused Emily chuckled. "Huh, maybe I should put my summer vacation to good use, make a little extra cash."

Everyone laughed except for Jester, who scowled at Emily

with an expression that looked remarkably possessive. The woman in Emily thrilled at the idea of this potent man wanting her for himself. But it didn't matter. She was here for one thing and one thing only. Information. If Jester wanted her, so be it. It would just make her job easier.

Chapter Seven

They stayed through the afternoon and well into the evening, and Emily found that she enjoyed herself more than she had for quite some time. In fact, they stayed so long that leftovers were reheated and eaten as dinner.

This group really was a family. Emily had a difficult time reconciling these people with Snake and his crew. Each man was a member of an outlaw motorcycle club, and she had no illusions—these men could be deadly if necessary—yet they didn't seem to be the type to prey on the innocent or terrorize women.

Suddenly, the food in her stomach settled like a lead weight. Yesterday the objective was clear: meet rival MC, get information for Snake, save Johnny. Thoughts of what Snake would do with the information didn't enter her mind. Now, as she sat with a group of people who were nothing like she'd expected, it was all she could think of.

Oh God. Snake would hurt them. He was a sadistic sociopath, of course he would use the information for some sort of retaliation. Emily would be responsible for whatever happened to these people who made her smile, made her laugh, and—for one of them—made her feel desirable.

But Johnny would be alive.

The thought didn't give her as much comfort as it had every other time she chanted it through her head.

She glanced at Jester where he interacted with his friends. The entire afternoon had been an extended form of foreplay. Jester touched her in some fashion every chance he got. Whether it was a hand that caressed her thigh under the table, an arm across her shoulders while they stood chatting, or fingers trailing up and down her spine when they sat next to each other on a chaise lounge, he was in constant physical contact with her.

Emily loved it. She loved his attentiveness, she loved his friends, she loved this entire day, and sometime during the afternoon her attraction to Jester blossomed into a full-blown crush. She was beyond screwed. Falling for him in any way was not allowed. Feelings already clouded her judgment and distracted her from the end goal. Save Johnny. The No Prisoners were a tough group of badass men. They could take care of themselves.

As the day wore on, and Emily observed Jester interact with his family, she learned a lot about the man beneath the muscles. Countless stories were told about his penchant for jokes and pranks, and how it had gotten him into trouble on more than one occasion. She also learned that everyone knew he used that jovial exterior to hide a core of intensity, and one did not want to cross him.

Wise advice. Advice she needed to keep in the forefront of her mind. If the truth of her presence was revealed, he would probably hurt her just as bad as Snake would.

"How you holding up, Em? You about ready to go?" Jester's whispered words made her shiver as his warm breath tickled her skin.

Not trusting herself to speak, she nodded. She worried

she'd beg him to touch her, or worse, sleep with her if she opened her mouth.

Jester stood and linked his much larger hand with hers, seeming to be in a bit of a rush. "We're gonna take off. Thanks guys. Lila, amazing as usual." He tugged Emily along as he bent to give Lila a quick peck on the cheek.

Emily hugged Marcie and Lila as she passed, feeling like she could be friends with these women. That was, if she wasn't here to screw their men over on her quest to protect her brother. A sense of sadness overtook her. By handing over the No Prisoners to Snake, she'd also be hurting these women. They knew who their husbands were. They knew the risks of being with men like Striker and Hook, right? Why didn't that thought ease any of her guilt? "Yes, Lila, thank you for everything. I really had a great time getting to know you all."

"I'm so glad you came, Emily. I really enjoyed getting to know you as well. We'll do this again really soon!"

"Definitely. Thank you again, you have an exquisite home."

Emily and Jester walked out hand in hand. Neither spoke. The air between them crackled with awareness. Her body felt primed, ready for whatever was going to happen, and she had a feeling something would happen. Jester was too sexual a man to have spent the entire afternoon teasing her into a state of arousal to let the opportunity slip by.

Would she allow something to happen? She had to. For Johnny. It was the easiest way to get close to the club. And easier to think along those lines than admit she just plain wanted Jester.

When they arrived at his bike, Jester lifted her, and set her down sideways on the seat, facing him. "I have to taste of you." The words left his mouth as it descended on hers, touching down with an explosion of heat.

The man could kiss. He made love to her mouth, using his lips and tongue to drive her crazy. He was highly skilled, and if he could make her feel so out of control with just a kiss, she imagined she'd lose her mind if he ever got that mouth on parts lower.

Emily was lost in the consuming heat of the kiss when a loud voice startled her so badly she nearly fell off the bike. "You better keep your clothes on in my damn driveway, Jester! This is a respectable neighborhood." Striker's laughter roared before he disappeared back into the house.

"Fuck off, asshole!" Jester called back.

Emily giggled and covered her face with her hands.

Jester sighed and rested his forehead against hers, stroking a hand up and down her spine. "Well, I suppose I had that coming. Bastard's probably been waiting for the opportunity all day."

"I've heard you have a nasty habit of catching them in the act," she agreed.

"Yeah, I've had the unfortunate pleasure of seeing way more of Striker than I'd ever wanted."

"Hmm," she said, feeling a bit mischievous. "Doesn't seem like that would be a bad thing."

Jester growled at her. "You checking out my friends, babe?"

"Who me?" She made her eyes wide with exaggerated innocence.

"You keep those gorgeous eyes trained in my direction so I don't have to kill one of my brothers." He laughed when she sent him a sassy wink, then his face grew serious. "You want to come home with me, Em?"

Her neglected body screamed at her to say yes, but her mind won out. Unable to meet his gaze, she stared at his muscular chest, which didn't help her resolve any. "I can't, Jester," she whispered. "This isn't me. I don't move this fast, and I can't have any complications right now."

Jester placed his fist under her chin and forced her eyes up to him. "I'm not a complicated guy, Emily. I want you and I can tell you want me. And I don't do anything beyond one night, ever." He shrugged. "I like you, which is new for me. Who gives a shit that it's fast? We can hang out and fuck our brains out until this burns itself out. Simple, uncomplicated."

It was the most unromantic proposition she'd ever heard, but Emily appreciated Jester's honesty. Their relationship had a shelf life; he may not realize it was only a two-week shelf life, but still, his suggestion alleviated some of the guilt she felt knowing she'd disappear from his life forever in a few weeks.

There was no doubt she'd experience things with Jester that she'd only read about late at night alone in her bed. The physical desire building for him all day had nothing to do with getting close to him for Johnny's sake, or did it? Which sin was worse? Whoring herself out to gain information, or taking the time for selfish pleasures when Johnny was in danger?

"What's it gonna be, Em?"

Two days ago in her living room, another biker asked her the same question. This time around, the question had an entirely different effect on her. She looked in his eyes, into a heat that promised ecstasy. Could she live with herself? She would have to. She'd get what she needed—an in with the MC, time to find the intel to save Johnny. Jester would get what he obviously wanted, and she would get what her body wanted as well. "Your house."

In two weeks, after Johnny was safe and they left Arizona, she'd have plenty of time for guilt and self-recriminations.

Now, she'd take what was offered and worry about the consequences later.

Five minutes later they were at his house, and he guided her off the bike, to the front door. Darkness from the desert night enveloped them, making the exterior details of the house difficult to take in, but the main shape was visible, and Jester's home was surprisingly large.

With speed and efficiency, Jester opened the door and ushered her into his house. She stepped into a large den with a plush, dark brown leather sectional and giant television.

The kitchen could be seen through a large window cutout in a wall that separated the two rooms. Tall cherry cabinets ran around the room with pristine granite countertops below them.

"That's the most unused room in the house. I think the oven's been turned on once in the five years I lived here, and that was two months ago when Lila brought me dinner."

Emily chuckled and stepped into the den. His home was warm, masculine, eclectic, and seemed to fit him well, at least what she'd learned of him so far. "Jester, this is really nice."

"Thanks. Glad you like it."

Emily trailed her hand across the top of the buttery soft couch and wandered around the spacious living area. Her attention was drawn to a framed print of a motorcycle with a vibrant, stunning paint job. It was true work of art, a showpiece that probably wasn't ridden on the road. "Wow, this picture is striking."

His smile was a bit sheepish. "Thanks."

"Did you take the picture?"

"No, but I did the paint job on that bike about three years ago. It's still my favorite."

Emily's jaw dropped. She stepped closer to examine the print. He painted that motorcycle? There was more to this man than she'd realized.

He turned and started up the stairs before she could tell him how impressed she was. "Follow me."

His bedroom fit the rest of the house, masculine without being macho. The room was quite expansive with an immense bed dominating the center of the space. The bed had to be custom made; it looked both longer and wider than a king size, and the mattress rested at least three-and-a-half feet off the ground. Not surprising, given the size of the man who slept in it. She had to be careful or she'd look like a fool climbing up onto it. Assuming of course, that she'd be in it at all.

All the furniture was dark and smooth, a modern style that complemented the rest of the décor. Stunning black and white framed photographs of desert scenes and motorcycles adorned the walls.

"Does it pass muster?" Jester's deep voice broke her out of her musings.

"Sorry, I don't mean to be so nosy." She shrugged.

"You're not. I want you to like it. Aside from Marcie and Lila, who helped me decorate, you're the first woman who's seen this room."

Emily's jaw dropped for the second time in as many minutes, and she felt slightly bad for not even trying to hide her shock, but she couldn't help it. "For real?" Butterflies flitted through her stomach, followed immediately by a herd of angry elephants. She couldn't find him sweet. Couldn't be touched by the fact he'd probably slept with hundreds of women but never brought one to his home. She was allowed two things: sex and information.

He laughed. "Yes for real. Why would I make that up?"

"Well, it's just…Marcie and Lila…well, they said," she stammered, and almost rolled her eyes at herself for sounding like a fifteen-year-old talking to the cool boy in school.

Jester stepped closer and brushed an errant hair off her shoulder, skimming her neck in the process, a look of amusement on his face. "What did they tell you?"

Emily shivered. Everywhere his fingertips grazed, goose bumps erupted. Like a cat, greedy for attention, she leaned into his petting. "Just that you've had your share of...female admirers."

He laughed, long and loud.

Emily scowled. It wasn't that funny.

"There is no way either of them said *female admirers*. I guarantee they said something more like skanky hoes."

Her face grew warm. "Okay, no, that was my phrase, but you obviously know what I mean."

He stared at her, and she got the distinct impression he was deciding how much he was willing reveal to her.

She chose not to wait for him, and forged on with her own admission. "Look, I don't want to be presumptuous in my guess as to where this evening is going, but I'm not the most, um, experienced person when it comes to certain things." Jester remained quiet so she continued. "I'm not a virgin, but...oh fuck it. I've only slept with one man, and only three times at that. Lila and Marcie alluded to the fact that you were on the other end of the spectrum. I'm just telling you this in case you want to back out. I'd rather you call this off now than be disappointed later."

She played with the edge of one of the patches on his cut as she chewed her lip, unable to lift her eyes to meet his. Could this be any less sexy? "Oh my God, I can't believe I'm saying all this. I want to die."

Jester scooped her up, and sat her on the edge of his mountainous bed. With a hand on each knee he nudged her thighs open wide, and stepped into the cradle of her body, before he yanked her forward so her still clothed sex rested right against the impressive bulge of his erection.

"What did I tell you about torturing that lip?" he asked as he flicked it with his finger. "Does this feel like I want to back out, Em?" His voice sounded gravelly, tense, like he was working to keep himself in check.

She shook her head and she stared up at him, trying to hold her hips still when what she really wanted to do was grind against him until the need was fulfilled.

"Thank you for being straight with me, babe. I'm gonna be straight with you as well. There's not much I haven't done when it comes to sex. Yes, I have slept with more than my fair share of women. What can I say? I like sex, a lot of it, and frequently. I'm pretty damn sure I've never been with a woman who's only had sex three times or only been with one man. Hell, you saw the women at the club the other night. Most of them have slept with so many guys they're one fuck away from professionals. That's what I typically go for, someone who knows the score, and can get the job done without expecting anything more. I've never had any interest in a woman who wasn't, let's say, well-practiced."

He paused and Emily looked away. She wanted to crawl under the bed. His next words would probably be, "So let me call you a cab." She shouldn't care. In fact, it was better this way. Nothing was supposed to happen between them anyway. This wasn't the reason why she was here, yet after spending the day with him and his family she wanted him, plain and simple, independent of her mission to save Johnny.

"Then I saw you standing at that bar," he continued.

Emily's eyes snapped back to his. Now, all the money in the world couldn't tear her gaze away from the captivating heat and desire reflected in his dark eyes.

"Baby, I could tell you were innocent the first second I saw you at the party, like you'd rather be getting a root canal. Last night, I lay awake all night hard as a fuckin' rock while I imagined all the things I could show you, teach you. All I can think about is taking you over the edge again and again. I want to watch your gorgeous baby blue eyes react when I do things to you no other man has done, and see them glaze over as you realize the capacity your body has for pleasure." While he spoke he lifted her arms above her head, and slowly drew her top up and off her body.

Emily's mouth dried up at the same time her pussy flooded. She was wetter than she'd ever been, and he'd done nothing but speak to her. A war waged in her head between her rational mind screaming, "Stay detached! Ask questions!" and the endorphin flooded part of her brain. The sound of his voice, the feel of his hands sliding up her arms trumped all other thoughts and she gave herself over to sensations.

Still on the edge of the bed, half wrapped around him, arms raised, she allowed him to remove her shirt, revealing her breasts encased in the black lace pushup bra she'd told herself she didn't wear for him.

"Say something, baby."

"I can't think of anything to say. All I can think about is your hands, and how I want to feel them everywhere." Her hips involuntarily moved and she rubbed against him, the movement not sufficient enough to ease the ache as she'd hoped, but perfect for enflaming the need.

She was going straight to hell.

Chapter Eight

Jester stared at the sweet, innocent, first grade teacher who had him so turned on his hands nearly shook. How was it possible to want one woman as much as he wanted her right now? Why her? He should be running away. This had commitment and shackles written all over it, but nothing short of the ground opening and swallowing him whole could pry him away from the gorgeous woman staring at him like he was a king.

Her breasts were magnificent, large and high; they sat plumped in the sexy as hell bra. He wanted to take his time, spend hours touching her and sucking her, showing her just what's she'd been missing. But his dick throbbed with a demand he couldn't ignore, and he wasn't sure how long he'd last without burying himself in her slick heat.

With an expert hand he flicked open the back clasp of the bra, and chuckled as her eyes widened.

"Pretty good at that, huh?" she asked on a shaky laugh.

"Just got lucky. You nervous, baby?"

"A little."

"Don't be." He lowered her arms drawing the bra straps down while brushing his thumbs over the indentations they left on her shoulders. One downside to having bigger breasts. "Soon you won't be able to think enough to be nervous." His mouth literally watered as he bared her breasts, and removed the bra, tossing it over his shoulder. Attention drawn to the hard points of her nipples, they looked as hard as he felt, and he appreciated the visual evidence of her want. "Fuck, baby, your tits—"

"Are way too big," she said with another tremulous laugh.

Jester scoffed, and traced a finger around one large areola, drawing a hiss from her. "First of all, Emily, there's no such thing. And even if there were, yours are not too big. I have huge hands, baby, and I like them to be full, almost as much as I like my mouth to be full."

He cupped a hand under each mound, demonstrating the fit. With a squeeze he lifted them as he bent his head close to blow a breath of hot air across one sensitive tip. Captivated, he watched as it tightened even further. Out the corner of his eye, he caught sight of Emily as she fisted her hands in the soft comforter on the bed. Her knuckles whitened with the force of her grasp.

Perfect.

He wanted her needy, out of her mind with desire for him.

"Jester." She moaned, her pelvis rocking against his hard-on as her body sought release.

"Tell me what you're feeling." As he spoke, he blew on the other nipple, and Emily whimpered. If she was this responsive when he'd barely touched her, she'd go off like a rocket when he really got down to business.

She flushed, and he could see the shyness warring with the desire to let go and be a little naughty. "My nipples." She swallowed hard. The movement drew his attention to the tempting line of her throat. He made a mental note to get to that spot at some point tonight. "They need something, I don't know. I can feel them. My breasts feel swollen but my nipples just ache."

Her back arched, as though she was trying to bring her enticing tits closer to his mouth since he was taking his sweet time putting it on her.

"Is this what you want, baby?" He dipped his head, and sucked a beaded nipple between his lips. He filled his mouth to capacity. His tongue laved the pert bud as he sucked with hunger. When he drew back, he raked his teeth over it and a loud cry was dragged from deep within Emily.

Her arms flew up to grip his protruding biceps, her small hands not even circling halfway around the thick muscles. When he released her, she held tight to his arms, not letting him pull back. "More." She gasped. "Please, I want more."

"Shhh, easy, baby. I promise I'll give you everything you need." He unbuttoned her jeans before he slid his hands under her bottom and gave a firm squeeze. "Lift up, Em."

When she complied, he eased the snug denim over her hips and down past her knees. She toed them the rest of the way off then lowered her hips back to the bed. With her arms stretched out behind her, she propped herself up.

Jester's attention was drawn to the black lacy triangle covering her mound. He lifted his gaze to stare into her baby blue eyes, trailing his open palms up the silky skin of her thighs. When he reached the apex he used one hand to pull the fabric to the side, while a finger on the other hand teased the slick folds.

She was wet, the lace of her panties soaked through, and a flare of satisfaction surged at the evidence of how much she wanted him. "Do you wax, Em?" he asked, noticing how smooth and slippery she was without any hair.

"Yes. I, uh, lost a bet to my best friend in college. Had to get a Brazilian. Turns out I like it, so…"

Look at that, a little naughtiness hiding in there. "Christ, it's going to be so good when I get my mouth on you. Nothing to blunt the sensation, for either of us. Not sure I have enough patience for that right now though."

As he rimmed her opening with his finger her eyes fluttered closed and her breathing increased. "Eyes open, Emily," he ordered. "I want to watch them as you climb, and I want to make sure you know who is taking you there."

"Trust me, I know it's you." She panted. "Never wanted anyone like this." Her cheeks tinged and she looked embarrassed, like she didn't mean to reveal so much.

Jester loved it. She wasn't schooled in the games men and women played. She wasn't trying to control him with her sexuality. She was real and honest in her desire and reactions.

A tiny spear of uncertainty hit him. Why was she here with him? She recently moved here, was she just stepping over the line on the wild side for a night? He almost laughed out loud at himself. What the hell did it matter?

With his eyes locked on hers, he slowly inserted one thick finger into her. She was tight. The walls of her pussy clasped at his finger as it sank in to the knuckle. Jester nearly came in his pants for the first time since he was a young teenager at the thought of how she would feel clenched around his dick.

He curled his finger, stroking deep inside her and she moved her hips. The pale blue of her irises darkened to a deeper shade, and small whimpers of pleasure escaped her throat.

"That's it, Em," he crooned. "Take what you need."

The pleasure on her face was exquisite. It did matter. He wanted to be the cause of that pleasure again and again, not just while she checked *sex with biker* off her bucket list. He didn't want to be her act of rebellion.

~ ~ ~ ~

Emily was on fire. The slow pace Jester set was enough to drive her crazy. She rocked her hips trying to find the speed and pressure she needed. His one finger stretched her to the point of feeling full, and she wasn't sure how she'd survive it once he got his cock in her.

The strong pull of his mouth on her breast had been amazing, and now that it was gone she felt deprived and achy once again. Wanton, and beyond caring if she sounded needy, she moaned. "Jester. Please!"

"What, baby?"

"My breasts."

"You want me to suck these pretty nipples again?" The thumb of his free hand brushed over one nipple and she shuddered in response.

"Yes! Don't tease me, please."

"My pleasure." He dipped his head and sucked a nipple back into the warmth of his mouth. This time he used his tongue to press the firm tip to the roof of his mouth and Emily nearly screamed.

It was exactly what she needed, and spurned her into a frenzy. Her hips pumped furiously against his palm, and she gripped his hair to hold him at her breast.

When he pressed his thumb against her clit, she saw stars. Emily was pulling his hair so hard it probably hurt, but he didn't seem to mind. Rather, the harder she fisted his mane, the stronger he sucked on her breast, and the louder her cries grew. The consistent pressure on her clit combined with a bite of pain in her nipple sent her flying into an intense orgasm.

The room spun out of focus as Emily shuddered, and she let out a sharp cry of completion. For several minutes, she shook, and waited to regain control of her limbs. Jester's mouth gentled, and he tongued her nipple with almost tender strokes. The contrast to the rough way he'd treated it seconds ago had her feeling more than just physical pleasure. His finger had calmed as well, but remained seated deep inside her.

When she finally stilled, Jester raised his head and pierced her with his intense gaze. His eyes had darkened with lust and unfulfilled desire. She groaned when he withdrew his finger and her stomach tensed in shock when he lifted the finger to his mouth and licked it clean.

He didn't utter a word, but took a step back from her and yanked his shirt over his head, dropping it on the floor.

Holy shit. She'd had a mental picture of what he might look like without his clothes, but it paled in comparison to the visual feast before her. He could be a cover model for a male fitness magazine, with smooth skin, perfectly sculpted muscles, and yards of vibrant tattoos.

Emily had never cared one way or the other for tattoos, but on Jester they were a work of art. Each arm was covered from wrist to collar bone, the designs intricate, but too far away for her to catch the details. She'd seen some of them, since he always wore short sleeves, but now that his upper body was bare, the ink registered in her mind where it hadn't before.

An evil looking court jester riding a motorcycle spanned his entire right flank while the left side was bare, tanned skin. She wanted to run her hands over every inch of him, explore every hard plane of muscle and study his ink. It would have to wait though; she was too eager to find out what came next.

"Jester, you are remarkable," she whispered, unable to tear her gaze away from his male perfection.

He chuckled as he shucked his jeans, leaving him clad only in black boxer briefs that hugged an immense bulge. "Ready for the best part?" he teased with a wink.

The comparison between him and her former lover was laughable. Chances were she couldn't handle him, but if this was her one opportunity, she'd give it her all. Emily licked her lips. "Oh yeah."

"Jesus, woman, you trying to end this before it begins?" He tucked his thumbs in the elastic band at his waist, and pulled down the underwear, revealing an erection that took her breath away. It was long, thick, and in definite proportion with the rest of his oversize body.

He shifted back to her and Emily reached out. She wanted to feel him throbbing in her hand. Jester stopped her fingers with a shake of his head. "Not tonight, I'm too close to the edge."

He lifted her under her arms and scooted her up to the head of the bed, resting her on the pillows propped against the headboard. When he lowered down on top of her, he kissed any protest she may have had about not having the chance to touch him right off her lips. Within seconds, the heat of the kiss mixed with his heavy weight pressing down on her and the need was ignited once again as though she hadn't just had a core rattling orgasm.

Jester tore his mouth away, and lifted off her enough to sheath himself with a condom she hadn't realized he'd procured. "I need to be inside you, baby. Now. I'll try to be gentle, but I'm close to losing my shit."

"Don't you dare." Emily surprised herself with her bold statement. Everything about this encounter was so far out of character. Some lusty alter ego had taken hold of her and now ran the show. In twenty-six years, no man had incited a fraction of the desire she experienced for Jester. Was this it for her? Was it possible to have this kind of chemistry with more than one man in a lifetime? Probably not. So she'd let that alter ego take charge and soak up every ounce of pleasure before it was ripped away from her. "Give it all to me, Jester, don't hold anything back." She reached down between them, wrapped her small hand around his girth, and positioned him at the opening of her sex.

Jester wasted no time. He pushed into her, working his cock in inch by inch. "Oh, fuck, you are so tight, Em. Jesus, it's like a vice." His voice sounded rough, tortured, and a thrill at being the woman to test the control of this formidable man zinged through her blood.

She squirmed as he seated his cock fully inside her. Her world felt…whole, like their bodies were made a perfect fit. Impossibly stretched and impaled, she tried to focus only on the physical sensations and ignore the accompanying emotional joy. It would only turn to sorrow later. "Oh God, Jester. I feel so full, it's amazing, but you need to start moving."

With a chuckle, he drew out slowly, until just the tip remained. "Yes, ma'am."

This time when he pumped into her, she squeezed her internal muscles around his shaft. The action drew a harsh curse from his lips, and seemed to be the nudge he needed to tip over the threshold. He growled and drove in and out her with near violent strokes.

A prickle of heat started at the base of her spine and traveled north as it grew in intensity. Jester fused his mouth to hers in a passionate kiss that conveyed tenderness in contrast to his fierce possession.

When the need for air became too vital to ignore, Emily ripped her mouth away. After she filled her starving lungs with oxygen, the pleasure crested and she cried out Jester's name.

His continued thrusts prolonged the pleasure, the orgasm

consuming her, as intense as the first one. Just when she sagged against the mattress in sated exhaustion, Jester stiffened above her, and thrust one last time before emptying himself into the condom.

He pulled out then collapsed on her, burying his face between her breasts. Completely crushed under his substantial weight, but not willing to let him move, Emily wrapped her arms around his upper back.

He stayed in place until his breathing calmed, then rolled to his side, anchoring her to him with a heavy arm and leg across her body like a longtime lover. In another world, what they shared could have been the beginning of something significant. But in this universe, it was the prelude to future heartbreak.

Neither spoke for long minutes. Jester's chest rose and fell in a steady, even rhythm against Emily's back.

Was he asleep? Should she leave?

She'd have put money on the fact that Jester did not spend the entire night with women after sex. Maybe she should wiggle out from under his arm and call a cab. The idea filled her with a sadness far more concerning than the fact that she was too tired to move.

With a mental shake, she shifted her body in an effort to worm her way out from under the large man in a sex coma trapping her to the bed. Focused on her task, she didn't realize he was awake and started when he spoke.

"Is this your way of telling me I'm squashing you?" Jester asked. He rolled her on her back and settled on top of her once again.

Her chuckled turned to a gasp when he placed a soft kiss first to her nipple, then to the side of her breast. A sigh of contentment threatened to escape at his attentive gesture, but she managed to hold it back. She needed to keep her emotions locked down. "I was just going to find my phone so I could call a cab."

Jester frowned. "Do you want to leave?"

"Well, I just assumed that's how this worked." She needed the escape. Being with him this way clouded her thinking. She had to come up with a way to get the information Snake needed, while dealing with the rising storm of her emotions.

He didn't say anything for a moment, just watched her with an expression she couldn't decipher. "Stay, Em. I'm not done with you, not near it. I'm going to want you again in a few hours, then a few hours after that, and again in the morning. Stay."

His words excited her in a way that was bound to lead to disaster. Not only did her body flare to life again, but her heart swelled with possibility. The rational part of her brain knew it was important for her to leave; there wasn't anything here but future heartbreak and pain, but the past twenty-four hours had led her to genuinely like this man.

Would it be so wrong to soak up what happiness she could while it lasted? She was almost able to convince herself that her sincere affection and desire for Jester outweighed the way she had to use him.

Hopefully, later when she thought back to this nightmarish period in her life, the hours spent getting close to Jester would be the one shiny spot. Most importantly, this closeness could lead to Jester opening up to her and sharing what, if anything, the No Prisoners had in store for the Grimm Brothers. Johnny's battered image flashed in her mind and any question about what to do evaporated. "I'll stay."

"Good." He nudged her until she was on her side, and tucked her close, with a hefty arm draped across her midsection. "We should sleep. I've got plans for you and you'll need to be well rested."

She settled against him with a dizzying combination of pleasure and guilt. None of this brought her any closer to saving Johnny. All she'd accomplished was two orgasms and a heart full of confusion. So much for uncomplicated. This was by far the most complicated mess she'd ever been mixed up in.

Chapter Nine

Emily awoke the next morning, her skin hot and sweaty like she lay next to a furnace. After a few moments, her sleep addled brain cleared enough for her to remember the night spent with the man giving off the heat. For the first time in her twenty-six years she finally understood what all the fuss was about. She smiled to herself when she recalled how insatiable they'd both been.

As promised, Jester had woken her after a few hours of sleep, entering her from behind while she lay on her side. He'd palmed her breasts and driven her to completion yet again. Afterward, he'd dragged her to the kitchen for a late night snack, which turned into another round of vigorous sex, this time on the kitchen counter.

Emily felt as though a sex-crazed alien had invaded her body and her mind. She ached all over, particularly between her legs, but found she enjoyed the physical reminder of how many times Jester had taken her.

Guilt overtook her blissful morning-after reminiscence. Thoughts of Johnny and the fear he must be experiencing invaded her mind. How could she possibly have had one of the most incredible days of her life, topped off by the most satisfying night of her life, when she was supposed to be working her ass off to help Johnny?

The devil on her shoulder told her she was doing what was asked of her, making connections, getting in with the club. They'd never reveal information to an outsider so she had to work her way in, and if that included sleeping with Jester, so be it. Her brother's life was at stake. The angel on the other side said she was taking advantage of a man who'd been nothing short of amazing to her, as well as neglecting her suffering brother.

Trapped in the middle, Emily's heart told her she was falling too hard and way too fast for a man she barely knew and had no business getting involved with. Panic flared, and constricted her chest making it difficult to draw in air.

Careful to avoid waking Jester, Emily extricated herself from under his arm—no easy feat since it was the size of a tree trunk. Naked, she rushed to the sanctuary of the bathroom to take care of business and deal with her racing thoughts.

When she was finished, she stood in front of the mirror, and her eyes widened in astonishment at the woman who stared back at her. The woman in the mirror bore signs of a night spent indulging in many forms of sexual play. Her hair was rumpled, her mouth slightly swollen and reddened, and her eyes glowed with fulfillment. She wasn't a woman Emily recognized.

The door opened and Jester burst in. He monopolized the space in the bathroom as he wrapped himself around her from behind and pressed his lips to her neck. "Morning, gorgeous. You hiding out in here?"

A shiver of delight originated under his kiss and traveled its way down her spine. "No, just needed a minute."

Their eyes met in the mirror, and he gave her a suggestive

smile she had no doubt dampened many a panty.

"I wish I had my phone in here. This would make one hell of a sexy photo. Me, so much bigger, my skin tanned and inked, wrapped all around you with your smooth, pale skin, light eyes and shiny hair. Not to mention your magnificent tits. It's sexy as fuck."

He was right. Sometime during the night his hair had come loose from its customary tie, and now fell nearly to his shoulders. One tattooed arm was banded across her stomach while the other rested over her chest, above her breasts, and his hand cupped her shoulder. The position made him look protective, feral, and mouthwatering.

"Purity and sin wound together." He smiled. "I'll let you guess which one you are."

She knew exactly which one she was, a liar and a betrayer, the sinner for sure. Certainly not purity as he mistakenly thought. But, since she was getting so good at deceiving, she smiled and played along, wishing they could be what he saw, wishing she didn't have to betray him or lose her brother.

A glimpse of something in the mirror caught Emily's notice and she gasped and shifted to get closer look. "Is that —is that a hickey on my breast?" A good-sized purplish mark marred her skin.

"Fuck yeah it is. You think I was gonna have you that many times last night without leaving my mark on you?" He snorted. "No fuckin' way babe. No other asshole is gonna get near you without seeing my mark."

Exasperated, she turned in his arms and frowned up at him. "Jester, it's on my breast. We already established my lack of experience. Who the heck is ever going to see it?"

A smug smile appeared on his handsome face. "Oh, well, that one's just for me because I couldn't resist, and it makes me hard looking at it. But I was referring to the one on your neck."

"What?" She spun back around, and leaned closer to the mirror. Sure enough another hickey screamed for attention at the base of her neck. "What are you? A Neanderthal?"

"Damn straight." With a laugh he gave her a playful swat on the ass. "Now get dressed. I'm sure you're sore as shit, and if I spend one more minute around your naked body I won't be held responsible for my actions."

Emily scooted out of the bathroom, hunting and pecking around the room for her discarded clothing. She needed a shower, but it could wait. It was time for her to go, to get away and put everything that happened in the past forty-eight hours into perspective.

Within minutes, Jester emerged from the bathroom, still gloriously naked. "You want to hang here today? I gotta work at the garage for a few hours, but I'm free later." He stretched and scratched at his chest.

Emily forced herself to focus on her task of getting dressed and not ogle him. She needed space and time to think. Maybe she should stay, she could snoop around his house, but she had the distinct impression no club information would be found here. "Actually I have a bunch of errands to run. I need to...uh...get a few things for my apartment." That was believable.

"You need help with it? I can't skip work today, but I can send a prospect to help you with any heavy lifting."

The offer warmed her heart. This would be so much easier if he'd turned out to be a jerk. If he was just another Snake. "Not necessary. I already have most of the big things. Would you mind dropping me at my hou—uh, apartment?" Jesus, she needed to be more careful.

"Sure, if you promise to meet up with me later."

Emily paused. This would be the perfect opportunity to

pull back a bit, put the brakes on this runaway train before it flew right off the side of the cliff. But as she looked at the stunning man who not only gave her such physical pleasure, but also seemed to be stepping out of character by asking to see her again, she couldn't deny him. "I'd love to."

~ ~ ~ ~

After seeing Emily safely to her shitty apartment, Jester rode straight to the garage that occupied the same lot as the No Prisoners' clubhouse. He had a big job coming due in the next week, and needed to put in a few solid hours of work today.

Jester specialized in custom paint jobs for cars and bikes. He was meticulous, demanding perfection of himself in his work, and had made quite a name for himself among auto enthusiasts. On more than one occasion he'd been commissioned to do work for cars featured in big screen movies.

Wealthy collectors and racers, of both cars and motorcycles, contracted most of the jobs he completed. He loved it. It was the perfect outlet for the artistic side of him that had never found the ideal medium to express itself. At one point he'd seriously considered becoming a tattoo artist —he'd designed nearly all the ink he wore—but while he enjoyed coming up with designs, he found he didn't care for the endless hours bent over some punk kid who wanted his girlfriend's name on his leg.

Currently, he was working on a bike that Striker had just finished restoring. A twenty something wealthy software mogul from the Silicon Valley with a thrill seeking side had crashed his Ducati in a race the year before. After a month in a coma, he was told not to expect much in terms of regaining his function and independence. Well, the guy showed everybody, and one year later, he was back to doing just about everything he'd done before.

Jester was in the middle of airbrushing a phoenix on the bike, symbolizing rebirth, pretty fitting for this client. The color palate was amazing, swirls of reds, golds and fiery oranges. He was really pleased with his progress so far.

Until today.

Today his concentration was shit. Visions of Emily's eyes, Emily's lips, Emily's unbelievable tits flashed through his mind like a sexual slideshow. Beyond the occasional, *ah she was a good fuck* thought, he didn't dwell on his conquests once they were concluded. He fucked them, enjoyed himself in the moment, then moved on to the next. On the odd occasion it was good enough to warrant a repeat performance, but even then he didn't fantasize about them all day long.

Now, he mooned over Emily like a lovesick teenage girl lusting after her favorite boy band. Disgusted with himself, he tried to purge thoughts of Emily's tight pussy milking his cock from his mind so he could accomplish some work today.

A sharp slap to his shoulder drew him out of his fantasy, and killed the boner that had begun to swell. With a muttered curse, Jester yanked the headphones off his ears, and shut off the airbrush machine before he peered up to see who interrupted him. He had to resist the urge to roll his eyes when he saw it was Colt who loomed over him. They hadn't spoken since Jester warned him off Emily.

"What do you want Colt?"

"I wanted to ask you about that chick you were with the other night."

From the corner of his eye Jester saw Hook and Striker stop working and tune into the conversation. "What about her?"

"She was a pretty hot piece. I was wondering if you were

done with her yet?"

Jester froze. He didn't want to clue Colt into his muddled thoughts, but was also unwilling to accept Colt thinking he could move in on Emily. "No, I'm not." His jaw ached with the force it took to refrain from saying more.

"She any good? Sometimes bitches that hot think you'll do all the work, and they can just lie there and look pretty. Know what I mean, brother?"

Colt looked like an overgrown little boy. Shaggy platinum hair sat atop his head, which also boasted a round, baby face. He was one of the youngest to patch in, just turning twenty-one three days before he finished prospecting. Rule was, you could prospect before your twenty-first birthday, but couldn't patch in.

Problem with Colt was that aside from looking like a child, he had proven to behave like one on more than one occasion, something Jester had no tolerance for. He'd been a heartbeat away from voting against him, but didn't want to be the only reason the man didn't patch into the MC.

Jester spun on this stool, stood to his full height, which was a good eight or nine inches taller than Colt, and leveled him with a stare that made most men question their next move. "What she is, is none of your fuckin' business, Colt. Got me?" The venomous tone of Jester's voice matched his pissed off stance.

Colt was either too cocky to care or too stupid to notice because he continued to run his mouth. "Hey, brother, chill out. I can wait. Plenty of fish out there in the meantime. Mind letting me know when you toss her back though? My dick gets hard every time I think about those sweet tits." He held his hands out in front of his chest demonstrating a huge rack.

Jester's vision went red at the thought of Colt getting near any part of the seductive body he'd explored all night. He lunged forward intent on grabbing Colt by the throat. Satisfaction rose sharp and swift when Colt's eyes bugged as he finally realized how furious Jester was.

Striker inserted himself between the two men, one snarling and the other grinning, and slapped a hand against each man's chest. "Colt! Shut the fuck up before Jester rips out your throat."

With a self-satisfied smirk, Colt raised his hands in surrender, and stepped backward out of the garage. "My bad. She must have some magic pussy to have your dick all tied in knots. You usually go through women like Acer goes through hair gel."

"What the fuck, man? Don't drag me into your shit. You may have a death wish, but I sure as hell don't." Acer grumbled from across the garage. He was a trust fund baby, came from some serious old family money. While he was prospecting, he'd tried everything to shed the wealthy, pretty boy reputation. He got tattoo after tattoo, wore chains and leather and adopted a *fuck off* attitude toward the world. Didn't matter. He still looked rich, something about the way he carried himself and spoke.

Acer was a bit of an enigma. He never talked about the real reason he'd left the white collar fold to join the MC. Jester had a feeling Striker knew, but both men remained tightlipped. Acer could do some scary shit with a computer, and rumor had it he was the proud owner of a computer programming degree from Harvard, but no sane man would ask him about it. He tended to get a bit testy when you brought up his past.

Despite his departure from the ivory tower, Acer still liked some of the finer things in life. He looked like a rich boy, with impeccable blond hair, good posture, perfect teeth, and the man kept some damn expensive liquor in his house.

"Colt, I'm gonna let him at you in five seconds, so you better get your ass out of here." Striker gave Colt a look that should have shut his mouth, but Colt's laughter trailed behind him as he left the clubhouse.

"Fucking child," Jester muttered, turning back to his work. He glanced over his shoulder at the three other men who stared at him with amused expressions. With a sigh, he gave up on being productive. "All right, get it the fuck over with."

Acer spoke up first, his enjoyment of Jester's discomfort evident in the way he rubbed his hands together. "I don't even know who the hell he's talking about, but I'm intrigued. Cupid been shootin' arrows your way, brother?"

Jester snorted. "I'm gonna knock that smug grin off your face if you don't shut up."

"Hmmm." Acer continued, undeterred, "Turning it around to be about me, classic avoidance behavior, boys."

Striker and Hook laughed, but wisely kept their thoughts to themselves.

"Acer, you can take that fancy college degree and shove it right up your ass," Jester said. "Told you once before if you tried to psychoanalyze me I'd take you out back and show you exactly how I deal with my shit."

"Okay, man, I'll lay off. Not like it matters anyway, since once she catches a glimpse of me, you'll be watching her walk away."

Jester ignored the teasing, not about to start vomiting his feelings all over the garage floor. Hell, he didn't even know what he was feeling at this point. He'd spent his entire adult life, and, let's face it, much of his teens, bouncing from one chick to the next. It wasn't so much that he didn't want to get to know a woman on a deeper level, but he liked sex and liked variety so there wasn't any point in sticking around.

This time, though he just wasn't ready to end it. He liked Emily. A lot. Both in bed and out of bed, though all he could think about at the moment was getting back inside her as soon as possible. That was pretty much as far as he'd thought it through in his head and as far as he was going to think it through at this point. Holding a high standing position in his club and dealing with the Grimm Brothers sucked up much of his time. Carving out a slot for all the demands that came with a woman wasn't something he was interested in.

"Jesus, Striker, I thought him bringing her to brunch was serious. Now he's sitting there all lost in his fuckin' thoughts." Hook howled with laughter. "He just might be a goner."

"He brought her to brunch?" Acer's voice was laden with exaggerated disbelief. "Woohoo. Is it even possible to be pussy whipped after just two days? Maybe Jester will set some kind of record. Fastest a woman has ever brought a man to heel. What do you think, guys?"

Jester chucked his airbrush onto a tool cart, disgusted with his inability to concentrate and finished being the butt of their taunts. "Fuck you all." He grumbled as he stomped out of the garage toward the clubhouse in search of a drink. Maybe if he drank her out of his mind he'd actually get something accomplished today.

Chapter Ten

Emily stared down at the menu, not paying attention to the words, and not sure why she was in the restaurant in a first place. She'd spent the past two hours sitting in her car outside her house in Sandy Springs. Despite her initial plan to go in her home and get some thinking done, she couldn't force herself to go in a second time. The quick trip she'd made for a few weeks' worth of clothes, toiletries, and other necessities following the No Prisoners' party had been bad enough. Snake poisoned her house, and if she entered it, she'd only be greeted by Johnny's blood on the carpet once again, so she stayed in the car writing out questions to ask Jester. She phrased and rephrased hundreds of questions and scripts looking for a believable way to get information without giving herself up.

She'd also tried to work up a list of alternative ideas. Things she could offer Snake in exchange for Johnny's life. So far all she'd come up with was selling her house to pay Johnny's debts. Couldn't hurt to try.

Now she sat at an outdoor table, part of a trendy new organic café that had opened a few months back in the small downtown area of Crystal Rock. It had been on her list to try, and seeing as how she was procrastinating going to her depressing apartment, now seemed like the perfect time to test it out. But as she watched the letters on the menu swim in front of her eyes, she realized what she'd really been hoping to escape were her swirling thoughts. Unfortunately, they seemed to have joined her in the restaurant.

Her phone buzzed from its position on the table next to the menu. As though connected to the phone, her heart rate kicked up, and the butterflies in her stomach did a happy dance at the thought it might be Jester. This was not good. She needed to maintain an emotional distance, and was completely failing.

She peeked at the phone. "Shit." Her stomach, which had been happily fluttering seconds ago, dipped with nausea and anxiety. Snake's name appeared on the screen with a message that read, *Tick tock, Emily. Any information for me? Poor Johnny's counting on you.*

Emily's vision swam with tears she furiously blinked away. There wasn't anything to report, and she wasn't even sure how to begin to obtain the information Snake wanted. All she had so far was a newfound craving for sex and a mess of emotions that muddied her thinking.

With her phone in her lap to ensure no one peeked over her shoulder, she tapped out a response. *Made contact. No info yet, but they seem to trust me. Please tell me if Johnny is okay.*

It vibrated in her lap just seconds later. *Fast work. You must have some skills. Johnny's fine. Uncomfortable, but fine.*

She ignored the sexual innuendo. *I have money I can give you to pay what Johnny owes. If you let him go you can have it.* It wasn't entirely true, but she could get it if she sold her house. He couldn't possibly owe Snake as much as a house, could he?

It vibrated again, but before she could read the text, a voice she recognized rang out.

"Emily? Oh my goodness, hi!"

She shoved the phone deep into her purse and looked up, genuinely pleased to see Lila standing next to her table. "Lila! How nice to run into you. Won't you please join me?"

"You sure? I'd love to chat but don't want to interrupt you." Lila gave her a warm smile.

"I'd really love it if you would. I could use a distraction from what's rattling around in my head."

Lila sat in the empty metal chair across from Emily while the hostess placed a menu in her hands. "Have you eaten here before? This is one of my favorite places to come for lunch."

Lila wore scrubs, and Emily assumed she was on her lunch break. "No, I haven't been here yet. What's good?"

"Oh gosh, everything." Lila groaned. "But my favorite is the grilled veggie sandwich on ciabatta. It has a pesto mayonnaise and goat cheese. Oh it's so good." She laughed at herself. "This is not Striker's kind of place, so I usually come with my coworkers."

"Well, that sounds delicious. I think I'll take your recommendation." The waitress stopped at their table, and they each ordered the grilled veggie sandwich with iced teas. She tried to imagine Jester in this restaurant and had to agree with Lila; its hippie, natural vibe wasn't quite biker approved. While they waited for their meals, they made small talk and got to know each other a bit.

They didn't have to wait long for their food. Emily bit into the sandwich with a hum as the smoky flavor of the grilled vegetables permeated her senses. Lila was spot on; the sandwich was delicious.

"So, Emily, now that we got the chit chat out of the way, I'm going to dive on in." Lila still wore a friendly smile on her face, but Emily knew her reprieve was over. This woman wanted to know what Emily had in store for her friend. "You said you'd like some distraction from your thoughts. I know we just met, but I hope you'll soon be able to consider me a friend. If you need to get some of those thoughts out in the open I'm more than willing to lend an ear."

Emily studied her for a moment. Lila appeared sincere, genuinely interested in what was happening with her, and not just about to give her the *I'll kill you if you hurt my friend* speech. She was so alone in this quest to bail out Johnny, and could use a friend, even if she couldn't give Lila any real details. Plus, maybe she could learn something useful about the club from the vice president's woman.

The thought of using Lila's generous offer of friendship against her made Emily feel dirty, but the alternative was Johnny's death, and that wasn't something she'd allow if she had any power to prevent it.

Emily took a fortifying breath. "I'm just feeling a bit overwhelmed. I went to that party because I'm new in town and didn't know anyone. I met Trixie and she talked me into it. Bikers are not my normal crowd, and I never in a million years expected to meet a man I was interested in at a party like that. I mean, aren't they criminals?" With a grimace, she realized she might have upset Lila by criticizing her friends and family. "Oh my gosh, Lila, I'm sorry. My head is all mixed up right now. Please know I didn't intend any offense."

Lila laughed and waved it away. "Honey, they weren't my crowd either. I was raised in Washington DC. I'm the daughter of..." She paused, seeming to consider what she wanted to say to Emily. "Okay, I'm going to trust you with something that doesn't leave this table. There are only a handful of people who know this."

Intrigued, Emily nodded. "I'll absolutely keep your confidences, Lila. I would also like us to be friends." Guilt crept up her back and settled on her shoulders, a heavy weight.

With a quick glance around, Lila leaned in. "My father just announced his intentions to run for governor of Maryland." She kept her voice low, and after dropping that bomb she leaned back and watched Emily.

Emily opened her mouth to speak, closed it, and opened it again. Lila chuckled and nodded at her. "True story."

"That is not anywhere in the realm of what I thought you were going to say."

"Well, now you know that these guys were nothing at all like what I was used to." She shrugged. "Now they're family, everything to me."

"Jester is just so…huge in so many ways."

One of Lila's eyebrows rose. "Reeeally?" She drew out the word in an evocative manner.

Picking up on what she said, Emily laughed and covered her face as it flamed. "I did not mean *that*. I meant his personality, his height, and his whole presence. Oh, hell… that too."

With a crack of laughter, Lila fanned herself with her napkin. "Trust me, Emily, I know how intense that aspect of these men can be. And I noticed that mark on your neck. My advice?" She winked and smiled. "Enjoy every damn second."

"I sure have so far." Emily's face burned and her hand flew to her neck. So much for her makeup job. "I can't believe I'm running my mouth to you like this. You must think I sound like a moron."

Lila stopped laughing and grew serious. "I think you caught Jester's eye, and that makes you pretty special. You're right, he's an intimidating and overwhelming man, but he's the best. He's loyal, protective, and trustworthy. You'll find that out soon enough."

Emily sipped her tea to stall before she delved into dangerous territory. "I've only been here for a few weeks, but I came because a college friend of mine told me about the area. She used to live in Sandy Springs." Emily swallowed the nausea generated by the lie. Part of what she worked on while sitting in her car earlier was her cover story. It was all on paper, tucked away in her purse. "She always told me she liked living there except for the motorcycle club in that town. I think she called them the Grimm Brothers. The stories she had were terrifying. Are they, um, are they friends with the No Prisoners?"

Lila's whole demeanor changed. She closed in on herself, leaned back in her chair, and crossed her arms as a haunted look entered her eyes. "They aren't friends at all. They're enemies, and the Grimm Brothers are a dangerous enemy to have, unfortunately. If you ever come across any of them, you need to tell Jester immediately. In fact, try to stay out of Sandy Springs as much as possible. The clubs aren't the same, not at all. The Grimm Brothers are evil, plain and simple. While I won't bullshit you and tell you the No Prisoners are choir boys, I can tell you with one hundred percent certainty they are nothing like the Grimm Brothers."

Emily nodded and stared down at her uneaten meal. The first bite had been delicious, but the second was like sawdust in her mouth. Her appetite fled the moment Lila told her to stay out of Sandy Springs.

Lila dropped her voice again. "Striker and I were ambushed by the Grimm Brothers last year riding from the clubhouse to our home. Six Grimms stopped us on the road, threatened us, roughed up Striker a bit, and Snake, their president, took me as collateral until some issues were resolved."

Emily's heart went out to Lila. She knew firsthand the fear Snake could instill. That fear had been with her for days. "Oh, Lila, that must have been terrifying. Were you hurt?"

She shook her head and stared off to the side. "No, thankfully. Anyway, it's long over, but I just want you to know that the two clubs are nothing alike."

Emily was torn. Part of her, the woman who'd just given her body to a man who made her feel things physically and emotionally that she'd never experienced before, was thrilled to hear Lila thought so highly of Jester. The other part of her, the part that had to sell him out to Snake, almost wished he was a monster. "Do you know a lot about what the No Prisoners do, business wise?"

Emily held her breath while Lila took her time answering. The question may have been too nosey. If Lila grew suspicious she might pass her concerns along to Striker. "I just, um," she rushed to explain. "I find them fascinating. And now that Jester and I are…whatever we are, I want to know as much about his life as I can."

"No, I don't know much, at least not details." Lila sighed. "I'm going to give you some important advice." She took a sip of her tea. "Don't expect Jester to let you in on much club business or secrets, now or ever. These guys are very protective of family, and once you're in the fold, you're considered family."

Emily's heart sank as she listened to Lila. The chances of getting any information directly from someone in the club sounded next to impossible. She'd have to find another way.

"Well, I need to get back to the hospital before they send a search party out for me." Lila stood and placed a few bills on the table. She met Emily's eye. "I'm really glad we had the chance to chat. Hopefully what I told you will help ease your mind. Enjoy the rest of your day, I'm sure I'll be seeing you soon."

"Thank you, Lila." Emily stood and embraced her before wishing her a good day.

Her phone buzzed again, reminding her she had an unread text from Snake. She stared at her purse as though the phone might attack when she reached for it. Snake's answer to her request to pay him off awaited her. "Suck it up and look, Emily," she muttered to herself as she reached in her leather handbag and pulled out the phone.

Nice try.

That was it. Nothing else. She dropped the phone to the table and stared down at the unfinished plate. Hot tears flooded her eyes. Deep breaths in and out helped to keep them at bay.

"Excuse me, miss, are you all right?"

Emily jumped and looked up at the waiter. Her mouth felt hot and dry. "Yes, um, I'm fine, thank you for asking. May I please have the check?"

"I'll be right back with it."

The phone buzzed against the table.

Conflicting emotions swamped her when she read Jester's name on the screen. Part of her was thrilled he'd contacted her, while another part of her had been hoping Snake had changed his mind. It was a long shot, but if he would have taken money, Emily would have sold her house in a heartbeat.

Can't focus for shit today. Keep thinking about how tight your pussy felt around my dick. I'll swing by to get you in three hours. Pack a bag.

Emily's mouth dropped open as she reread the text. She'd never been around anyone as free and confident with their sexuality as Jester. And why shouldn't he be confident? He certainly had the goods, and the skills to back it up.

As Emily read the text for the third time, she reached for

her iced tea. Suddenly the air felt hotter than it had only seconds before. She was also wet, again. Jester could turn her on like nothing else. Emboldened by his obvious desire for her, she typed out a response. *If you thought last night was hot, you should know I'm not wearing panties...*

Not true, but it was fun to play with him.

Christ woman, you'll pay for that. I'm rock hard in a garage full of men.

Emily laughed out loud which drew the attention of the few other diners eating on the patio.

Three hours and she'd get more of the pleasure from last night. Three hours until she'd be alone again with the man who had the information she needed to save Johnny's life. Emily pushed her plate away. There was no way she could stomach any more food.

Chapter Eleven

Jester groaned in satisfaction and flopped to his back, taking Emily with him. She lay sprawled over him, her head nestled in the crook between his neck and shoulder. Legs intertwined, they remained silent for long moments, allowing their breathing to normalize.

The heat of her pussy around his bare cock was incendiary; there was no way in hell he'd ever wear a rubber inside her again. Hours ago they'd had the conversation. Emily was on birth control, and he'd never gone bareback before. The chicks who hung around the club weren't exactly clean and couldn't be trusted. The orgasm he had without the rubber nearly melted his brain.

Emily didn't speak for long enough that Jester assumed she'd fallen asleep. Christ, he liked the feel of her naked body entangled with his. Soft breasts were cushioned against the hard wall of his chest, and her slender, yet strong arms held tight around his body.

She startled him when in a drowsy voice she asked, "Don't you think it's about time you told me your real name? And how you got your nickname?" She lifted her head so she could see his face as she spoke and he smiled down at her.

"Hmmm, I'm not sure we know each other well enough yet." Teasing her was becoming one of his favorite activities.

"Jester, we've spent the better part of the last week naked together. I think we know each other well enough."

He didn't quite agree. Emily was guarded when it came to sharing information about her life and it didn't resonate well with him. She'd been introduced to all of the important people in his life, and she hadn't so much as hinted at a friend or family member on her side.

He'd promised her, and himself, uncomplicated, so he shouldn't give a shit what she talked about, but he did. "I'll make you a deal babe. I'll tell you my name and how I came to be Jester if you answer two questions for me as well."

Emily stiffened. It was impossible to miss, but it didn't last long. In two heartbeats time she was back in the game. "Okay, sure, two questions all around. Sounds fair to me." Her voice wasn't as confident as the words.

Still looking down at her he grinned his approval. "Let's see, my name, I need to think about it for a minute. No one's called me by it in so long I think I forgot it."

"Come on!" Emily gave him a playful pinch on his stomach. There wasn't much to grab so it wasn't very effective and he swore he heard her mutter, "Stupid six-pack," under her breath.

Chuckling, he conceded. "My name is Mason, Mason Sterling."

"Mason? Seriously?"

He laughed. "Yes, babe. Seriously."

"Huh."

"Huh what?"

She peered up at him with a sheepish look on her face. "Sorry, but there's no way I could ever call you that. Nothing against the name. Mason is a good name. It is just not at all a name that fits you. It's not...hmm." She traced a tattoo on his chest as she thought.

"Crazy enough?" He tugged her hair.

"No, no, it's not big enough. You are an imposing character, Jester. You're insanely tall, your personality is substantial, and you have so many giant, hard, sexy muscles that..." She laughed at herself. "Okay, once I started thinking about your muscles I completely forgot the point I was trying to make was."

She was hilarious. Jester couldn't believe how much fun he had just talking with Emily. Aside from his friends' wives, the sum total of his conversations with women usually entailed, "Top or bottom?" With Emily, he not only craved her body, but he found himself eager to be with her at all times. At least ten times a day he made mental notes to remember to share something with her. "You were talking about my giant and hard body parts."

"Ha, you do have a few of those. I'm done talking. Somewhere in there I was supposed to prove how the name didn't fit you."

He nodded. "That's probably because it's literally been over ten years since anyone has referred to me as Mason."

"Where did Jester come from?"

He groaned. "It's a really dumb story. You know I like to joke around a lot, pull pranks and shit, bag on everybody?"

With exaggerated disbelief Emily gasped and her face took on a feigned look of shock. "You do? I must not be paying enough attention, because I didn't pick up on that at all."

"You want to hear the story or not, smartass?" He pinched her on the rear, much more effectively than she'd pinched him, and she yelped out a giggle. He smoothed his hand over the sting, any excuse to get his hand on her luscious ass.

"Anyway, I bought this coffee pot after I moved in my then apartment, and the thing didn't fit under my counter, so I had to return it. I dragged Acer and Hook with me to the store to get my money back. The clerk behind the return counter was this pissed off looking old hag, so I decided to have a little fun with her." He smirked recalling the day.

"Oh, the poor woman. Please don't tell me you did anything to scar her for life."

"Shush, I did no such thing. I made up some elaborate story, to be honest I can't even remember all the details anymore, maybe Acer does. That guy's got a memory like a steel trap. I do remember I delivered it with an Oscar quality performance. The story was something about how I had a Great Dane who was the perfect height to turn the machine off, and I could never have a cup of coffee because he turned it off every time I tried to brew some."

At Emily's skeptical look Jester laughed. "I told you the story was dumb."

"You were right."

"Gee thanks. Anyway the ol' battle-axe looked me up and down with her stern wrinkly face and disapproving eyes and said, 'Surely you jest, sonny.'" Jester mimicked an aged female voice. "And that was that. Acer took the story and ran it right back to the club. I was a prospect at the time, and Jester was born."

"Well, it's more you than Mason is." She shook her head. "How did you get involved with the No Prisoners?"

"Uh uh, that's a third question. You willing to pay the price?"

She hesitated and Jester began to wonder if there was something in her past, or hell maybe in her life now, that was causing her trouble. Maybe something she was ashamed of. Why else would she be so hesitant to share? He'd have to find a way to draw it out of her. "Okay, yes, I am."

Interesting.

"I moved here with my old man when I was sixteen. My mom passed the year before so it was just us boys. He was a violent, drunken asshole. I'd been obsessed with motorcycles since before I could ride a tricycle, the love of bikes was the one good thing I inherited from my old man. Anyway I started hanging around at the clubhouse, helping with shit, running errands etc. Shiv took pity on me. When I was old enough, I prospected. That's all she wrote."

He didn't bother to tell her that his dad had borrowed money from the club, money he never intended to pay back. He got worked over real good, and sank even further into a drunk and drugged out state, completely unable to care or provide for his teenage son.

They'd never spoken about it, but Jester was pretty sure that was the reason Shiv let him hang around at such a young age. He was beyond grateful. The club had become his family and they had one hundred percent of his loyalty.

"That satisfy your curiosity, baby?"

Emily nodded.

"Good. My turn to ask the questions." Was it his imagination, or did she tense and shift away from him a fraction of an inch?

~ ~ ~ ~

Emily swallowed down her nerves, praying Jester wouldn't ask her anything she would have to lie too badly about. The thought of being further dishonest with him made her stomach clench and her head throb. She'd already decided to keep any information she gave him as close to the truth as possible. For one thing, it would be easier to keep her story straight if she wasn't making up wild tales, and maybe when this was over, he could find some comfort in the knowledge that she told him as much of the truth as she felt she could.

"Well, what would you like to know?" Despite the impending doom of their future, she loved being with him like this, their bodies drained and sated while they quietly spoke well into the night. It was an intimacy she'd never shared with a man before, and she found it both comforting and arousing.

"You never mention any of the people in your life. Do you have family, friends?" The look in his eye was one of genuine interest, not nosy curiosity or mistrust. It helped to relax her. Maybe it would be okay to share a little of the truth with him without putting herself at any further risk.

"My parents died when I was eighteen. Car accident. A drunk driver hit them as they were coming back from some work dinner of my father's. They were only two miles from our house." She shook her head and lowered her eyes, a familiar sadness swamping her. It surged whenever she recalled that time in her life, which she tried not to do often.

"Jesus, baby, I'm sorry." Jester brought his arm up to stroke her hair and down her back, providing more comfort than she'd received from another human being in the eight years since their passing.

"It was a long time ago now, but I do have a brother. He's five years younger than I am."

Shit! Why did she say that? She'd meant to leave out any mention of Johnny. When this was over, and she was gone, she didn't want the No Prisoners to know about him. Jester may be a generous and attentive lover, but he'd make a deadly enemy.

Jester's powerful hand caressed her bare back and she wanted to purr like a contented kitten. Unfortunately, her racing thoughts won out over her desires.

"Where is he?"

Emily's mind spun and she shrugged. "Still in…um… Colorado, where I moved from. We're not that close." The lie tasted bitter in her mouth. Denying him when he needed her most felt wrong, even if it was to protect him. She wanted to spill every last detail to Jester and beg for his help, but she was too afraid. Johnny wasn't an innocent victim in all this. He was a prospect for the Grimm Brothers. The risk of coming clean was too high. "So there's one answer. Next question?"

He was silent for a moment and she held her breath. Did he not believe her?

"Why did you move here?"

This she could handle. This she'd prepared for. "I was spinning my wheels in L—uh, Colorado. The school I worked at underwent major budget cuts, and since I was one of the younger teachers, I was laid off. A college friend of mine grew up around here, and I was always intrigued by what she told me of the desert, so here I am."

Short, sweet, succinct. Maybe too succinct, if Jester's raised eyebrow was any indication. Again, he remained silent for a minute. Did he believe a word of it? The story was so flimsy she could tear it in half with her bare hands.

"I know it's summer, but do you have a job lined up for the fall?"

There it was, a sliver of an opening, a window cracked open just an inch, but it was more than she'd had so far. "I have an offer at an elementary school in Sandy Springs." She'd taught there since she and Johnny moved to the area. She loved that school and the staff that worked there. "I'd really like to take it, but I'm not sure. I've heard the town has some trouble with, uh, well, with their own MC."

She bit her lip and waited for his reaction. It was swift and fierce. Jester sat straight up and she tumbled off his body. He turned to stare down at her, an angry scowl on his face. "There is no fucking way you're working in Sandy Springs."

Ookay...that was not what she expected. "What? Why not?" She sat up as well, not that it put them on an even level; he still towered over her. The sheet fell to her waist and she pulled it back up. Having this discussion naked left her too vulnerable.

Jester placed his hands on the bed, caging her against the headboard, and leaned his face close to hers. "It doesn't matter why not, it's just the way it is." Warmth and teasing were completely absent from his voice.

Despite the ferocious look on his face, Emily laughed out loud. "I'm sorry, what?" She should probably be intimidated by him in this moment, but she found it so ridiculous that he felt he could order her around after knowing her for a week. "If there's a real reason you think I shouldn't work there, I'm more than willing to listen, but you're going to have to do better than 'because I said so.'"

Some of the tension seeped out of his shoulders and he rested his forehead against hers. "You do realize that most of the MC steers clear of me when I make that face, don't you?"

"Guess I don't find you that scary." She rubbed a hand up his firm inked arm.

Jester snorted and tugged at the sheet covering her breasts. She allowed him to draw it away from her body, and her eyes drifted closed when he traced a thumb around one nipple. It stiffened immediately. She was so easy when it came to him.

"I can't, and if I'm being honest, won't, give you details about it, because I don't want you tainted by that world. Sandy Springs does have problems with their MC. The Grimm Brothers. We hate them as much as they hate us. They are a group of sadistic motherfuckers who wouldn't

106

blink an eye at harming you if they thought there was a sliver of a chance it would hurt me or the No Prisoners. I wouldn't be able to function if you were spending all day in Sandy Springs. It's their turf, we have no power or control there."

"Jester—"

He cupped her face between his hands and kissed her, hard. "I know it's crazy, baby. We've known each other a week, but I need you to trust me on this. Please don't take a job in Sandy Springs."

Her heart ached so bad she almost couldn't speak. The lies wouldn't matter. She needed to remember that. In another week she'd never see him again and none of this would matter. Johnny would be safe and that's what did matter. "Okay, I won't take the job."

"Thank you, Em. Lila knows quite a few people on the school board here in Crystal Rock. I bet she could get you an interview, easy."

"Sure, thank you." She wanted to cry. Why couldn't she have met him under different circumstances? Why couldn't Johnny have stayed away from drugs?

"It's getting late, let's just get some sleep. You've been wearing me out, I need to recharge." Jester laid back on the bed, drawing her down next to him.

She forced a laugh and tried to get back to where she'd been before they started talking about her job. "That's because you're so much older than I am."

He scoffed, "No way. I bet I'm not that much older than you."

She raised an eyebrow at him. "How old are you?"

"Thirty-seven, you?"

"Twenty-six." She chuckled as his features transformed into a look of astonishment.

"You're shittin' me! Eleven years? I'm eleven years older

107

than you? I didn't realize you were *that* young. Huh, I'm practically robbing the cradle."

Emily shoved down the last of her sadness and tweaked his nipple. "How old did you think I was? And I'll advise you to think before you answer."

A playful growl erupted from Jester's massive chest and he rolled her to her back, hovering over her with a hand on each nipple. "That how you want to play, baby?" He pinched her nipples, giving just enough pressure to have electricity shooting directly to her clit.

She gasped and pushed her hips against him as a punch of desire slammed into her. "I'm not playing anything. Oh God." Her eyes rolled back in her head as he increased the pressure on her nipples. "I'm…just…ah…saying, thatyou'reold!" The last part came out in a rush as he bent his head and lightly raked his teeth over one nipple.

"I'll show you old, missy." He rumbled, sliding into her in one fierce thrust.

"Oh!" She cried out, a mixture of shock and pleasure.

"Ain't nothing old about this, baby." Jester pulled out and pushed in, starting a heavy rhythm.

Emily gave herself over to the power of their connection. She wanted to forget about dead parents and MCs, drugs and everything she needed to do and hadn't been able to yet. She wanted to feel peace, even if just for a few minutes.

Chapter Twelve

The next afternoon Emily sat at her kitchen table staring at her cell phone. Snake had texted her earlier in the morning, saying he'd be calling to discuss their business around noon. Jester was due by to pick her up around two and she was relieved that she didn't have to make up a reason to delay him.

Her fingers drummed on the table at the same time her right foot tapped out an anxious rhythm on the floor. She was no closer to finding out any club business. Did Snake know this would be an impossible task? Was it all part of his plan? Play with her until she failed, then kill Johnny? Nausea swamped her and she breathed through her nose to calm herself.

The shrill ring of the phone caused her heart to skip a beat even though she'd been expecting it. "Hello?" She answered before the first ring ended.

"Hello, sweet Emily. What'd ya got for me?" His voice gave her chills and she rubbed her free hand over a bare arm.

"I...I'm not going to speak to you until I talk to my brother." Her voice shook, betraying her nerves.

He laughed and she wanted to throw the phone across the room, but that would only anger him. "Emily, I think you watch too much TV. You don't have any power here. I hold all the cards and you'll jump when I tell you to."

She pinched her eyes tight and held her breath, determined to speak to Johnny. As the seconds slipped by in dreadful silence her resolve began to slip. Just as she opened her mouth to speak, Snake beat her to it.

"All right, Emily. What could a little chat with your idiot brother hurt? Here he is. You have thirty seconds."

"Emmie?" Johnny's voice sounded so dejected she wanted to cry.

"Johnny, are you okay?" Tears thickened her voice, but she refused to let them fall. She had to be strong for him. She'd always been the strong one, the one he could depend upon. And he needed her to be that now, more than ever.

"Emmie, listen to me. You have to get out of town. Forget about me. It's not worth it. Snake won't—" His voice disappeared, replaced by a thud and a low moan.

Emily couldn't prevent the cry of distress from leaving her throat.

"Satisfied? You got what you wanted, now give me what I want." Snake's voice replaced Johnny's.

Emily started to shake. The situation was beginning to seem hopeless. "I—" She choked on a sob. "I don't have anything yet. You have to know they don't tell women any club details."

"Then I suggest you fuck someone. Men tend to let things slip when their dick's are happy."

Not Jester.

Snake laughed when she didn't respond. "No? Well, I guess you better get creative. Break into the clubhouse at night. I don't give a shit how you do it, but you have a little under a week to get it done."

He hung up without waiting for a response and Emily dropped her forehead to the table. Break into the clubhouse. If the situation wasn't so dire, she might have laughed. First of all, she'd have a hell of a time getting away from Jester for one night, the man wanted her with him all the time. Secondly, she wouldn't have a clue how to break into the clubhouse.

Emily wouldn't allow her mind to fathom what they would do to her if she was caught in the clubhouse when she wasn't supposed to be. Breaking in was out of the question, but maybe she'd be able to find a time when no one else was around and do a little snooping. It was so risky, she didn't want to entertain the idea, but her options narrowed by the second.

She stood and paced the apartment, her breath coming in shallow pants. All of a sudden the room spun and her chest tightened to the point of constricting her breathing. On shaking legs, she stumbled to the den and sat on the couch, bending her head forward to rest between her knees.

After a few moments of forcing one slow, deep inhalation after another, the panic attack subsided. She was going to need therapy, or maybe medication if she survived this. A glance at the clock on the DVD player revealed there was still over an hour until Jester was scheduled to arrive. No way she could wait in this state of stress for an hour.

Emily stood and stripped off her shirt and pants, leaving her clad only in a sports bra and bikini panties. She grabbed the remote control and turned on the television. Her favorite yoga DVD was still in the machine. Physical exertion was exactly what she needed to calm her nerves and give her mind a chance to think of a plan and not just of how terrified she was.

~ ~ ~ ~

At one thirty, Jester jogged up the cracked concrete steps toward Emily's hole of an apartment. He hadn't been inside yet, but he was astounded she lived in this complex. Surely as a teacher she made enough money to rent in a safer and slightly more upscale neighborhood, didn't she?

Maybe the move drained her finances. She didn't act like someone who was acutely worried about paying the bills. But she did act like someone who hated sharing personal information. He shouldn't make assumptions about her financial situation when he really didn't know that much about her life.

For the foreseeable future, she'd be staying nights at his house. He made that executive decision on the ride to her place. While whatever this was between them lasted, he wanted to spend every spare second of his day with some part of his anatomy deep inside her. There was no way he was staying in this dump when he had a perfectly good house with a perfectly comfortable and very large bed. That left one viable option: Emily was coming with him.

He reached the door to her unit, and rapped a meaty fist against its dusty surface. When she didn't answer after a few seconds, Jester glanced at the unit number to make sure he had the right place. Apartment 2C, just like she'd said. Muffled voices, what sounded like the television, came from inside the unit.

Maybe she just couldn't hear him knock. Pounding on the door would only annoy the neighbors, so he tried the knob.

It turned easily. Jesus, he had to talk to her about keeping her door locked. Especially in this shit neighborhood.

"Em?" he called as he strolled down the hallway, taking in the sparse decorating and minimal furniture.

The white walls were bare, and what little furnishings she

owned were worn and shabby. This place didn't jive with Emily's warm and fun personality at all. He'd have to ask her about it, after he got on her about that unlocked door.

His list of items to bring up to Emily flew right out of his head as he stepped into her living room and took in the sight before him.

Holy.

Shit.

Emily lay on a towel on the floor, eyes closed, doing what he assumed was some kind of yoga, while a woman on the small television screen voiced encouragement in a soothing tone.

All of the blood in his body surged and traveled to one throbbing location as he shifted his gaze from the TV to Emily, drinking in the sight of her where she lay on the floor. She was in a bridge position, with her shoulders and arms on the ground, and her back and hips in the air. One shapely leg was extended straight up, yet, somehow, she balanced without wavering.

All she wore was a black sports bra and a tiny pair of hot pink panties. She must have been at it for a while. A sheen of sweat coated her skin. He pressed his tongue to the roof of his mouth, wishing it was running over her body instead.

Christ, she was every hot yoga fantasy come to life. Forcing his feet to unglue from where he'd been stunned to immobility, Jester walked until he stood in front of her, gazing down at the erotic picture she made.

As though she sensed his presence, her eyes popped open so wide he almost laughed. "Oh, Jester." She gasped on a breathless whisper. "You startled me, I wasn't expecting you for another half hour. Do you mind if I finish this? I'm supposed to hold this pose for two minutes per leg. I've been close, but haven't made it the whole time yet."

He didn't respond and her face took on an apprehensive expression.

"Sorry," she said. "I can do this another time." Emily started to lower her hips, but Jester reached out to hold her shapely leg in its place in the air.

"Don't," he said with a shake of his head.

"Thanks. I only have—" She turned her head to look at the television where a timer counted down the remaining minutes. "—three minutes and thirty seconds until I'm done. At least I hope I can make it that long."

Emily was almost unbearably sexy in that position, with her small but toned muscles straining to maintain the posture. A faint outline of muscle was visible on her flat stomach, subtle enough to still be feminine but it showed what great shape she kept herself in.

Jester didn't like a woman with a six-pack and rippling muscles. He preferred his women have softness to counter the hardness of his own body. Speaking of hardness, his dick was so stiff he could feel the teeth of his zipper digging in.

"You know, it's kind of cheating if you hold my leg up for me," Emily quipped with a sassy grin.

Jester still didn't speak. He wasn't sure he could, but he speared her with a molten look that left no question as to his desire. Then he slowly slid his hand down her leg pausing to caress the smooth skin of her inner thigh before he released her. With a glance downward, he noticed a dark spot on her panties, directly over her pussy. She was wet.

That knowledge was all Jester needed to kick him into action. No way would his woman lie there wet and wanting while he was in the room. He'd take care of her, and enjoy the hell out of it.

In a move so fast he must have shocked her, Jester dropped to his knees and tore her panties off. Her yelp followed the

114

sound of ripping fabric. Mesmerized by her heady aroma, he lowered his head. Just before his mouth made contact with her weeping slit, Emily squeaked and started to lower her leg. "Jester, what are you doing?"

"I have to taste you, Emily." His voice sounded strained to his ears. One hand pushed her leg back into position.

An idea popped into his head. This was going to be fun. "Don't drop your pose, Em. I'll stop if you fall out of position."

She raised her head and met his eyes with a hesitant look. "Um…I've never…I mean no one has ever…" Her face reddened, but she kept her light eyes locked with his.

He stared at her, mouth inches away from taking her to paradise. "You trying to tell me no man has ever eaten your pussy?"

"Jester!" she shrieked, turning even redder at his explicit words than she'd been seconds before.

"Well, that's a damn shame, baby. And not a problem you have to worry about anymore. I'll eat you out any damn time you want. I would have gotten to it sooner, but every time I get near your naked body I can't seem to keep my dick out of you. Now, lie back. I've got—" He shifted his eyes toward the television. "—two minutes and forty-five seconds to make you come."

Emily started to lay her head back when Jester thought of one more thing. "Oh, and, babe? Don't hold back. I want to hear you lose control."

She dropped her head on the carpet with a soft thud. "Oh my God," she whispered.

Jester chuckled as he dipped his head, swiping his tongue through her folds from the base of her pussy up to her clit, in a long, slow lick.

"Oh my God." This time it came out on a moan.

Oh my God was right, he thought as the taste and smell of her assaulted his senses. She was intoxicating. From the corner of his eye Jester caught her fingers flexing against the carpet as though trying to grab onto the fibers. She thought she needed something to anchor herself now? Just wait until he really got going. Damn, this was going to be fun.

Jester got back to work, licking, sucking and nibbling, just grazing over her clit. Emily's breathing increased, and she rotated her head from side to side as though trying to clear her mind. *Not gonna happen, baby,* Jester thought.

He swirled his tongue once around her swollen nub before wrapping his lips around it and sucking it into his mouth. Emily cried out and her legs began to tremble. The combination of the intense pleasure, and the physical strain of holding the yoga pose made her overworked muscles quiver.

She cried out again when he licked into her, fucking her tight channel with his tongue. The leg that had been held up in the air now rested over his shoulder, the heel digging into his back.

Damn, her pussy was sweet, he could keep this up for hours, drawing her right to the brink and backing off, suspending her in a sexual limbo until he finally let her crash over the edge. It was a shame he had less than two minutes to finish this little game.

Emily's hips moved with purpose now, and Jester knew if their positions had been reversed, and she was on top, she'd be riding his face like a rodeo queen. He filed that idea away as a must try in the very near future.

Jester was so hard he spared a second to wonder if his cock could split through the zipper on his jeans. He felt like a fuckin' king, being the first man to introduce Emily to oral sex. Her responses were honest and unguarded, and she did nothing to hide the fact that she loved the feel of his mouth on her, in her.

She didn't play games, didn't use her body to manipulate him. Emily was a woman who didn't have much experience, but who seemed to revel in her sexuality as she discovered the power of it. He couldn't wait until the day she was confident enough to demand what she wanted from him, and take what her body needed to be satisfied.

The walls of her sex began to flutter around his tongue. She was getting close. After one last thrust of his tongue, he moved back up to her clit, flicking it over and over as her cries grew louder and more desperate.

Chapter Thirteen

Emily was lost in the intense sensations rocketing from her pelvis. Her entire body shook with the strain of holding the pose. She'd lost the battle of keeping her leg in the air, but there was no way she was lowering her hips and risking Jester stopping. Nothing had ever felt this good.

She was making a lot of noise, probably sounded like a wild animal, but she couldn't control it. The sounds poured from her throat, and Jester seemed to enjoy hearing how much she enjoyed his efforts.

Lifting her spinning head, Emily peered down her body and her stomach tightened at the image of the powerful man who worshiped her with his head buried between her thighs. The sight was humbling. He was so gorgeous, so strong and sexy; he could have, and did have, any woman he wanted. Yet he chose to kneel between her legs to bring her tremendous pleasure. Her heart clenched with an unfamiliar emotion and a longing that would never be fulfilled.

Jester slid his tongue from inside her, licking back up to her clitoris. Emily couldn't have stopped the orgasm from ripping through her if she tried. Somewhere in the back recesses of her endorphin swamped mind, she registered the sound of a woman's voice counting down *five...four...three...two...one*, and sure enough, just as the instructor reached, one Emily exploded. Her muscles clenched and her vision clouded as she literally screamed with the force of her release.

Feeling physically sated and emotionally dazed, Emily finally allowed her limp legs to collapse to the ground. There wasn't any point in trying to stand, her legs couldn't possibly hold her after the workout they just had.

"Did that really just happen?" she asked, glad her voice still worked after all that screaming.

"It sure did, babe, and it was the sexiest fucking thing I've ever seen." Jester scooped her up off the floor and carried her to the couch, arranging her so her legs straddled him and her torso rested intimately against his when he sat.

Where just seconds ago she thought she was too drained to do much more than breathe for the rest of the day, she now felt a prickle of renewed desire forming as Jester's hardness nestled into the junction of her thighs.

The ridge pressed against her flesh, sensitive from her recent orgasm, and reminded her of exactly how well-endowed Jester was. She snickered out loud, and the movement caused her sex to rub against his erection.

"Care to share? I know there is no way you are laughing at my skills," Jester said, giving her hair a tug.

Emily lifted her head from his shoulder so she could see his face. "Never that. I was just thinking that I've barely had any sexual encounters, but when I do finally get some it's with a man who is packing this monster." She giggled again rolling her hips to emphasize exactly which monster she was referring to.

Jester laughed along with her. "What can I say, babe? Looks like you were just holding out for the big boys."

Emily smiled at him, and reached out a hand to trace a

finger along his smooth jaw. Her eyes drifted closed in contentment as Jester's hands traveled up and down the bare skin of her back. His hands were so large they spanned her entire back and wrapped part way around her rib cage. His palms and fingertips were roughened and callused, and Emily shivered at the slight tickle they evoked everywhere he trailed them.

She grew restless as need pumped through her blood, and suddenly the light touching was no longer sufficient. Opening her eyes, she found Jester watching her, matching desire burning in his own gaze. This time when his hands smoothed up her back he helped her remove the sports bra, and let it drop to the floor forgotten.

His hands moved around her body and up to her breasts, and his thumbs rubbed over her pointed nipples, making her pussy clench almost violently with need. Emily forced her eyes to stay open; mesmerized by the yearning she saw reflected back at her.

If she didn't get him inside her soon, she might cry, so with shaking hands she reached out and unzipped his jeans, careful not to injure his cock where it strained against the metal. She rose up on her knees and helped him wiggle the denim down over his hips. It didn't matter if they went down farther, just as long as he was free enough to get inside her.

Emily didn't waste any time. Jester's swollen length sprang free from its confines, and she immediately lowered herself onto him. Wet from her previous orgasm and current arousal, he slid in easily. He went incredibly deep, the sensation so intense it bordered on painful, and Emily wanted him to stay there forever.

Jester hissed out a curse as she descended, and his hands locked on her hips once he was fully seated. "Christ, Emily, you're so tight, so hot." He leaned forward and captured her mouth in a hungry kiss.

Emily could taste herself lingering on his tongue as he took his time exploring her mouth. She tried to move. She needed to feel the friction of him sliding in and out of her, but he held her firmly anchored to him, and she was no match for his strength. The only movement she could manage was small rocks of her pelvis against his. She shifted her legs, shoving them between the cushions of the couch so she could wrap around Jester's body and lock her ankles together. The action sunk him even deeper, and each time she tilted her pelvis forward her clit dragged across his pubic bone.

She gasped, breaking the kiss; shocked by the power of the pleasure she was feeling. Lifting her lashes, she met Jester's eyes and was captivated by the force of the emotion blazing in them. Emotion welled in her also; emotion that felt very close to love.

No. No. No.

This was not supposed to be happening. She couldn't afford this. Emotional attachment had the potential to get Johnny killed. It could get her killed. And it could destroy Jester. Emily shifted her gaze, hoping to halt the growing connection between them. She could allow herself the physical pleasure but nothing else.

Jester, however, wasn't having that. "Emily," he ground out, the command in his voice unmistakable. She hesitated for one second, staring at his heaving chest before she lifted her lashes and met his eyes once again. She tried to harden her heart, but the effort was futile.

"Come with me, baby," he said before he kissed her again. A bone deep orgasm rolled through her, as consuming emotionally as it was physically. Jester's hard body shuddered beneath her arms as he came with a rough groan.

Spent, she collapsed against his heaving chest. Snake's words invaded her mind and ruined the intimate moment. *Men tend to let things slip when their dicks are happy.* She opened her mouth, prepared to ask him for some details on the club's business, but the words died in her throat.

She would do it. She'd find a way to get Snake his information. Despite Jester's talk about being an uncomplicated man and keeping things simple between them, Emily had no doubt her betrayal would cut him to the bone. There just wasn't any way she could bring herself to use information Jester shared with her in an intimate moment.

She was a fool, acting like she could preserve her relationship with Jester and give Snake what he needed to release Johnny. Emily blinked furiously, refusing to let the tears that flooded her eyes fall. She felt tortured, divided in her feelings of complete happiness and abject misery.

Chapter Fourteen

"How's it going?" Jester asked Acer with a grunt as he released the barbell and rubbed a muscle that twitched in his chest. The flicker reminded him of yesterday's yoga session with Emily. If he wasn't careful, his muscles wouldn't receive enough blood to complete the next set.

"You need me to spot you?" Acer raised his gaze from the laptop he'd been plugging away at in silence for the past fifteen minutes.

"Nah, bro, I'm good. One more set." He wrapped his hands around the heavy metal bar lifting it straight up from the supports and lowering it toward his chest as he exhaled. He was tired, but the burn in his muscles felt good, and they weren't near the point of failure so he didn't need a spotter.

With a shake of his head Acer returned to his work. "If the club had known you were such a meathead jock when you were prospecting, you'd have never been voted in."

Jester waited until he'd powered through his ten reps before answering. It was hard to carry on a conversation while he raised and lowered more than three hundred pounds of metal directly over his chest. The weights clanged back into the holder as he sat up and stretched his arms behind his back loosening the tight muscles in his chest. "Hey, man, don't hate just because you're a puny thing."

Acer snorted without looking up or missing a keystroke. While Acer didn't have nearly the bulk Jester did, he was no slouch and could certainly hold his own in a fight. He just had a leaner build.

"Besides," Jester continued, "the ladies love how huge I am. They're drawn to my guns like a baby to the teat."

"First off, you're more drawn to tits than any baby. And second, ladies? Don't you mean lady? Because it seems to me there is only one of those these days. This Emily chick getting under your skin, bro?"

Jester opened a bottle of water and guzzled the entire contents, allowing himself a chance to consider Acer's question.

"All kidding aside?" He pulled up the hem of his shirt to wipe the sweat off his face. "She's sunk her claws in deep. I'm sure this makes me a complete dick, but I can't remember ever wanting to spend time with a woman after I've fucked her. I can count on one hand the number of times I've fucked a broad more than once, and it's not like I stuck around for conversation afterward."

Acer shrugged. "We're all like that, man. With the amount of willing and able pussy that hangs around the club we've no reason to be anything else." Even though Acer spoke, his attention was still firmly on the monitor in front of him.

"Hook and VP seem to like what they've got now," Jester said, referring to the monogamous relationships of their friends.

Acer stopped typing and gave Jester his full attention. "Shit, you thinking along those lines?"

With a self-deprecating grunt Jester sat up on the weight bench, and leaned forward, resting his forearms on his powerful thighs. "No. Fuck no. I just..." He rolled his eyes. "Oh fuck it. I can't stop thinking about her. All day. Every day. I'd rather be with her than just about anywhere else, and I can't seem to fuck her out of my system. She's smart, she sweet, she gets me, she's just...good."

Acer cracked up, not appearing phased by the dark scowl that his laughter brought to Jester's face. "So why don't you just quit whining and enjoy it? Seriously man. We don't meet many women like that. Most who come through the club are hardened, bitter, and used up. Seems to me, you find one who's all that shit you mentioned, plus she's as fuckable as your Emily, you should hold tight and enjoy the ride."

Jester glowered at Acer's description of Emily, but he couldn't argue with the man. He wanted inside her every chance he got. Even now, just hearing her name he was semi-erect.

"She doesn't seem in any hurry to kick your overgrown ass to the curb either, brother. Consider yourself one of the lucky ones and roll with it."

Jester nodded, and let Acer's words sink in. His brother was right, he just needed to shut up and enjoy her. To his surprise, he didn't miss the revolving door of easy women he'd had before. Emily was more than satisfying his sexual needs. On top of that, she calmed him and soothed his rough edges. She was accepting of his lifestyle, but as Acer mentioned, she wasn't a washed up biker whore. He liked talking to her, and liked hearing what she had to say as well.

"There's just one thing."

"What's that? She doesn't let you be on top enough?" Acer laughed at his own joke.

"I'm serious, asshole."

"All right, what's the thing?"

"Sometimes I feel like she's hiding something. She doesn't

tell me much about her life. It's like she's holding something back."

"You may be the only man in history to complain that his woman talks too little."

Jester flipped him the bird. "Forget it, asshole."

Acer laughed again. "Okay, I'm done bustin' your balls. You worried she's not into a relationship?"

Jester rubbed a hand across his chin. "Maybe, but I think it's more than that. I can't shake the feeling something's bothering her, maybe some kind of trouble."

"So, why don't you just ask her?"

He shook his head. "I doubt she'd tell me. I can't get her to talk about much of anything personal."

"Give it time, brother. You forget that you just met her. Trust takes time to build." Acer shrugged. "Maybe it's just too soon for her to put her burdens on you."

He made a good point.

"Thanks, Dr. Phil. Next time you need help with a woman, you know who to call."

Acer snorted. "Fuck that. You'll just grunt and beat your chest."

Done with the sensitive bullshit, Jester nodded toward the computer. "How's that going?" he asked again.

Acer studied him for a second or two before he shifted topics to what he'd been working on for the past few hours. "I'm nearly done. I have plenty of satellite imagery over the mountain pass. There's really nothing around for miles. We shouldn't attract any unwanted attention."

Acer was using his many and varied computer skills to assess the area where the Grimms were supposed to meet with the cartel. Recluses frequently moved to remote parts of the desert to disappear from the law, to live off the grid for various reasons, and they settled in lone shacks in the middle of nowhere. The club needed to be sure some random nosey bastard wouldn't catch them in the act of hijacking the Grimms' money.

"We should be good. Doesn't look like anyone will stumble across us that day. I'm also working on the money piece. I have a few irons in the fire as far as distributing it and laundering it so we don't flag any interest. That's way too much green for us to handle any other way."

Jester smiled at him. The club could do a lot with the money they'd get from the Grimms. He was looking forward to this on so many levels, not the least of which was the straight up thrill of seeing Snake taken down a few pegs.

"Have you run this all by Shiv?"

Jester nodded. "Yeah, he agrees that we should be at the meet site in place of the cartel. This way we can get there early, set up our shit and be ready when the Grimms show. Too many things can go wrong if we try to intercept the Grimms on the way there as we originally planned. The chance of being caught is way too high."

Acer leaned back in the chair and interlaced his fingers behind his head. "You have a way to keep the cartel from making the meet?"

Jester rose from the weight bench and tossed the empty water bottle into a small trash can across the room. "Still working on that piece. I'll let you know. Gonna grab a shower before Em gets here."

"Take your time. I'll keep your woman company," Acer called with a smirk.

Jester flipped Acer off over his shoulder as he strode from the room.

~ ~ ~ ~

Emily let herself into Jester's house and sighed with pleasure as the cool air enveloped her. Near one hundred and ten degrees today, the temperature was so hot outside she grew sweaty and overheated walking the short distance from her car to Jester's front door. Thankfully Jester was expecting her and had left the door open,

Noises could be heard coming from the study at the back of the house, a room Jester had converted to a gym of sorts, with a universal weight machine and treadmill. She didn't bother announcing her presence. He knew she was on her way so she just headed back to the study.

Stepping in the room, she came to a complete stop when she was greeted, not by Jester, but by one of his club brothers. "Oh! Sorry, I didn't realize anyone else was here. I didn't see your motorcycle."

"Hey, hon, it's in the garage. That sun is murder on the paint job. Jester's in the shower."

"Okay, I'll just leave you to it." She started to back out into the hallway.

Acer sat on the small loveseat sofa in the corner of the room with a laptop open on his lap. He looked up at her and closed the computer. "No need to leave, I'm done. Come sit and I can tell you all sorts of dirt on your man." He patted the empty cushion next to him.

Emily hesitated. She hadn't really spoken to any of the other guys in the MC. Sure, she had brunch with Striker and Hook, but their wives were there as a buffer. Truth be told, she found most of them intimidating. But, they were important to Jester so she'd make the effort. Plus, there was always the chance someone would let something slip she could pass along to Snake. Too bad he'd closed the laptop.

"Thanks. It's Acer, right?" Next to him, she put her back against the armrest and sat facing him, cross-legged on the loveseat.

He nodded. "Jesus, girl, how do you fold yourself up like

that? This couch is tiny."

Emily laughed, his teasing putting her at ease. "Yoga."

"Ahh, that explains a lot of things."

Her brows drew down as she tried to determine what he was referring to. "I don't follow."

He lifted one sandy-colored brow and smirked at her. "Jester's had the look of a very satisfied man lately. I'm sure the yoga has something to do with it."

Heat rose to her face as visions of the yoga session with Jester from the other day flashed in her mind. "I cannot confirm or deny that statement."

Flawless skin and sharp features gave him an almost regal look. The dark blond hair atop his head was impeccably styled and she swore she'd never seen more perfect teeth. He had the look of old money, like someone who should have *the third* at the end of their name, at least from the neck up. From the neck down he had nearly as many visible tattoos as Jester, and who knew how many more were hidden under his No Prisoners T-shirt and jeans.

While his body wasn't as powerfully built as Jester's, Emily wasn't under the impression that he was weak in anyway. There was an intelligent air about him, and she had a feeling he could use that to be very deadly, if the situation called for it.

With a grin, he raised a brow at her. "You can put away your microscope and just ask me anything you want to know."

Emily flushed. She'd been openly studying him while he sat just two feet away from her. "Sorry. That was rude. And I believe I could ask you anything, but I don't believe you'd tell me much of anything."

"You got me there, Emily." He reached out and ruffled her hair like she was his kid sister. "I think I like you. Jester sure seems to."

"He talked about me?" She bit her lip to hold back a groan. Could she have asked a more sophomoric question? Next she'd be asking Acer to pass Jester a note in class.

"Your name may have come up once or twice."

She refused to ask what they were talking about, even though she was dying to know.

He stared at her, and she understood what he'd meant by the microscope comment. "Can be a tough life," he said breaking the momentary silence.

"Excuse me?"

He pointed to the No Prisoners patch on the front of his cut. "MC life. For a woman especially."

"You trying to warn me off your friend, Acer?"

Her comment brought the grin back to his face. He was devastatingly handsome, and she imagined he didn't lack for female attention. "No, darlin', quite the opposite. I think you might be just the softness he needs in his hard life."

Emily couldn't prevent the smile from expanding on her face. The more time she spent with Jester, the more she wanted to be just that. She had a feeling there were times his life was full of violence and misery, and she'd love to be the one he came to when he needed to chase away his demons. What was that expression about wishing in one hand?

"Thank you." Emotion thickened her throat and made her voice deeper than usual. Maybe it was a good thing that she wouldn't be around to see the fallout from her deception.

Acer put a hand on her knee and gave her a gentle squeeze.

"Hands to yourself, asshole." Jester growled.

Emily started.

He stood in the doorway wearing a pair of navy basketball shorts and holding a gray T-shirt in his hand. The sight of his sculpted chest had her forgetting all about the man sitting on the couch next to her. Jester moved into the room, straight toward her. When he reached the couch, he shot Acer an annoyed look and hauled Emily to her feet.

He pulled her flush against his hard body, still slightly damp from the shower, and lowered his mouth to hers. He kissed her. And kissed her. And kissed her. The room spun and she melted against him with a sigh.

"You start ripping her clothes off, brother, and I'm gonna take that as an invitation to join in."

Jester broke the kiss long enough to say, "Get the fuck out of here Acer."

"Jester, that's not nice. He doesn't have to leave." She started to pull back but only made it about one inch before Jester crushed her close.

"Yes, he does. And he has to leave now."

Acer laughed, and shoved the laptop in a computer bag on the floor. "Okay, I'm leaving. I can take a hint."

If anything else was said, Emily didn't hear it. Jester returned his mouth to hers as he lifted her off the ground. She wrapped her legs around his waist, and he turned and backed her against the wall. The hard planes of his body pressed against her as he lifted his head and whispered to her. "Missed you today, baby."

In these moments of softly spoken words and intimacy, Emily could pretend they were a couple. Imagine this relationship had a future, and that there was no guillotine above her head just waiting to drop.

Jester rocked his erection against her saturated sex.

Damn her clothing.

"You ready for me, Em?"

With a moan she looked him straight in the eye. "Always Jester. Anytime you want me I'm yours, just take me."

How was it possible for her heart to be so full at the same time it was breaking?

Chapter Fifteen

The days passed in a combined haze of sexual satisfaction, fear, and frustration as Emily spent her nights with Jester and her days hitting walls with every attempt to uncover the No Prisoner's plan for the Grimms. Before she knew it, ten days had blown by, and nearly three quarters of her time limit imposed by Snake had vanished.

Jester was a locked vault when it came to club business and if she wasn't careful he'd soon grow suspicious of her inquiries. A few times when she'd been alone in Jester's house she was able to do a bit of snooping. Betrayal burned, a tight ball in her stomach the entire time. To her everlasting shame, she was actually relieved when she didn't uncover anything.

She needed that information for Snake, but the idea of it coming from a direct betrayal of Jester was nauseating.

Today they were spending the afternoon at the clubhouse. The MC was hosting their annual Memorial Day Barbecue. This was the first time she'd been back at the clubhouse in a week and mutant butterflies had been fluttering in her stomach all day. She had to find some intel for Snake. With four days left, she was approaching desperate, and the once ridiculous idea of breaking into the clubhouse at night would be her only option if she didn't catch a break soon.

She stood with her back resting against the bar, gazing at the room full of bikers. Jester stood against the bar as well, facing her, one hand absently playing with her hair as he sipped a beer.

"You better knock that shit off before I take you right here on this bar." Jester growled in her ear.

"What?" Emily cast an angelic look his way. "What am I doing?" It took all her strength to stay in character and not break down right in the middle of the clubhouse.

"Jesus." Jester groaned. "I've created a monster. Baby, don't ever play poker. Every raunchy thought is written clearly on your face." Leaning in close, he whispered, "You're thinking about last night. Which time? When I went down on you in the kitchen? Or maybe when I bent you over couch and fucked you from behind? Damn your ass looked good. Maybe it was when—"

She stopped him with a hand over his laughing mouth as moisture pooled between her thighs. The man was lethal with words, but he needed to shut up before she died of embarrassment. There were at least ten other people bustling around the clubhouse.

Jester wrapped his arms around her. Palming her ass with both hands, he lifted her and spun around, setting her down on the bar top, which put her almost at eye level with him.

Still holding her ass, he nudged her thighs open and stepped between them, planting his mouth on hers in a searing kiss. As his talented tongue filled her mouth, the fact that they were in the middle of the clubhouse among other people fled her mind. Jester trailed his lips across her jaw, down the column of her throat, to her chest.

Before she caught on to what he was planning, Jester removed his hands from her bottom, and brought them around to cup her full breasts outside her clothing. She wore a dark purple tank top with a scooped neck that showed off a hint of cleavage, or it had until Jester pushed her breasts up and together with his hands, exposing more than was acceptable for mixed company.

"Jester!" She gasped, scandalized, as he placed biting kisses across the flesh he'd plumped up toward his face. Mortified that people were watching, she tried to swat him away.

He lifted his head slightly, but didn't release her. "What babe? You started this, thinking about how many times I made you come last night. Now you have to deal with the consequences." He dropped his head back down, dipped his tongue in her cleavage, and Emily had to bite back the moan threatening to escape. Part of her wanted to rip off her clothes and let him do whatever he wanted right here, not caring who saw, but luckily that was just a small part.

She needed to get through to him so she grabbed a handful of his hair, and gave a hard yank.

"Ouch! Shit babe! You know I like it when you pull my hair, but usually we're both about to come so the pain is kind of erotic. That hurt like a son of a bitch." He stood back up with a wince and rubbed the back of his head.

"There ya go, girl," a man called from across the room. "Don't you let him treat you like a piece of meat. You gotta teach him how to be a gentleman. He doesn't get a free pass just because he made you come all night long, or so he says."

Jester turned and flipped off Acer, who was snickering from the other side of the room.

Emily decided to shove the discomfiture away. Sure they were in a room full of people, but all of these men were highly sexual, and what Jester just did didn't come close to the exhibitionist acts they were used to seeing around here.

Besides, she had to admit it was fun to be a little naughty and let her inhibitions fall away.

She peeked around the large tattooed body blocking her view, and directed her words at Acer. "I'm trying, but he's been a wild beast for so long that it's taking quite a bit of work." She hopped down from the bar and turned toward the kitchen, which was through a door behind the bar.

As she passed Jester, he bent and whispered in her ear, "I'll show you how much of a wild beast I can be later tonight. Then we'll see who has the last laugh." Straightening he gave her a sharp slap on the ass as she strutted by.

A sad smile that he couldn't see formed on her mouth. How she wished everything was as simple as the fun and games he thought it was.

Emily entered the kitchen and sought out Lila and Marcie, finding them busy getting all the food ready to be transported out to the parking lot. The day would get cooler as the evening approached, and they'd have the barbecue out in the lot.

"Oh my God, that smell is intoxicating." Emily groaned as she stepped into the kitchen and gave each woman a quick hug. "What can I do to help?" The food had been brought in from a local barbeque joint. Trays of ribs, pulled pork and chicken were stacked high on the counters while the women uncovered additional platters filled with macaroni and cheese, greens, and potato salad.

"Hey, girl! Pick your poison. Everything needs to be opened and then the prospects will lug it all out for us."

Emily salivated as she uncovered a foil pan loaded high with ribs falling off the bone. The ribs were swimming in a sauce and emitted a sweet and spicy aroma, that made Emily's stomach growl in a decidedly unladylike fashion. "Oh, man, I am starving. Can I just eat this whole tray right here?"

Lila threw her a snarky grin. "Nonstop sex with a triple H man will do that to you."

Emily felt her face heat, but her curiosity beat out her embarrassment. "Okay, I'll bite. What's a Triple H man?"

"Hot, hard, and huge." She flexed her muscles like a body builder on the word huge.

Emily shook her head, the denial on the tip of her tongue. But, what the hell? These women were both involved with men cut from the same cloth as Jester. They probably knew exactly what it was like to be on the receiving end of all that focused sexuality. "Damn right it will."

Marcie whooped with laughter as Lila held up a hand for a high five. "Damn girl," Lila said. "I'd tell you it gets less intense, but I'd be lying."

"Amen, sister," added Marcie. "And we wouldn't have it any other way."

Emily smiled. She loved the bond between these two women, and felt grateful for the way they included her so effortlessly. The three chatted as they uncovered all the dishes and sent them outside with a few of the prospects. When all the work was done, Marcie and Lila made their way outdoors in search their men. Emily used the excuse of needing to make a trip to the bathroom to hang back for a moment.

Noise from inside the clubhouse had dimmed. Most of the members were outside drinking and getting ready to dive into the feast. There was a chance she could poke around for some information, and she'd take any chance she could get at this point.

The more time she spent with this group, the harder it was to envision selling them out to Snake. Guilt was a constant companion, but it burned particularly bright when she imagined Lila and Marcie's reaction upon discovering she was working for Snake. But what choice did she have?

Emily poked her head out of the kitchen and peered into the main room of the clubhouse. It was as silent as death. Not one club member remained. Her gaze landed on the double doors leading to the room the club used for meetings. That's where she needed to be. If any information was to be found it would be in that room.

With a deep breath, Emily pushed the door open, stepped out of the kitchen and walked in the direction of the meeting room. Her heart rate increased with each step and the butterflies in her stomach turned into a pack of angry vultures. The closer she got, the heavier her feet grew and before long she felt like she was slugging through thick muck.

By the time she reached the doors, she was sweating and dizzy. The paralyzing fear had to stop. She conjured up the image of Johnny from ten days ago and felt anger replace the fear. Anger she could use. Anger could fuel her.

She reached for the door handle and yanked.

The heavy door swung out toward her body. Yes! It wasn't locked. Finally, she had some hope. Emily was halfway through the doorway when footsteps pounded on the floor above her.

Shit! Someone was seconds away from descending the steps and catching her.

She let go of the door like it was on fire and dashed toward the bar.

"Emily?" a man called her name.

Her heart seized in her chest "Y-yes?"

A lanky man whose limbs had a rubbery appearance stood five steps from the bottom of the stairs. What was his name? Stretch? No. Gumby? That sounded right.

"What are you doing? I think Jester's outside."

Well, I'm just trying to break into your meeting room so I can give your enemies information about you. "I…um…" She scrambled for a cover, the words sticking in her dry mouth. "I wanted a drink." She pointed to the bar.

He didn't answer, but pierced her with a steady look. "I think they've got anything you could want outside."

"Right," she answered. "Guess I better get back out there."

Gumby's focus shifted from her to the meeting room doors.

Emily held her breath. If he questioned her, if he mentioned it to Jester, the game would be over.

"Go on then, girl. I'm gonna hit the can then be out there myself. I'm fuckin starved."

Emily scurried toward the door.

Gumby remained in his spot on the steps until she'd left the building.

Bright sun assaulted her eyes. Squinting, she scanned the parking lot for Jester. Dozens of large, leather-wearing men milled around, eating, drinking, and smoking. The scene was definitely tamer than the party from the previous week, but there was still an abundance of women in barely-there outfits flitting around the men.

"Hey, girl! We're over here." Marcie's voice rang out from about twenty feet away.

Emily hadn't spotted Jester yet, so she walked to Marcie, Lila and two other women. Thank God they couldn't see her still racing heart, and hopefully they'd attribute her sweaty brow to the heat of the day.

"Let me introduce you. Emily, this is Jaz and Betsy. Jaz works part time at the reception desk in the garage," she said of the woman who looked like a female version of the bikers. Jaz was about Emily's height, with spiky hot pink hair and myriad tattoos over her widely exposed skin. Leather short shorts and a black halter finished off the biker chick look. "And Betsy here is trying her damnedest to pretend she's not over the moon in love with Gumby."

"Marcie!" Betsy, a tall, willowy blonde with caramel colored eyes, swatted her arm.

Marcie laughed, and slung an arm around Betsy's shoulders. "Girls, this is Emily, Jester's ol' lady."

The two women didn't bother to hide their surprise at that news, blatantly assessing Emily with shocked expressions. Emily was quite stunned by the label herself. She wasn't Jester's ol' lady. They hadn't discussed what they were to each other. It was a conversation Emily avoided like a communicable disease.

"No, I'm not...I mean we're just..." she stammered, not having a clue where to go with this. They were just what? Spending every night together? Spending hours every day naked and pleasuring each other in ways Emily hadn't even know existed a week ago? Spending time with his friends and family? She had no idea what to say.

"Girl, you may not have given it an official title, but that man is off the market." Marcie blazed on, oblivious to Emily's discomfort. "Trust me on this. I've known the guy for years. Years! And I've never once seen him look at a woman with a fraction of the emotion he looks at you with Emily. You're his ol' lady."

Lila took pity on her and changed the subject. "We were all just talking about what we have planned for the summer months. Besides hiding from the outrageous heat that is."

Grateful for her sensitivity, Emily mouthed a thank-you to Lila. Pretending to be a smitten women hanging with the girls was a struggle when her mind was still inside that meeting room. She had one more chance before drastic measures would be taken. Wednesday night the boys had a meeting, then they all went out partying afterward. Now that she knew the doors weren't locked, she could use the time they'd all be away to go snooping.

Emily grabbed a beer from a cooler, pasted a smile on her face, and tried to act normal. God help her if she didn't find anything Wednesday night.

Chapter Sixteen

Jester stood across the asphalt lot, his back against the exterior wall of the clubhouse, drinking in the sight of Emily. She blipped on his radar as soon as she exited the building, but he didn't go to her, letting her have some time to connect with the women.

She fit in well. For someone who seemed so skittish and apprehensive when he first met her, she adapted to his world like a natural. People were drawn to her kind and genuinely warm, accepting personality.

Emily had no clue how gorgeous she was, standing there in a pair of white denim cutoffs with a fitted purple tank top. Brown cowboy boots topped off the outfit, and did amazing things for her legs. The clothes were typical desert attire, but she wore it well, and looked insanely sexy. He intended to have those booted legs wrapped around his waist as he pounded into her later tonight.

Taking a drink of his beer, he watched as she laughed at something Marcie said. Her head was thrown back, exposing the creamy expanse of her neck and his dick twitched in his pants. Jesus, he was like a horny teenager who'd just discovered sex. He could have her three times a day, and still want her like a man starving.

This was an entirely new situation for him. Sure, his sexual appetite had always been on the excessive side, but he usually lost interest in a woman five minutes after he came. It was crass, and probably made him an asshole, but it was what it was.

With Emily, however, he not only continued to want her body again and again, but he genuinely enjoyed every second of time he spent with her, fucking or not.

"You've got that look." Striker ambled up next to Jester, handing him another beer.

Jester tossed his empty bottle in a nearby trashcan as he took a pull from the fresh one. He snorted in response to Striker. "Go ahead. I'm sure you're dying to tell me exactly what look it is."

He smirked. "I sure am. It's the look of an animal who found its mate."

Christ. Is that what this was? Was Emily his mate? Jester wasn't sure he could handle that. He wasn't finished with her, but did he want something permanent?

Striker laughed. "It's also the look of a man who knows he's fucked."

"Yeah, that sounds more like it."

"She sure is pretty. It's those light eyes, they pull you in something fierce. Tits ain't bad either."

Jester turned and scowled down at Striker who stood just three inches shorter than he did, still over six feet, but Jester had the height advantage. "I'm sorry, VP, Lila ain't enough for you?"

Striker laughed, and Jester knew he'd fallen right into his trap. "Brother, Lila is more than enough for me, but that don't mean my eyes are busted. Emily's a gorgeous woman. Every man here can see that. But you sure did react like a male animal protecting his mate."

Jester grunted, somewhat pacified by Striker's words. "Christ, I feel like a wild animal half the time I'm around her."

Striker shrugged. "We all are, man. At least until a good woman comes along and tries to domesticate us." He lifted his beer in a toast toward Jester. "To being domesticated. I'm living proof that it can be a damn good thing, bro."

Jester lifted his own beer toward Striker, taking a long drink while he thought about his VP's words. At some point they'd have to figure out what they were doing with each other, but it could wait until after the club was just about one million dollars richer. Emily didn't seem to be in any hurry to get away from him, a few more days wouldn't matter.

"What's that about?" Striker pointed at Emily.

She had her phone to her ear and was walking away from the group of women, but what caught Jester's attention was how her entire demeanor changed. Her posture was rigid, gait jerky and the light had gone out of her eyes. Fear was written all over her face. The conversation didn't last more than a few seconds, but Emily was affected by it.

She shoved her phone in the back pocket of her shorts and bent her head forward, pinching the bridge of her nose between her thumb and middle finger. Then she took a deep breath and seemed to rally, making her way to the food table.

That's it. Jester was done. Something in her life wasn't right, and she was going to tell him was it was. This wasn't the time or place, but he'd get it out of her soon. If there was something she was afraid of, he could sure as fuck fix it for her, no matter what their relationship was.

"Oh shit," Striker muttered.

Jester glanced at him. His jaw had clenched and eyes narrowed.

"Food table. Look." Striker pointed in the direction he was referring to.

Emily picked up a plate to fill with food. Colt had wandered up to her, and was saying something Jester didn't stand a chance of hearing from his distance. Emily's back was to him so he couldn't see her reactions, either.

"No fucking way." Jester stepped forward intent on showing Colt exactly what he meant when he'd ordered him to stay the fuck away from Emily. A firm hand on his arm stopped his forward progression.

"Hold on a minute, brother. I want to see what he does. He's been a dick ever since he patched in, and Shiv is starting to get pissed. Might have to take some action soon. I just want to see what he's going to do."

"Striker, there is no way in hell I'm standing by and allowing him to put his hands on her."

"I'm not asking you to, Jester. If he looks like he's about to cross a line you can go over and beat the shit out of him."

After glowering at Striker, Jester took a step back, but he did not relax. Fists clenched, he bounced slightly on the balls of his feet like a boxer in the ring. He was ready to spring forward and tear Colt away from Emily if need be. Wild animal indeed.

Emily turned, and set the plate she was holding down on a table to give Colt her attention as he spoke to her. She was too damn nice to tell him to fuck off. Her face was impassive, and she held herself rigid, but spoke with him and didn't appear afraid. Then Colt said something that had her frowning and shaking her head. She shifted her body slightly, angling away from him, giving the impression that she was growing distinctly uncomfortable.

To the rest of the partiers at the barbecue, the scene might look like two people chatting, but to the man who knew her body as intimately as he knew his own, he picked up on how uneasy she was.

Just as Jester reached his limit—he wasn't going to stand by and watch as Emily grew distressed—Colt lifted a hand, and with one finger, traced the neckline of her top, right across the hint of cleavage that peeked out. She immediately slapped his hand away, and took a step back with a firm shake of her head.

"That's it," Jester ground out. "I hope you got what you needed because he's a fuckin' dead man."

"Right on your heels, brother." Striker shadowed Jester's lengthy stride.

As Jester neared the table, and could make out their conversation, he itched with the need to plow his fist into Colt's smug face.

"Come on now, Emily. Don't be like that. Jester already told me I could take a turn."

Emily looked crushed, and Jester rushed to get to her.

"You don't think you're the only one Jester's fuckin', do you?" Colt laughed, a nasty sound, and Emily took another step back. "He fucks any and everything with a snatch. You're a fool if you're loyal to him."

Jester rammed his fist into Colt's face with a satisfying crunch. The powerful blow knocked Colt off his feet and into the table, sending trays of food flying in all directions.

"Jester!" Emily stepped forward. She didn't get more than one step toward the fray when Acer slid an arm across her shoulders, and pulled her back from the ensuing fight. Jester briefly met Acer's gaze and Acer nodded once, an unspoken promise among brothers to keep his woman safe.

"Get up, Colt. You need help understanding what stay the fuck away from my woman means? I'm more than happy to educate you."

146

Colt stood. He spat a mouthful of blood on the ground, and gave Jester an unrepentant smirk. A crowd had formed by now, a rowdy half-drunk group looking to egg on the fight. Jester didn't care. A number of members had issues with Colt. Most would be more than happy to watch the little shit get pounded.

Right now, he wasn't interested in Colt's overall behavior since he'd patched, but he planned to make sure Colt knew to keep far away from Emily from here on out. As an added benefit, it wouldn't hurt a few of these other assholes to see what happened if they poached on his property.

"What the fuck's up with you, man?" he asked Jester with a sneer. "You used to talk shit and joke all the time. You seem to have lost your sense of humor. What's wrong, brother? Emily not keeping your dick happy?"

"I've got a sense of humor. What I don't have is patience for you touching what's mine. Especially after I warned you what would happen if you didn't back the hell off." Jester was through talking to this piece of shit. He lunged and slammed his fist into Colt's stomach before hitting him in the face again.

~ ~ ~ ~

Queasy over the idea of Jester fighting because of her, Emily tried to break away, but an immovable arm remained locked across her chest, anchoring her to the man who looked too pretty to be an outlaw. "Please let me go." She turned her head to Acer. "I need to stop this before someone gets hurt."

Acer stared down at her, his eyes alight with amusement. "No can do, baby doll. Jester will have my ass next if I let you get anywhere near that fight."

"This isn't funny. Someone is going to get seriously hurt."

They traded punches, Colt's face now sporting a black eye. Visions of Johnny's bruised face invaded her mind. Would

Jester beat Colt like Snake had Johnny?

She thrashed in Acer's hold, increasing her efforts to get free. Why didn't anyone intervene?

With a chuckle Acer gave her a teasing squeeze, as though her efforts to loosen his grip were humorous. "Relax, honey, it's not acceptable for a man to pee on his woman, at least not in public," he added with a wink. "So we mark our territory in other ways."

"So this is a male ego thing?" Colt's fist connected with Jester's jaw and she winced. "I don't like this at all. Please let go of me. I need to stop this." Her voice rose as panic started to take hold. All she could think of was Colt lying on the floor, looking exactly like Johnny.

Was Jester the kind of man who would do that to a brother?

Acer finally tuned into her distress. He bent down so his face was next to hers, watching the brawl, his mouth near her ear. "Honey, he's fine. Trust me, your man can handle himself."

"But I don't want Jester to hurt someone because of me. He's not like that. He looks so scary right now." Her voice was nearly a sob.

It must have finally clicked for Acer. "Take a deep breath and stop fighting against me. I'll face Jester's wrath next if I bruise you."

Emily gasped and stopped all her struggles.

"I was kidding, but at least it got you to stop. I was the one who was going to be bruised."

His attempt at humor was lost on her.

"Watch him, Emily. Really watch your man. He's not a bully. Look how he's holding back. This ain't all about you. Colt's been a little shit ever since we patched him in, which is why no one's breaking it up. He needs to be taken down a notch or ten. It will be over in just a second."

Sure enough, Jester clocked Colt once more, and he went down face first in a heap on the ground and didn't stir. Jester turned and marched straight toward the clubhouse without a backward glance.

The crowd hooted and hollered before dissipating, the show over now that one of them wasn't able to fight back.

Lila pushed through the throng of bikers until she stood next to Colt's prone form.

"Nice, Jester," Lila muttered with a roll of her eyes. "Someone carry him into the bunk room so I can check him out. Make sure he didn't rattle his brains around too much."

Emily, stared down at the man on the ground, unable to make her feet move in any direction. Her insides twisted with the thought that she was the reason behind this and Jester was the man responsible for it. It was only then she realized Acer had disappeared.

"You'll get used to it, Emily. Sometimes these guys need to beat on each other to get their points across. I think it's in their DNA or something." Lila laughed, and Emily hoped that meant the man on the floor wasn't seriously injured.

Was she crazy for getting involved with a man like Jester? Maybe he was more in line with Snake than she'd originally thought.

What was she supposed to do now? She couldn't leave, Jester was her ride. She wasn't convinced she should be around him either. Casper hit Johnny in front of her face, but aside from that she'd never witnessed violence up close and personal like this. Was he even safe to be around right now?

As she stood there feeling stupid and confused, Striker strolled over. "You okay, hon? You look like you want to puke or try to break the Olympic record for fastest female runner."

"I'm so sorry to have caused trouble. I'll call a cab and clear out of here right away." There was a good chance she'd start crying and that couldn't happen here.

"No need, hon. That's been brewing a long time. Besides, you need to go in and see to your man."

Emily shook her head. "He may not want me there right now, and I don't know how to handle him like…that. He looked—" She swallowed a lump in her throat. "—dangerous."

Striker cocked his head and leveled her with a hard stare. "I'll say this once, Emily, since you don't know Jester very well, but just once, so listen good. Whatever happens here." He pointed around to the men still drinking and shoveling in food. "That's one thing, between brothers. A very different thing than will ever happen with you. He can be as mad as a rabid dog, but he'll never lay a hand on you. He's a man, not a hot-headed little boy. He knows how to control himself, doesn't pick on people weaker than he is, and he doesn't go off the rails. Ever. It's just not him. I promise you have nothing to be afraid of."

She stared at him, struck dumb by his impassioned plea for his brother.

"He'll want you. Here, take this." He placed a silver key in her hand. "It's a spare to my room on the second floor. Jester knows which one. I keep it locked during parties. Never know who'll show up here looking to make trouble for us."

Wasn't that the truth.

"Take your time, no one will bother you in there and Jester can get cleaned up. And Emily? Don't listen to what Colt told you. You have Jester's loyalty. He's not screwing around on you."

Guilt swamped her. She didn't deserve his loyalty. She didn't deserve his trust.

She glanced down at the key, and thanked Striker before making her way toward the clubhouse. The metal in her hand was more than a room key. It was a possible key to information for Snake. Her heart beat an uneasy rhythm, and she wondered exactly what she'd encounter when she got in there, both with Jester and in Striker's room.

Jester sat at the bar taking a swig directly from a bottle of amber liquid. Emily wasn't very well versed in liquors and couldn't begin to guess what it was. He turned when the door slammed behind her and their eyes met. Emily's gait faltered at the strength of the emotion shining out toward her.

There was some sorrow in his gaze, but mostly desire, and a vulnerability so unlike him. Any other time that stare would have warmed her body and her heart, but today her attention was divided. Part of her wanted to rush to Jester, to comfort him and ease burdens, but the key was burning straight into her palm.

Walking straight to him, she gently removed the bottle from his bloodied hand and rested it on the bar. With a light tug on his arm she coaxed him off the barstool and directed him up the stairs. "Striker gave me his key."

With a nod Jester walked down the hallway and stopped in front of a closed door. Emily slid the key in the lock, twisted the knob, and pushed the door open. "Go lie down on the bed, and I'll grab something to clean up your hand." She nudged him toward the bed.

"Emily," he started.

With a shake of her head she cut off what would most likely have been him telling her he was fine.

As she walked toward the bathroom, her gaze darted around, taking in as much of the room as she could without being obvious in her search. There wasn't much to see. Aside from the bed and a small dresser, the room was basically empty. Striker probably didn't spend much time here, now that he had Lila.

In the Spartan bathroom, she fished around until she found a washcloth, and wet it with warm water from the sink.

When she returned to the room she found Jester lying close to the edge of the queen sized bed, one booted foot resting on the ground while the other was stretched out on top of the blankets. A pile of pillows propped his head up, and his astute eyes followed her every movement.

He showed no signs of falling asleep as part of her hoped he would. Now her chances of searching the dresser and nightstand were next to zilch. Emily sighed. This day was wrought with repeated failed attempts and frustration.

Chapter Seventeen

Emily went to the bed and sat on the edge, her side pressed into the masculine slope of Jester's body where his hip met his flank. She picked up his hand, which was slightly swollen with three split knuckles. The blood was already drying, but the sight of it bothered her. Careful not to restart the bleeding, she dabbed the area with the wet washcloth. Neither spoke, the air between them thick with unvoiced emotion and uncertainty.

When she was satisfied the cuts were clean, Emily tossed the washcloth on the floor and made a mental note to wash it for Striker. With a delicate hold, she raised Jester's injured hand to her lips and placed a soft kiss on each damaged knuckle.

"Emily." He pierced her with an unsmiling stare. "Colt's full of shit. I'm not fucking around on you. Jesus, you're all I can think about, your eyes, your voice, your tits, and the way your pussy feels gripping my cock. And it's more than just physical. It's everything you are. I haven't so much as thought of another woman. You've hijacked all the space in my head. To be honest, I'm not exactly sure what to do about it."

Emily's eyes filled with tears. She wished she was deserving of his affection. "Shh, Jester you don't have to explain anything to me. I didn't believe him."

"I'm sorry I scared you."

How did he know? "You didn't," she lied.

His face was a mask of disbelief. "You're a shitty liar, babe."

If he only knew.

"Okay, you scared me."

"I don't go looking for fights. If I'd wanted to, I could have left him in a bad way. He's probably already up and cursing my name."

She gave him a small smile. It was the same speech both Acer and Striker had given her, and they were right. Jester was twice the size of Colt. The fight could have been a massacre, but he'd controlled himself.

He wasn't like Snake in any way. Snake preyed on the weak and innocent. He manipulated people and situations to serve him no matter the consequences.

"And, Christ, honey, please tell me you don't think I'd ever lay a hand on you for anything other than pleasure. Is that what happened to you? Did some asshole hurt you? Is that really why you moved here, and why you don't talk much about your life?"

The lie would have been easy to perpetuate, but it died in her throat. Instead, Emily slid off the bed, and knelt on the floor next to Jester. She unlaced his boot, tugged it off and dropped it to the ground with a heavy thud. She rose on her knees, and removed the boot from the leg resting on the bed as well.

"Emily…" he cautioned.

She shook her head. "No, no one has ever hit me." She couldn't talk about this now. Couldn't talk about why the violence of the afternoon scared her. The truth was too likely to slip out. She needed to get his mind on something else.

From her spot on the floor, she shifted her attention to his pants. Her eyes met his, darkened with arousal, and she gave him what she hoped was a seductive smile as she slowly lowered his zipper.

With a few awkward and fumbling tugs Emily had his jeans and boxer briefs down. She willed her hands to stop shaking. Jester was used to sexually confident women who were probably masters in the art of blowjobs. She'd done it twice before, with another man, but it had been quite some time ago.

When his pants were out of the way she climbed on the bed, knelt next to him, and drank in the sight of him. His legs were long and powerfully built, with toned muscles encased in tattooed skin. From a thatch of dark hair between his thighs, his shaft rose, thick and swollen, to rest against his belly, and Emily licked her lips in anticipation of tasting him.

"Emily."

Jester's voice was dark, strained, and she immediately froze, lifting her gaze to meet his. Had she done something wrong already?

"I'm not a good man Emily. I've done shit that I will never tell you about because you shouldn't even know such things exist in life. There will be more in the future. It's just who I am. But I'm not a bully and I'll never hurt you. This is your one chance to walk away, because if you stay, you are mine. Fucking mine. And I will tear apart any man who touches or threatens what's mine."

Her eyes widened. This wasn't their deal. They'd agreed to enjoy it until it fizzled out, and now he was changing the rules. Here she was using sex to distract him from probing too deep into her life, and hoping for a chance to search Striker's room after he passed out. Whatever happened, whatever heartbreak she would endure as a result of her deceptions, she fully deserved.

Jester was ignorant to the fact that Emily had recently been introduced to the uglier side of life. She wasn't his, couldn't be. The desire to be his woman was so strong it was a living presence within her, but for one more week, she belonged to Snake. Maybe not her body, her body she could give to Jester, but her actions and motivations, they were owned by Snake.

The lines between right and wrong, good and evil were becoming so blurred she feared it would never be clear again. The two things she now wanted most in this world were mutually exclusive, and yet here she was trying to make the impossible happen. Trying to make a relationship work with Jester *and* save her brother. When this was over, and she was left with the shattered pieces of her soul, would she find comfort in the recollection of Jester's words? Or would they just make the guilt and regret burn brighter?

Emily lowered her head, and licked along the length of him from root to tip, taking her time before she opened her mouth wide and drew him in. As with all her actions in the past weeks, she was torn. Split in two between the desire to show Jester just how much he meant to her, and need to tire him out and search Striker's room.

There was a special place in hell waiting just for her.

~ ~ ~ ~

Jester hissed out a breath as the searing heat of Emily's mouth surrounded his cock. Her cheeks hollowed with a tentative suction and she drew her lips along the hard shaft, swirling her tongue around the sensitive head when she reached the tip.

He felt a bit shaken and vulnerable after his confession to Emily. Fuck their original deal. He wasn't tiring of her;

156

rather the intensity of the desire to be with her grew strong each day. She wanted him just as much, he could see it in her eyes, but she hadn't said anything. Emily kept her emotions close and he still had the impression there was something in her life that troubled her, something she wasn't yet willing to share.

He lost thought of everything besides the heat of Emily's mouth as she grew bolder and slid her lips back down his shaft, sucking him deep this time, and with more vigor. Jester had to fist his hands in the comforter to keep from plunging his fingers into her hair and taking control of the pace. It was obvious she didn't have much experience giving head, and he didn't want to overwhelm her with his demands.

Jester had received countless blowjobs by innumerable women, most of whom were practiced experts on the subject. Typically, he rested his head back, threw an arm across his eyes and let the woman go to town. This was an entirely different experience involving all of his senses. His eyes were riveted to Emily's head, bobbing up and down in his lap. Every few seconds she would lift her lashes, and he'd catch a glimpse of her beautiful eyes, smoky with desire.

She made tiny sounds; light little moans that alerted him to the fact that he wasn't the only one affected by this act. And her smell…Christ, he swore he could smell her arousal permeating the air. He groaned low and long, and her mouth tightened as she worked him up and down, her inhibitions fleeing at his obvious enjoyment of her efforts.

Emily didn't need proficiency; in fact, he was thrilled that she hadn't been spending her time with men buried to their balls in her mouth like he was now. The notion of her with another man brought out his murderous side.

She was a natural. The wet heat of her mouth, her generous nature, and her enthusiasm gave her an advantage over the most skilled of lovers.

When she reached out and cupped his balls, giving them a soft caress, he could no longer hold still. His hips surged up and drove him deeper into the cavern of her mouth. For a moment she hesitated, and he worried he'd gone too far, that she'd gag and pull back, but she readjusted and went right back to her task.

She sucked him with passion now, completely engrossed in the act, using her tongue, lips and teeth to take his breath away.

"Emily," he warned on a gasp. "I'm not going to last much longer." The next move was up to her. He wanted nothing more than to watch her swallow all of him down, but since this was new to her he wasn't sure if she'd be into it.

For a moment she lifted her head, replacing her mouth with the sure, steady stroke of her hand. "I absolutely love coming in your mouth. I'm hoping that means you'll feel the same." She removed her hand, opened her swollen lips wide, and took him back in.

The memory of her losing control against his mouth did him in, and within seconds he was coming, harder than he had in a long time. His hips jerked, and Emily grabbed onto them to stabilize herself as he bucked and grunted beneath her.

She kept her mouth still around him until the shaking subsided. He gasped, overly sensitive, as she let him slip from between her lips. Jester felt drained, extremely sated, and just plain happy.

Still fully dressed, Emily crawled up his body and placed gentle kisses along the way on his thighs, his quivering abdomen, and his pecs.

When she completed her journey, she wrapped her arms around his sides and laid her head on his chest, draped over him like a warm, sexy blanket. Jester reached down, grasped the backs of her thighs and drew them up so her arms and legs were on either side of him, cradling his body.

He left his hands wrapped around her legs, and stroked the tender skin of her inner thighs. "That was indescribable, Em, and if you give me three minutes I'll be more than happy to return the favor."

She shook her head and squeezed him tight with her slight arms. "Just hold me like this for a while, if you don't mind."

He slid his hands up and cupped her ass, holding her flush against his body. A hint of sadness whispered in her voice. Something wasn't completely right with her, and he hoped she would soon be willing to confide in him.

Loud pounding on the door killed any chance for post-orgasm bliss.

Striker's voice poured into the room. "You two have thirty seconds to get your clothes on and then I'm coming in. No way are you guys going at it all day while the rest of us are stuck at the barbecue. Twenty-four seconds now."

Emily scrambled off Jester with a mortified look on her face. She smoothed the front of her rumpled clothes and tried to restore order to her hair. Her lips were slightly swollen from sucking him off, which gave her a sultry look.

Jester swung his leg over the edge of the bed and came to a stand, pulling his pants back up. He didn't really give two shits if Striker busted in on him.

"Fifteen seconds, asshole. And I better not see your hairy ass when I get in there."

"Striker!" Lila exclaimed. "Jester does not have a hairy ass."

"And how the hell would you know?" Striker snarled, crystal clear, through the closed door.

"Well, I guess I don't know for sure, but come on."

"Ten seconds and counting."

Emily's eyes widened. "I can fully attest to the fact that Jester's ass is a perfect specimen, not at all hairy," she called, loud enough to be heard in the hallway.

Deciding to have a little fun of his own, Jester released his hold on his pants, and let them drop back down to the ground. He turned his back to the door, bare ass on full display, and struck a pose, flexing his extraordinary muscles just at the door flew open.

Lila released a low whistle.

Striker wasn't quite as impressed. "Oh, hell no!" He shoved Lila back into the hallway. "Close your eyes, woman. You take one more look at his fuckin' ass, and I'll redden yours so bad you won't sit for a week."

"Hmm it might be worth it. Did you see him? That is one fine piece of man meat." The couple disappeared down the hallway. The sound of Striker's hand landing on Lila's bottom was followed by a high-pitched shriek.

Emily had a small smile on her face, but it didn't reach her eyes, and it wasn't the reaction Jester would have expected from her.

Feeling quite pleased with the outcome of that exchange, Jester tugged his jeans back up. He wrapped an arm around Emily's shoulders, bringing her close to him as they exited the room.

He couldn't keep the satisfied smirk from erupting on his face. "Well, a beat down, a blowjob, and I got one over on Striker. I think it's safe to say I am today's grand prize winner."

Once again, she didn't laugh and he frowned down at her. At some point he'd need to have it out with her. If she was going to be with him—

Shit.

Maybe that was it. Maybe she didn't want him like he wanted her.

Chapter Eighteen

On Wednesday evening, Jester stepped outside Emily's apartment, and jogged down the steps to his parked bike. It wasn't dusk yet, but the sun had dipped in the cloudless sky, taking with it the sizzling temperature that often made summers in the desert intolerable.

As he approached the bike, Jester glanced at his phone. Six forty-five. Church was at eight tonight, the last one before the Grimm's meet up with the cartel on Friday. The club hoped to finalize the details of the takedown, and if all went well, they'd have a solid plan to rid the Grimm Brothers of hundreds of thousands of dollars while keeping the drugs out of Crystal Rock, and keeping the club off the radar of the cops.

The No Prisoners had a very comfortable relationship with the local boys in blue. A strategic few of them were paid to look the other way. But border crossing drug shipments worth upward of a million dollars tended to attract the attention of the Feds, and that was the last thing the club wanted.

Jester's ears twitched as the rumble of motorcycle pipes cut through the quiet of the evening. Four bikes, if he was

162

correct. Outside the club, there weren't any bikers in town who traveled in groups. The riders were probably out of towners passing through, unless the club had sent some guys out to meet him at Emily's. His guys would only come if there were some kind of trouble.

The roar grew louder. Emily stepped out of her apartment and started down the steps. The skirt of her teal summer dress—with thin straps he wanted to rip right off her—flowed around her thighs. She looked edible, like a cool treat, the perfect ending for a hot summer day, and he fully planned to indulge later.

The noise swelled to a thunderous level, whipping Jester's attention away from Emily and back toward the street. Four Harleys peeled into the lot leaving a cloud of dust and sand in their wake.

Shit.

He was so distracted by her, he'd lost his radar sense for danger.

Grimm Brothers.

This was not good. Jester spun and speared Emily with the most serious and lethal look he could muster. Pointing, he said, "Emily! Get back in the apartment, now. Lock the door."

She turned and fled up the steps to the second floor landing. He had to trust she'd listen and lock herself in the apartment, because his focus need to be on getting rid of the Grimms.

Snake and his lackey Casper dismounted their bikes. The other two remained seated on their bikes with helmets and sunglasses on, concealing their identity.

"You take the wrong exit, Snake?" Jester relaxed his stance and kept his palms at his sides facing outward in an attempt to assume a non-threatening pose. Sure, he was huge and could fight like a gutter rat if need be, but Snake was no slouch, and four to one were never good odds.

Snake focused on something beyond Jester.

Risking a lack of attention on Snake, Jester peeked over his shoulder.

Emily stood two steps from the second floor landing. She held the railing, her knuckles white. Her normally fair complexion had paled even further, and her light eyes displayed pure terror.

Motherfucker!

A gentle breeze had her hair floating across her face, and her skirt swirling around her bare legs. Innocence and sweetness radiated from her, amid the potential violence. His moral, child-loving woman couldn't possibly know how much danger she was in just by being a witness to this exchange. He wanted to pin that entirely on the reptile before him, but he was the one who'd let the darker side of his life invade her world.

He had the urge to sprint up the stairs and drag her into the apartment, but he couldn't risk leaving without learning the reason for Snake's presence.

He turned his attention back to Snake. "You got something to say, let's hear it. I have shit to do." He needed to pry the man's eyes off his woman. Either that or gouge them out.

Snake's mouth twisted into a lecherous grin as he moved his attention to Jester. "I can see what it is you have to do. Quite a tasty morsel you've got yourself there." He shifted lifeless eyes toward Emily again before giving Jester his focus.

"That what this is about? You running out of women in Sandy Springs? Have to come here to eye-fuck mine?" Jester's patience was running thin. If there was a reason for this little visit, Snake needed to put it out there soon.

Snake laughed. It was an unnerving sound Jester had heard on more than one occasion. It had a chilling quality to it that made him wonder if Snake was really all there. Next to him, the bald as a baby Casper snickered as well.

Jester smiled as he imagined snapping the twig of a man in half.

"You live up to your name well, Jester. We were in town visiting a friend, but they turned out to be otherwise engaged." He shrugged. "When we saw you, we decided to stop by and say hello. That's all."

With one last look at Emily, Snake turned and walked back toward his bike, Casper trotting alongside him like the well-trained pet he was. Without turning, Snake yelled, "Don't be too rough with that one, Jester. Emily's quite the looker. It would be a shame if you damaged her."

A chill traveled down his spine. How the fuck did he know Emily's name? Jester wanted to tear after him, and slam his smug face into the ground until he spilled the real reason for this visit. But it was still four on one and if he was injured, Emily would be left totally unprotected.

He didn't buy Snake's story one bit. Did Snake come here just to fuck with him about Emily?

He turned around and saw that Emily remained in the same spot on the steps, just shy of the landing. Suddenly full of burning rage, Jester stormed toward the steps, taking them two at a time until he reached her.

~ ~ ~ ~

Emily was frozen, she couldn't have moved from her spot on the steps if her life depended on it. Snake's presence brought a terror so strong her muscles seized and blood pounded in her ears so hard she couldn't make out a word the men were saying.

She wanted to do as Jester commanded and run to the

safety of the apartment, but her feet wouldn't respond.

Why was Snake here? Had he come to see her, not expecting her relationship with Jester? She hadn't breathed a word of it to him, remaining vague in all her communication, mostly via text message. Maybe he'd decided he wasn't going to wait two weeks. Perhaps her time was up and he'd intended to…to what? She didn't even want to entertain the possibilities. Worse was the fear that he'd tell Jester everything.

Emily looked on astonished when, after a quick exchange, Snake returned to his motorcycle. Breathing out the air she'd trapped in her lungs, her muscles relaxed a fraction, until she took in the look on Jester's face. Six-foot-five inches of furious male stormed up the stairs toward her.

With her heart in her throat, and her stomach about to revolt, Emily forced herself to stand her ground. When Jester reached her, he grabbed her under her right arm and propelled her into her apartment. His grip was rough and uncomfortable, but he wasn't actually hurting her.

After he propelled her through the door, he kicked it closed with excessive force, the loud slam echoed through the sparse apartment. Emily jumped at the noise, and yelped when he turned her, and backed her forcibly against the door. He caged her in with an arm on each side of her head. Darkened with fury, his eyes bore into hers.

Emily held his gaze, and swallowed back her alarm, praying he wasn't about to tell her he knew about Johnny. She started to shake, and no amount of contracting her muscles could stop the trembling.

Jester leaned down, his face inches from hers, dwarfing her where she rested against the wall. He was purposefully using his size to intimidate her.

When he spoke, his voice was low, menacing, and left no

doubt as to the degree of his anger. "Don't you ever fucking disobey me like that again, Emily. Is that clear?"

Part of her wanted to scoff at his use of the word disobey, like she was a petulant child who didn't listen to daddy. "Y-yes." Now didn't seem an intelligent time to challenge him.

This was the intensity she'd sensed was always lurking under Jester's joking façade. She'd glimpsed it when he fought with Colt at the barbeque. Now that she was on the receiving end, she realized just how formidable the man really was, and it scared her to death. If this was his reaction when she didn't jump at his command to move away from Snake, the reaction to her betrayal would be unimaginable.

"He knows your fucking name, Emily. Somehow he knows your name, and now you're on his radar. That is not something you want. He is a ruthless sadist." With a roar of frustration Jester slapped his hand against the wall next to Emily's head, a loud crack that reverberated through the quiet evening. Emily's entire body jolted and her hand flew up, pressing against her racing heart.

The knowledge of exactly how dangerous Snake could be was burned into her soul in the form of images of her brother's beaten face. Jester didn't need to spell it out for her. But she couldn't share that with Jester.

Snake had come to check on her progress. Maybe to exert a little extra pressure, she was sure of it. And now he'd dropped hints to Jester, infuriating him and creating a link in Jester's mind between Snake and herself. Each time she thought this nightmare couldn't get any worse, it did.

The fear of Snake combined with the guilt over angering Jester, the fear over Jester's eventual reaction to her betrayal, and the ever present fear for Johnny slammed into her all at once. Suddenly, it was too much to bear.

A harsh sob escaped from deep inside her, and she sagged

against Jester's chest, hot tears pouring from her eyes. Once it started, she couldn't stop it, and she clung to him for many minutes as she sobbed out her fears.

Some of the starch leeched out of Jester's stance at her obvious distress. He wrapped his strong arms around her back and engulfed her with his massive body.

The masculine scent of leather, smoke, and Jester surrounded her as he held her close. She felt safe and protected in his arms, and allowed herself that comfort for a few seconds.

"Shit. I'm sorry, Em. I didn't mean to scare you. The idea of him touching you, fuck, the idea of him even thinking about you makes me absolutely insane. It's my fault. I should have been more careful about you being seen with me. The Grimm Brothers are our enemies and there's a nasty history between us. He's trying to fuck with me by throwing your name around. We won't have to worry about him for much longer though."

Emily froze, her breath coming in hitches as her tears ebbed. It was the most he'd ever said about anything related to club business, and he offered her an opening on a silver platter.

"What do you mean? Why won't we have to worry about him?"

"Shit," he said and rubbed a hand over his face. "You've got my head all fucked up, woman. Forget I said anything. Nothing you need to be concerned about."

She pressed on, no way could she let this drop so easily. "Is something happening? Are you in danger?" She didn't have to work to instill any panic into her voice, it was just there.

He hugged her close again. "Babe, I can't give you details about club business. I've told you that."

She banged her forehead against his chest. "I know, but

168

—."

"But nothing, Emily." He sighed. "Look, I know you can keep your mouth shut, it's not that."

Guilt hit her sharp and fast, but she shook it off, hanging on every word he spoke.

"Knowing shit about the club can get you killed. All I'm going to say is that we are taking care of our problem with the Grimms. I shouldn't even tell you that much, but I feel like I owe you that after what happened tonight, so you won't be afraid all the time."

She wanted to ease his conscience, tell him that Snake's visit had nothing to do with him, and everything to do with her. But she couldn't. Not yet. Not until she was sure her brother wouldn't die.

If she'd known what she now knew of Jester when she first met him, she would have spilled her guts that first night. Now, it was too late. She was in too deep. The lies and betrayal were a bottomless pit, sucking her further into the murky depths with every passing second.

"I'm sorry I didn't go back into the apartment."

Jester pulled back, and peered down at her. One large hand cradled her face, and his thumb swept across her cheek, wiping an errant tear away. "I'm not an asshole, babe. I don't need to order you around or have you bend to my will all day long. But if we are ever in a situation like that, and I tell you to do something, I need to know you'll listen. If you're going to be with me, this needs to be agreed on now. I'd give anything to tell you there will never be another incident like that, but the truth is I have enemies, babe. The club has enemies. I will always do everything in my power to shield you, but sometimes shit happens."

Guilt, and hatred for Snake twisted her insides. "I understand, truly I do. I promise if we're ever in a situation like that again I'll do exactly what you say." It was a promise she'd never get the chance to keep. She'd be gone in a few days, but the statement seemed to ease his worry.

Jester leaned in, laying a whisper of a kiss on Emily's lips, a gesture meant to comfort rather than arouse. When he ended the kiss, he rested his forehead against hers, and emitted a deep sigh. "It was four to one, Em. If something happened to me you'd have been a sitting duck up there on the stairs in that dress that just screams, 'rip these straps off and suck my tits.'"

Normally she would have laughed at his comment, but her mind was bogged down with worry for Johnny. Not knowing what Snake had wanted to tell her made her twitchy.

"Come on, trouble, it's safe out there now, and as much as I'd rather stay so I can show you exactly what that dress is doing to me, we have to get over to the clubhouse."

Emily trailed behind Jester as he exited her apartment. He was hyper alert and consistently scanning his surroundings for danger.

Time was ticking away, and Snake was getting more impatient. She had to get into that meeting room tonight. There just wasn't any other option at this point.

Chapter Nineteen

Jester leaned back in his chair as one by one the patched members filed into the meeting room. Normally the guys would banter, rib each other and generally be loud and rowdy until Shiv barked at them to shut up and called the meeting to order. Tonight, however, the mood was somber, everyone aware they were there to finalize the details for a takedown that had the potential to result in injuries or worse.

Bubbling under the serious mood was a ripple of anticipation as well. The Grimm Brothers had been a thorn in the No Prisoners' side for more than a year now and a part of each member was looking forward to the confrontation.

Now, with the memory of the way Snake leered at Emily fresh in his mind, Jester was more determined than ever to take the man out.

Emily's reaction at the apartment had startled him. He'd expected some fear and maybe a negative reaction to his own anger, but her breaking down in heaving sobs seemed over the top. Her terror was so intense it was almost palpable. Jester made a mental note to pry for answers from her once and for all, the moment this business with the Grimms was over. It was time to find out what in her life had her afraid.

Once everyone's attention was on him, Shiv addressed the men. "Jester's going to walk us through the plan thus far. Keep your traps shut until he's done. Then you can let us know if you see any holes." He turned to Jester and nodded for him to begin.

The map they'd been using to draw out their plans lay unrolled on the table. "Okay, we know from our source in Mexico that the Grimms are set to meet with the Fuentes Cartel at noon on Friday just beyond the mountain pass, here." He tapped a spot on the map just beyond where the highway traversed the mountain.

"Originally, we planned to take the Grimms before they got to the meeting spot. But our guy, who is with the Caballeros de Sangre MC down in Mexico, is planning to hit the Fuentes Cartel for the drugs before they even cross the border. Which means no one will be coming to meet ol' Snake and his band of assholes.

"That puts us in the perfect position to stand in for the cartel and intercept the money. Of course it won't be quite as easy as it sounds. No way will Snake fall for a trap and hand the money over to us. We're still going to have to take it by force. But the roads down there are windy as fuck and the mountains afford us plenty of hiding spots." He glanced at Shiv who nodded and stood to take over.

Rising from his seat at the head of the rectangular table, Shiv pointed to a series of red circles on the map. "These six locations are where we are going to have guys hidden. Striker, Jester, and Acer will be waiting at the meet up spot, as though they were the cartel. Prospects will have a van with three guys in the back. Plan is for everyone to jump out, weapons drawn at the same time. We'll overtake 'em with sheer numbers."

Jester resumed the explanation. "They will obviously have a van or truck as well. They ain't gonna carry upward of a million in cash on their bikes. Our guys here—" He pointed to the mouth of the mountain pass. "—will come around and jack it open, snatch the money, and load it into our second van, which will have been stashed off the road here. Van takes off immediately and goes to the warehouse, not back here."

The club owned an old broken down warehouse off the main drag that was used for more sensitive matters. Few people outside the club knew it was anything more than an abandoned warehouse, and those people wouldn't run their mouths, knowing the club would come knocking on their doors if word leaked out.

Shiv ran through additional details, then opened the discussion to the members. "Okay, let's hear it." He rubbed the back of his neck. Now that they'd ran through it once, his face relaxed, and he looked pleased with the plan. "Concerns, questions, comments?"

"We have any idea how many of them will be showing up?" Gumby asked.

Shaking his head, Acer answered. "We do not, which is why we are going heavy on the artillery and heavy on our own numbers." He was an intelligent bastard and had been integral in helping Jester devise the plan.

Gumby nodded.

"Where the bikes gonna be stashed?" an old timer named Buzz asked. Named for his buzz haircut, he had a giant belly that was as round as a ball. The old guy blew out his knee a year ago, and couldn't handle participating in something like this anymore, but he was still an active member of the club. "You're gonna have to hide them so Snake don't see them as he rides in."

One corner of Shiv's mouth curled up in a smirk that held a hint of evil joy. "That's the best part, boys. You ain't taking 'em. Everyone's riding in the back of the vans. Striker, Jester, and Acer will have theirs, everyone make sure you shower cuz you're gonna be in close quarters for the toasty ride out and back."

A chorus of dissatisfied male swearing erupted around the room, and Shiv just laughed. Jester knew he didn't much give a shit about the comfort level of the guys, not when the end goal was such a high payday.

~ ~ ~ ~

Emily sat at the bar with Marcie, nursing a beer while anxiously tapping her foot on a rung of the bar stool. Lila had planned to join them, but a coworker was ill and she'd ended up taking an extra shift at the hospital, much to Striker's very vocal dismay.

Tonight was the night. After the meeting the guys were heading to Black's, a local dive bar and strip club on the edge of town. Jester had some paperwork to complete over in the garage and they'd decided he'd skip out on the festivities so they could go home and have their own strip show.

If all went according to plan, Emily should be left alone, or close to it, in the clubhouse for a few minutes. She planned to use whatever opportunity she'd be granted to snoop for information on what was happening Friday. That had to be what they were in there meeting about.

It was impossible to spend time with these guys and not pick up on the fact that something was going down on Friday, but that was as far as it ever got. Every last one of them was completely tightlipped about any club information.

She hadn't eaten anything all day, unable to bear the thought of food. The few sips of beer she'd forced down mixed with the acid in her empty stomach, causing a gnawing pain.

Emily wasn't sure if she wanted to know the details or not, but that didn't matter. She had to try and find something. This morning she'd received a picture via text of Johnny, bruised, bloodied and obviously going through some kind of withdrawal.

His battered face looked so awful Emily spent the next half hour crying, grateful Jester hadn't been around. It was one less lie she had to tell him.

Not that that would be of any comfort to him in two days when she disappeared.

"Did you hear me, Emily?" Marcie's voice permeated the cloud of despair threatening to engulf Emily.

Emily blinked, and dragged herself back to the here and now. "I'm sorry, Marcie, I'm terrible company tonight."

"Everything good with you and Jester?" There was legitimate concern in Marcie's voice, which only served to make Emily feel worse.

She swallowed down the lump that formed in her throat, and gave Marcie what she hoped was a convincing smile. "More than good. I just have some family stuff weighing on my mind." It was the truth, or as close to the truth as she could safely get.

"I'm sorry to hear that, girl. We haven't known each other long, but I hope you know you can talk to me if you need to. Us ol' ladies need to stick together around here, what with all the testosterone and whores flying around." She winked.

Emily forced an unconvincing laugh. Marcie was a doll for making such an effort to cheer her up, but nothing could accomplish that this evening. "Thank you. I appreciate your concern. I'm just not quite ready to put it out there yet."

Marcie nodded, and tipped her head back to drain the last of her beer. "Fair enough."

The doors flew open and a hoard of loud, boisterous bikers spilled out into the bar area, much more animated than the group that had gone into the meeting room. Things must have gone well.

Marcie, ever bubbly, giggled and hopped off her chair as Hook drew near. He wrapped his arms around her, leaned in close, and Emily was near enough to hear him whisper in her ear. "Let's go home, baby, I've been dying to see what you've got on under that skirt all night."

Yes, they all needed to leave.

Emily glanced down at the pieces of ripped beer label that sat on the bar in front of her, unaware that she'd been picking it off.

She was so caught up in her own head, she didn't notice Jester approach her from behind until he enveloped her in his strong arms.

"They ain't got nothing on us," he whispered, nodding in the direction of Marcie and Hook, who shared a passionate kiss. He nipped her ear lobe before drawing it into his mouth and sucking briefly. "To be continued."

Normally, she'd love his affectionate mood and teasing, but tonight it fell flat. "You heading to the garage?"

Jester frowned down at her. "You trying to get rid of me?"

Yes.

"No, of course not." She took his hand and gave it a squeeze.

He stared at her with an unreadable expression. "Everything okay with you, babe?"

She cleared her throat. "Me? Yes, of course. Just...just a little tired tonight."

"You want me to take you home? I can come back and work."

"No!"

176

His eyebrows drew down.

This was not going well. She wrapped her arms around his waist and rested her head on his chest. "I'm totally fine to hang out here while you get your stuff done. It's no big deal."

He pressed a kiss to the top of her head. "Ok, babe, but if you want to go, just come find me in the garage."

The clubhouse was emptied in record time, none of the guys bothering to linger when the alternative was booze and an abundance of naked women. Marcie and Hook remained, having spent the time making out like teenagers. One prospect milled around behind the bar, cleaning up, but that was it.

"You guys walking out?" Hook asked as he steered Marcie toward the door.

"I have about twenty minutes of paperwork to get done. Jaz has been riding my ass all week, so I'm just going to run over and take care of it now." He turned toward Emily. "You sure you're okay to hang here? Jacko should be here the whole time."

Shit. She hadn't factored in the prospect behind the bar. He was missing a front tooth like a jack o' lantern and the poor guy was teased mercilessly. He'd only been prospecting for about two months, according to Jester, hence why he was stuck at the clubhouse cleaning when the rest of the guys were at the strip club.

"I'm good, Jester. Go! The faster you get over there the faster we can get home and on to other activities." She gave him a wink. It was nearly impossible to continue the façade of the happy girlfriend when she felt like crawling out of her skin with nerves and guilt.

Jester smiled as he bent down to lay one on her. "I like the way you think, baby." He turned and exited, heading toward the garage.

"Bye, girl," Marcie said as she gave Emily a tight hug. "Call if you need a girlfriend."

"Thanks, Marcie. You two have a good night."

"We plan to." Hook bobbed his eyebrows as Marcie rolled her eyes and grabbed his hand, dragging him out the door.

Alone with the prospect, Emily glanced at her phone. Nine fifteen. Jester said he'd be twenty minutes, so Emily gave herself until nine thirty to hopefully have a five-minute buffer. She rolled her shoulders and stretched her neck to the side. The muscles were cramped from prolonged tension.

"Damnit!"

"Something wrong?" Emily asked.

"I forgot I have to bring these crates to the storage room out behind the garage. You mind if I leave you here for five, ten minutes tops?"

Her heart sped up. Hell no, she didn't mind, in fact she insisted he leave. Finally, something was playing out in her favor. "Oh please, I'll be totally fine. Don't worry."

"Thanks, Emily. Ten tops."

She nodded and absently waved him off, her attention on the upcoming task. The second the door clicked shut, Emily darted toward the meeting room, almost dropping to her knees in relief when the door swung open and granted her entry to the chapel.

A round clock on the wall read nine eighteen. Each second ticked by louder than a gong in her mind. Less than ten minutes to find information she didn't know where to begin searching for.

Chapter Twenty

Emily stood in the doorway to the meeting room trying desperately to ignore the voice in her head screaming at her over and over what would happen if she were caught.

There wasn't a single acceptable excuse for her presence, and most likely she wouldn't walk out of this building alive if she were discovered snooping. She shut down the voice. She had to do this regardless of the possible consequences. Johnny's life was in her hands, and while he may have decided his own life was worthless, she'd still fight for him.

Her right hand began to ache and she forced herself to unclench her fist. Five angry red crescent shaped gouges marred her palm, one dotted with blood. The pain barely registered, her brain too full of fear for any other sensations.

Emily scanned the room for something, anything that could contain the information she needed more than her next breath. The clock read nine-twenty. Two minutes since the prospect left her alone. In her haste to explore her surroundings, Emily almost tripped over a long, laminated cylindrical object on the ground.

Heart pounding like a runaway stampede, she retrieved the object. Her hands shook and she fumbled with the rubber band holding the tube closed. Once she worked the blasted rubber band off, she unrolled what appeared to be a large map of Crystal Rock onto the table.

The document was a schematic of some sort, but she couldn't make sense of what it meant. There wasn't time to waste deciphering it, so she whipped out her phone and snapped a photo of the entire map. Later, when she was alone, she would attempt to interpret the meaning.

With clumsy hands, Emily struggled to return the map to its rolled up state. Her phone chimed in the pocket of the denim jacket she'd thrown on over her dress, and she let out a small shriek. One hand flew to her chest, over her racing heart, and she dropped the map and shot the rubber band into the corner of the room.

"Shit!" she muttered to herself as she sneaked a peek at the phone.

Text from Snake. Again.

It was crunch time and he was turning up the heat. The clock on the wall read nine-twenty-eight. No time to read the text. Her chest heaved and her breaths came in short, insufficient gasps. Where the hell did the rubber band go?

From her pocket the phone vibrated again, mocking her. Any time now, Jacko would walk back into the clubhouse. If Emily was found in this room it was all over, and there was a very good chance it would literally be over for her if they discovered what she'd been up to.

Black spots swam in front of her vision as her breathing grew more erratic. Finally, she caught sight of the rubber band peeking out from under the table. Emily rolled the map up as fast as possible, not caring that it was sloppy and shoved the rubber band around the cylinder. After tossing it under the table close enough to where she'd stumbled upon it, she bolted out the door.

›

The very second the meeting room door clicked shut behind her, the main entrance to the clubhouse cracked open.

Shit!

Getting caught just outside the meeting room was only one step away from being caught inside.

She stepped away from the door. Her right knee buckled, but she slammed it back and held her ground. In her chest, her heart galloped as though she'd been running for her life, and sweat ran down between her breasts as they rose and fell with the force of her breathing. All things Jacko would pick up on, if he weren't totally oblivious. Not a chance she could take.

Emily yanked her phone from her pocket and slapped it to her ear. She began paced in front of the double doors, tightening her thigh muscles with each step to keep her legs from collapsing. She elevated her volume in feigned anger and spoke to no one. "If it was working, I wouldn't be calling again!" she shouted, putting some huff and frustration into her voice.

Jacko made eye contact with her and she mouthed, "Sorry," before she pointed to the phone and rolled her eyes.

He waved her off. "No worries," he mumbled and resumed his duties behind the bar.

"You've been to my apartment three times to fix it, and it's still not working. This is the last chance, if it's not resolved after this I'm switching my service." She pulled the phone away from her ear, let out an aggravated sigh, and pretended to jam the end button. After a quick prayer that he fell for it, she turned toward Jacko and rolled her eyes again. "Damn cable company." She fanned herself. "They get me so flustered and pissed off. I know I shouldn't let them get to me, but they keep screwing up my service."

Jacko was quite obviously not interested in her problems, but he also didn't seem remotely suspicious of her actions. Goal accomplished.

With a shaky breath, Emily returned to the barstool she'd occupied earlier, and chugged her now warm beer.

Since Jacko was busy sweeping the floor, and paid her no attention, Emily opened Snake's text to see what threat he'd made this time.

Nice to see you today Emily. Loved the dress. Gave me all kinds of naughty thoughts.

The hairs on the back of her neck rose to attention and she shivered. Jester had been right about the dress. She'd never wear it again. Knowing Snake had noticed her body in the dress and commented on it made her want to burn the thing.

The door opened again and Jester strode in. She flinched and shoved the phone in her pocket. His eyes zeroed in on her immediately. He'd notice something was off. Unlike Jacko, Jester was observant, especially when it came to her.

With just a few steps of his extended stride, he was next to her and kissing her like a starving man. Her head spun as he stole her air and fired her blood.

"What's wrong?" He whispered against her ear when he broke the kiss. "You're shaking. I should have taken you home."

Emily forced her lips into a smile and stroked a hand up his chest. "I just want you." Normally it was true, she wanted him constantly. But tonight, the picture on her phone was all she could think about. She had a compulsive need to understand what it was before she sent it to Snake and betrayed Jester.

"You have no idea how much I want you. I can't go much longer without being inside you, so we need to leave now."

Words that normally flooded her panties and warmed her heart left her cold. A bone deep exhaustion crept over her and she leaned against Jester for support. "Let's go home."

"Babe." His body was relaxed against hers. "You sure you're okay? I'm not asshole enough that I can't go one night without if you're tired."

"I'm good," she lied. "Promise."

He studied her for a second more and she held her breath. Those warm brown eyes seemed to stare into her soul. God help her if they could, because he'd find nothing but betrayal and regret.

As the pair left, Jester called back to Jacko over his shoulder. "See ya, prospect. Too bad you got stuck on house duty tonight. Rest of the guys will be buried mouth deep in stripper tits by now. Ahh, but such is the life of a lowly prospect."

On any other night their banter would have made her laugh, but tonight she couldn't even drum up a chuckle.

"Looks like you've got your own cross to bear, man." Jacko fired back with a wink for Emily. "The little woman keeping you chained to the house? Won't let you go play with the boys?"

Never one to be outdone in the ribbing department, Jester laughed. "That may be, prospect, but she'll thank me real nice for all the orgasms I'm about to give her. Takes some of the sting out of it."

Jacko lifted his hands in surrender, conceding defeat.

Jester gave her a curious look, no doubt wondering why she didn't appear to enjoy their byplay.

"Maybe I am a little off tonight. I'm sorry, I'm just feeling a little out of sorts."

"Come on then, babe. I'll tuck you in and tell you a bed time story."

Despite her morose mood, a warmth settled in her stomach and she allowed herself one second to enjoy being cared for by Jester. After all, the sun was quickly setting on their time together.

***

An hour later—once Jester was finally asleep—Emily crept from the bed toward the bathroom with the stealth of a ninja. She'd retrieved her phone from the dresser on the way and held her breath as she closed the door without making a sound.

The toilet lid was down, so Emily used it as a seat while she pulled up the picture she'd snapped in the clubhouse. After several minutes of staring at it she felt her stomach drop to the floor. The map itself was confusing, but she was able to zoom in and read the hand written notes in the margins.

The details were still fuzzy, but Emily got the gist. They were planning to steal a huge sum of money from the Grimms, on Friday, at this spot indicated on the map.

Oh my God.

Her chest tightened until she couldn't draw in a breath. She bent her head between her knees and tried to inhale without making any noise. Jester couldn't find her in here like this.

Silent tears coursed down her cheeks and her body shook so violently she had trouble maintaining a grip on her phone. Despair overwhelmed her.

Snake could not get his hands on this map. If Snake found out what the No Prisoners were planning, the retaliation would be nothing less than devastating.

He would kill them.

All of them.

Lila's man could die. Marcie's husband could die. How

would she ever live with herself knowing she was responsible for harming these amazing women's husbands? She couldn't. That was the bottom line. She wouldn't survive the guilt of knowing she caused something horrible to happen to Striker or Hook, and it would be horrible, she had no doubt.

And the most horrifying thought of all, was the very likely possibility of harm coming to Jester. Every cell in her body wanted to protect him, to stay with him.

She'd fallen in love with him over the last two weeks. She wasn't under the illusion that they could maintain any form of a relationship after tomorrow, but she was completely in love with the man. Her mind refused to contemplate what would happen to him if Snake knew what the No Prisoners had planned.

But the alternative was Johnny's life. She would be sentencing her brother to death. Her only living relative, her flesh and blood, would cease to exist any longer if she didn't hand over the information to Snake.

She was dying inside. The extraordinary weight of this decision ate at her with each second that passed.

As she stared at the wall of Jester's bathroom an idea began to form. She needed time to flesh it out, something she was short on. She and Johnny would have to leave immediately and start over somewhere new, but they'd survived a move like that once before and could again.

Agony sliced her heart at the thought of moving and never seeing Jester again. She wanted to shove the pain into the dark corner of her mind and avoid it for now, but she forced herself to embrace it. Getting accustomed to the pain of losing Jester was imperative, because a life without him was the one constant in every scenario she played out in her mind.

Decision made, Emily opened her phone. *I have what you*

need.

The seconds ticked by slower than sap dripping from a tree as she waited for a response. Just as tears began to fill her eyes once again, the phone vibrated in her hands.

That's my girl. 4pm. Your house.

His girl. The phrase turned her blood to ice.

Emily blew out a breath and buried her face in her hands. If he didn't go along with the request she was about to ask of him, her entire plan was shot. It took her several tries to tap out the text, her unsteady fingers had trouble making contact with the correct letters.

I'll be there if you bring Johnny. I need to leave town with him. The NPs will kill me.

She hit send and closed her eyes, waiting to feel the vibrations of the phone in her hands. An eternity passed, in which she felt every second tick by like she was standing with a noose around her neck just waiting for someone to open the trapdoor beneath her.

The phone finally buzzed against her palm, causing an almost violent jolt through her body. So many lives rested on whatever was in this text message.

Emily forced her eyes open and read the screen. Relief hit her like a slap in the face.

I'll bring Johnny.

The nightmare was almost over. In less than twenty-four hours she and Johnny would be…somewhere. It didn't really matter where they were, as long as they were gone, never to return.

Never to see Jester again.

She buried her hands in her face to muffle the sounds of her tears. "I'm so sorry, Jester," she whispered. "It was the only way I could keep you safe."

After her tears subsided, she tiptoed back to bed. Jester

didn't stir when she slipped back under the covers, but when she curled herself around his broad back, securing an arm around his waist, he linked his fingers with hers and pulled her to his warmth.

Emily lay awake for most of the night, memorizing the feel of Jester's body held tight against hers while she rehearsed what she'd tell Snake.

Tomorrow it would all be over.

The staggering sense of relief combined with the crushing knowledge of what she'd lose overwhelmed her and kept her awake until morning sun shone through the blinds.

Chapter Twenty-One

Something was off with Emily.

She acted subdued and anxious, more in line with the girl he'd first met weeks ago. Jester tried coaxing a few laughs out of her, but wasn't successful. She staggered around his kitchen, the dark circles under her eyes evidence of a poor night's sleep.

She knew something big was going down tomorrow. Most likely she was nervous for him and would snap out of it later in the day.

Jester sipped his coffee only to choke on the burning liquid as a different thought invaded his mind. Could she be done with him? The idea shouldn't have been the air-stealing punch to the gut that it was. Women came and went from his life all the time. No big deal. Another was always waiting in the wings, eager to please him.

Why then, did the weight of an elephant crush his chest at the thought of Emily leaving him? She brought so much lightness and pleasure to his dark and sometimes violent existence. She softened him, maybe too much by the way his thoughts were going.

"You look exhausted, Em." He stood from the table and

poured his coffee down the sink, his mouth suddenly filled with a bitter taste.

She shrugged. "I didn't sleep well, no big deal."

"You know why that is, don't you?" He moved toward her and drew her into his embrace. A bit of his unease evaporated when she melted against him.

At last, she chuckled, the sound muffled in his chest. "No, but don't keep me in suspense."

"It's because you're used to at least two orgasms a night now. Best sleep medicine there is."

That had the desired effect, and a genuine laugh bubbled up from her. "You're right. Maybe I could get a little of your sleep therapy now."

He hardened as though there were a direct link between her words and the blood flow to his cock. "I think the doctor can spare a few minutes for you." He scooped his woman and jogged toward his bedroom with her in his arms.

"I can walk, you know."

"I know, baby, but I didn't get to touch you all night so I'm making up for lost time." He set her on the edge of the bed and captured her hand when it went to the waistband of her shorts. "Let me."

He locked eyes with her. She nodded and he gripped the edge of her sleep shorts. Emily lifted her bottom and allowed him to draw them down over her shapely hips. As he slowly worked them off her legs, his fingertips grazed the silky skin of her thighs and she shivered.

Next, he reached for the hem of her flowery tank top, lifted it, and pulled it over her head when she raised her arms. A sheer red bra overflowed with her generous breasts and a tiny swatch of red lace covered her pussy. He raised a questioning brow at Emily.

She smirked, bracing herself with her hands propped on

the bed behind her body, arching her back so her breasts were even more prominently displayed. Gone was the nervous, shy woman he'd met just a few weeks ago. In her place was a sexy siren who knew exactly how to drive her man wild. "I was too tired to bother taking it off last night. See something you like?"

He loved her like this. "Fuck yes, I do. Christ, Em, you are the sexiest woman I've ever seen. Each time I have you I want you more. Someone just has to mention your name and I'm hard and aching for you, counting down the minutes until I can touch you, taste you and hear you moan my name. You've done something to me, baby."

"Jester," she whispered, the flirty playful twinkle gone from her eyes as deep emotion filled them, darkening the pale blue.

He pulled his T-shirt over his head before stripping out of his sweatpants.

Emily's eyes roamed over his body as the soft material dropped to the floor. Jester loved the way she looked at him, always with a little awe in her gaze like she was continually surprised by what was revealed when he disrobed.

"Let's take a shower," he ordered, pulling her from the bed. "I smell like the clubhouse."

Emily took the lead heading to the bathroom, and he watched her walk away, mesmerized by the sway of her hips and the twitch of her ass.

"You coming?" She peeked over her shoulder, catching his eyes on her curves.

"Right after you do."

She laughed, and continued into the bathroom while he grabbed both of their phones and switched the ringers off. There would be no distractions this morning. The outcome of tomorrow's takedown loomed ahead, uncertain, but today,

today he would seal them away from the rest of the world, until nothing existed but pleasure.

When he joined Emily in the bathroom, he found her standing in front of the mirror much as he had the morning after they'd first been together. God, he liked her here. In his room, in his space. This was where she belonged, and he planned to tell her as soon as tomorrow was over and successful.

She stood there in that sinner's red bra and panty set, and his cock twitched at the picture she presented.

Jester slid into place behind her. He cupped her breasts in his large hands and trailed kisses along her neck. She tilted her head to the side, giving him unhindered access to the line of her throat, which he took full advantage of. When she sighed in contentment, he slid his thumbs into the cups of her bra, rubbing them over her nipples. He was pleased, but not surprised, to find them already drawn tight.

Emily squirmed, and he slid a second finger into each cup of the bra, pinching her nipples with the exact amount of pressure she liked. His baby loved for him to play with her tits, almost as much as he loved to do it, and she didn't require a light touch.

They both kept their eyes open, watching in the mirror, as the sexy couple reflected back at them grew more and more frantic with need. Jester controlled the pace, keeping it slow and just shy of what she needed. He wanted her on the edge, thinking of nothing but her need for him and the pleasure only he could give her.

"Jester." He sucked on the spot where her neck met her shoulder and she moaned. "It's not enough. I need more, please give me more."

"I know, baby, believe me I know. I want to be inside you so bad it hurts."

"Then why are you waiting?" Her voice sounded desperate, a near whine.

"Because I want you completely out of your mind before I take you."

"I'm there."

He chuckled. "No you're not, but I'll let you know when you are." He removed his hands from her breasts, and chuckled again when she protested. "Don't worry, I promise I'll get back to your tits. I know how much you love me to suck them." When she groaned again, he unclasped her bra, letting it fall to the floor.

His eyes immediately lowered to her breasts, watching in the mirror as they rose and fell with the increasing pace of her breathing. They were gorgeous, large and heavy with beaded nipples he loved to feel against his tongue. Despite the number of times he'd already had his hands and mouth on them, he still fantasized about them daily.

Watching themselves make love in the mirror was unbelievably erotic, but he needed to feel her tits in his mouth, and hear the sounds she made as he sucked them. Without warning he spun her around and lowered his head, latching on to a nipple and sucking with a force that had her crying out.

"Yes, Jester, you always know exactly what I need." She clutched his head, and held him close as she tried to grind her pelvis against him. He knew she ached, he did as well, fiercely, but he held his lower body away from her, prolonging the sweet torture just a bit longer.

He moved to the other breast and treated it to the same efforts he had the first. Emily moaned, a combination of frustration and ecstasy as he both delivered and denied what her body was begging for.

"Please, I can't take much more." She shook her head, her

control slipping.

"We're almost there, baby. Just a little bit more." He moved back to the original nipple and sucked harder still, knowing he'd be leaving a mark on her. The sound she emitted was almost animalistic in its intensity. There we go.

~ ~ ~ ~

Emily wanted to cry. This was the last time she'd be with Jester like this. It was impossible to commit every touch, every sensation to memory, but that's what she tried to do. The memories would be all she had to cling to after she and Johnny left town. No man could ever compare to Jester in her eyes.

She needed this final connection, this final bout of pleasure more than she needed air.

Her hips moved of their own accord, pumping against nothing, seeking friction and relief from the most intense arousal and need she'd ever experienced. Her entire body began to quake as Jester sucked her nipple, pain and pleasure mixing in a way that had her out of her mind. If he didn't fuck her soon, she might not survive this encounter.

Just as suddenly as he'd spun her the first time, he turned her once more so she was again facing the mirror. A firm hand on her back pushed her down, bending her over the sink, her forearms coming to rest on the counter top. Her pussy clenched in anticipation, knowing that anytime now she would have the relief she so desperately sought.

Both sets of eyes were riveted to the mirror, the voyeuristic factor adding to the passion of their joining. Emily could see Jester's cock behind her. A bead of fluid dripped from the purple head. She met his gaze in the mirror and held her breath as she waited. She loved that he wanted her so much.

"You wet for me, baby?"

Emily almost laughed at that. Wet didn't come close to

describing her state at the moment. Jester placed one hand on the inside of each thigh, and nudged her legs open wide. His hands encountered the cream that had spilled from her sex and run down her thighs.

"Oh, fuck." The masculine growl of approval had more fluid easing from her body. "Jesus, baby, you are fuckin' drenched. You need me bad, don't you?" As he spoke he used his hands to rub the moisture into her thighs.

Just a few weeks ago Emily would have been mortified by her body's uncontrollable response to him, but now she loved for him to know how much she wanted him. "I need you."

His fingers trailed up, pulled her thong to the side, and danced over the entrance to her core. Her body clenched, trying to pull his fingers inside, but he kept the touch light and shallow. "Only you, Jester. You're the only one I could ever want like this."

His eyes dilated and his nostrils flared in the mirror. Her words brought out the animal in him. This would be more than sex, it would be a mating, a claiming. He fisted his cock, pumping it twice before he rubbed it through her soaked folds.

"Look at yourself, Emily," he commanded.

She shifted her eyes to the woman in the mirror, a woman she barely recognized. The woman staring back was flushed, her normally pale eyes darkened with desire. Two substantial breasts hung low, the nipples swollen and reddened from Jester's earlier ministrations. She looked wanton, like a woman who couldn't get enough of her man, and as it turned out, that's exactly who she was.

She darted her eyes back to Jester and watched, captivated, as he continued to tease her with his shaft.

"Fucking beautiful," he ground out, his eyes so dark they looked black. He'd removed the tie from his hair, so it fell around his shoulders making him look wild and dangerous.

"I'm gonna fuck you hard, baby. I can't be gentle right now. I need to mark you, brand you, make you mine in every fucking way." He stopped moving, his erection poised right at her entrance.

"Yes," she whispered. "That's what I want." This would be the last time, and she needed to be claimed by him no matter how much harder it would be to heal from the broken heart.

With a roar, he slammed into her in one fierce, almost violent thrust, his big body moving her forward so she had to brace herself with her arms to keep from flying into the mirror. They both watched as he pounded into her without finesse, possessing her.

Her heavy tits swayed and she noticed his attention drawn to them. Bending forward he surrounded her with his large frame, and brought his hands up to grab her breasts, using them as a handhold while he continued to pummel her from behind.

Emily was completely dwarfed by the dominant position. She pushed back against him as best she could, but his thrusts were so powerful it took all her strength to hold on for the ride. Pleasure like she'd never known shot from her pussy with every ram of his hips. This was the man, hidden under the jokes and wit, the animal he didn't let many people see.

Her legs began to tremble, out of her control, as her mind went fuzzy, swamped by the physical sensations rioting through her. When Jester pinched her nipples, hard, between his thumb and forefingers, an earth shattering orgasm overtook her.

"Jester, oh my God," she cried out as her body soared to new heights. "Jester, Jester," she cried out again and again. It was almost too intense. The physical pleasure combined with her overwhelming emotions brought tears to her eyes.

"Let go, Em. Let it take you. I've got you, I promise," Jester crooned, his low voice at her ear, a soothing contrast to the wild actions of his body.

She gave herself up to it, and a second orgasm rushed over her before the first had even calmed. Her body was out of her control, and after two more thrusts Jester buried himself deep inside her coming with a savage cry of his own.

Neither of them spoke, there were no words to capture what had just transpired between them. Emily barely had enough energy to remain standing as Jester turned her in his arms and kissed her deeply. She realized the shower was running and wondered absently when he'd turned it on.

Jester lifted her into the shower stall. She was thankful he kept an arm around her the entire time, or she may have collapsed exhausted to the ground.

With an almost tender hand he washed them both, his mouth on hers nearly the entire time. He paid extra attention to her breasts and between her legs.

She sighed, wishing she could tell him how much she loved him, but the words stuck in her throat.

When they were both clean, he turned off the water and lifted her back out into the bathroom, gently drying her with a fluffy towel. He then scooped her up again and carried her to the bed. Before he laid her down, he pulled back the covers.

Jester climbed in behind her and she immediately turned into his embrace. Still naked, they wound themselves around each other, and within minutes Emily could feel the even rise and fall of Jester's muscular chest against her ear.

She was helpless to do anything but wait until her meeting with Snake. Despite her physical and emotional exhaustion, Emily knew sleep would elude her once again.

Chapter Twenty-Two

Emily slowed her car and turned into her driveway. The street was quiet and peaceful, but the flutter of her curtains indicated that horror and fear awaited her despite the beauty of the day.

Good thing she planned to move. No way could she live in this house again, knowing how easily Snake came and went. Her next house would rival the security of a military base.

Three deep breaths in a row did nothing to calm the furious beating of her heart, or settle the angry butterflies in her stomach. With a final breath she stepped out of the car and toward her and Johnny's fate.

The door to her house swung open before she reached it and a pale hand pulled her inside. The creepy egg-like man stood before her with a twisted smile on his pasty face.

"So lovely to see you again, Emily. It was unfortunately that we couldn't speak yesterday, but I'm so glad you've been successful in your task." Across the room, Snake leered, tall and imposing.

She didn't respond, her attention riveted to her brother, sitting in a kitchen chair much as he had two weeks ago. This time, thought, he wasn't bound to the chair. There was no need. He didn't look like he could manage to blink, let alone escape from Snake and Casper.

If he hadn't been sitting somewhat upright in a chair with his swollen eyes partially open, Emily would have thought he was dead. Corpses looked better than Johnny.

She would have a difficult time getting him out to her car, and they couldn't risk a stop at a hospital until they were well out of town. It would be the first place anyone would look. Emily sent up a quick prayer that he'd make it that long.

"As you can see, I brought Johnny for you. I can't say I'm sorry for the condition he's in." He shrugged as though he were telling her he broke a dish in her kitchen. "It's really no more than he deserves. Now, I played nice, tell me what you know."

Emily swallowed past the lump in her throat and rubbed her damp palms on her thighs. She just had to get through her rehearsed speech, then she could take her brother and go. The car was gassed up, her suitcase in the trunk. Whatever Johnny needed, they would get on the way.

"They know about the drugs you're buying tomorrow, and they plan to steal them."

If it was possible, Snake's black eyes grew even darker.

"Do they know where?"

"No." She drew in a shaky breath. "And they're pissed that they can't figure it out. They are aware it's happening at eleven tomorrow morning. They know you need a lot of manpower so your clubhouse will be unprotected. The plan is to invade and be waiting to ambush you when you arrive back with the drugs."

He had to believe the lie. She'd given him just enough truthful information to seem plausible. If he left men back to guard the clubhouse, the No Prisoners had a better chance at success in their plan. The deception was the only idea she'd had that stood a chance at protecting Jester after she left with Johnny. She'd still lose Jester, but at least the two men she loved would be alive and unharmed.

Of course, Snake had to buy into the deception first.

He drew in a deep breath, the expansion of his chest filling the space in the room. He glowered as he blew it out. "And I'm supposed to believe they want my drugs. You should know by now, teach, that they don't deal in drugs."

She nodded, forcing herself to relax and sound uninterested. "Money is a powerful motivator and I hear the drugs are worth a lot. I imagine a saint would be tempted."

Snake grunted, still piercing her with an assessing glare. One wrong move, one extra blink and she'd be caught. "How'd you find out? How'd they find out for that matter?"

As she'd lain awake all night, every possible question he could ask had rolled through her head. She was prepared. "I sneaked into the chapel when everyone was partying." She shrugged and looked Snake right in the eyes. "By the end of the night everyone was passed out. Maybe you have a rat."

If he didn't believe her soon her false bravado would fade. Throwing up at his feet would be a dead giveaway that something was amiss with her story.

After a few more tense moments of scrutiny Snake shifted his focus over her shoulder, she assumed to his eggy minion. They men seemed to communicate silently until Snake nodded and addressed her again.

"You've done good work. But how do I know this isn't all bullshit? How do I know you didn't tell Jester everything, and he fed you this story to lure us into a trap? He sure seemed protective of you yesterday. I'm supposed to believe you'd betray him?"

Tears filled Emily's eyes and spilled down her face. Pretending wasn't necessary anymore. She had betrayed

Jester. She met him under false pretenses, lied to him for weeks, spied on his club, and now she'd leave him without a word. The sorrow was real and deep.

"Yes." A sob broke from her chest and her knees knocked together. The upside to her breakdown was that Snake appeared satisfied.

"You wouldn't have lasted anyway. Too soft for our world. At one tomorrow you can pick up your brother, here." Snake smirked, completely unaffected by her emotional outburst.

Emily staggered backward as though she'd received a physical blow. "What?" She didn't even try to disguise the panic in her voice. He wasn't leaving Johnny?

Snake laughed and Emily's world crashed around her.

"I told you that you'd get Johnny back after my business was done."

"No. No please, you can't." She took two steps toward Johnny, but halted when she caught the look on Snake's face. He'd have no problem ending Johnny right now.

Casper gave Johnny a nudge and, to her amazement, her brother stood and stumbled toward the door. He hadn't uttered a word, or even looked in Emily's direction. The boy she knew was gone.

"Count to sixty before you leave the house, Emily. You go running out of here making a scene and I'll shoot Johnny right in your driveway. Got me?"

She nodded. Speaking was impossible. She was too busy screaming at the top of her lungs inside her head.

What the hell was she supposed to do now? She stood frozen, staring at Snake. If she told him she'd lied, he'd kill Johnny, probably kill her and he'd have the information about the No Prisoners' plan. If she didn't tell him, he'd find out tomorrow, after his money was gone. He'd kill Johnny for sure and probably hunt her down.

Either way, Johnny ended up dead.

There was one final option. She had to come clean to Jester. Come clean and beg him to help Johnny. He'd never forgive her, and she wouldn't ask him to, but there was a chance he'd be willing to help rescue Johnny if he knew she'd tried to steer Snake off their trail.

Snake disappeared and she started to count. When she hit sixty, she wiped at the drying tears on her face and raced out of her house. There wasn't enough time to think about what a bad idea confessing to Jester really was. She was out of hope and would get on her knees and beg if need be.

~ ~ ~ ~

Jester rolled his bike to a stop out of view from the quaint house Emily disappeared into. Who the hell lived there? The quiet street reminded him of a nineteen fifties movie—or at least it would if any of those had taken place in the harsh desert climate.

Grateful it was the middle of a work day, and no one seemed to notice the large biker slinking down the street, he made his way toward Emily's house. Questions came in rapid fire succession.

Who owned this house?

Why was Emily keeping secrets?

Was she in some kind of danger?

The vibe Emily had given since the previous night screamed trouble. For some reason she didn't trust him enough to share her burdens. Maybe it made him an asshole, but he was a man of action and felt compelled to follow her today.

Jester stepped around the side of a house diagonally across the street from the one he spied on. The house had a raise porch with a wooden railing he pressed himself against. Hidden from view, he waited.

Of course Emily didn't trust him with her problems. They'd known each other for two weeks and he'd given her no reason to believe she was anything more than a passing fuck. He shook his head at himself and refocused on the house.

After just a few minutes the door swung open and his stomach dropped to his booted feet.

Christ, no.

His first instinct was to charge across the street and wrap his hands around Snake's throat for daring to be in the same space as Emily, but he gripped the wooden rail of the porch and held fast. Snake wasn't stupid, he'd have back up stashed somewhere.

"Load Johnny in the car then go back to the clubhouse. I'll be there soon," Snake instructed his bastard VP, Casper.

Jester's entire body vibrated with a rage he hadn't known was possible. He gripped the rail so hard his hand ached, but the pain was welcome. Physical pain to match the emotional.

After Casper shoved a man who looked like he'd been worked over good into the waiting car, they sped off. The door to the house flew open a second time and Emily raced down the walkway to her own car. She gunned the engine and peeled out of the driveway. She wasn't here under duress. No gun was pointed at her. No one held her down. She walked in and out of that house of her own free will.

Emily was working with Snake.

He let the words roll around in his head, but they were hard to comprehend. Jester's vision blurred as his world crashed around him. A loud crack startled him out of his trance and he glanced down at the broken porch rail in his hand.

With a primal roar he threw the splintered lumbar toward the street and ran, full speed toward his bike. Blood seeped from a small shard of wood embedded in his palm. The sun scorched him, and sweat poured off his body like rain. He ignored it all. Nothing mattered beyond getting to the clubhouse before Emily could destroy what was left of his life.

Chapter Twenty-Three

Emily slammed her car into park and shoved the door open. Desperation and panic overrode her fear of revealing the truth to Jester.

A bike peeled into the parking lot spraying dirt and gravel all over her car. Inconsiderate asshole. "What do you think you're doing?" she yelled as she climbed out of her car. "Jester?" One look at his face and her thoughts froze. "Wha-what's wrong?" Her voice trembled.

He didn't answer and dread washed over her.

"I need—" She swallowed. "I need to talk to you." Her eyes darted around, unable to make contact with his.

~ ~ ~ ~

Fury like he had never known erupted from within him. "Who the fuck are you?"

Emily stumbled and stopped moving toward him. Her mouth turned down and her eyes were as wide as bike tires. "What do you mean? You know who I am."

"I don't know shit. Snake, Emily? Really? He send you here?"

She paled and her arms dropped limply to her sides, her purse hitting the ground with a thud. "Oh my God. Jester, please let me——"

He cut her off again, so furious he could barely tolerate her presence. "Are you fucking him?"

"What? No! God, no, never."

"And who the fuck is Johnny? You fucking him too?"

"Johnny? H-how do you know about Johnny?"

He stared at her, letting all the hatred show in his glare. "What have you told him, Emily?"

"Lies. I've told him lies to protect you. To protect your club." Emily bit her bottom lip, something he'd teased her about countless times. Now the memories made him want to vomit.

"Does he know about tomorrow?"

She shook her head, opened her mouth then closed it again. Tears flowed down her face.

"I asked you if he knows about tomorrow?" Jester screamed, unable to tamp down the rage and feeling of betrayal. Christ, he'd fallen in love with this woman and she'd played him for a fool. The internal admission only made the gnawing pain more intense.

"No! No! He only knows enough to make it believable. I lied to him, to throw him off track. I swear it on my life."

"What was that last night then, Emily? Did you forget we had plans and invite Snake over so you could have a good laugh while you fucked him? Or maybe you were just going to suck him off? With all that I was fucking you, I can't imagine you needed any more."

Emily trembled. "No, I could never…he's horrible, Jester. Please listen to me."

A crowd had gathered. Club members stared at them in horror and confusion. Striker and Lila stood at the periphery. Lila appeared to be crying, though not nearly as hard as Emily. Her tears did nothing to soften him.

"You sure played me, didn't you? I fell hard for your little innocent act. You're good, babe. I'll give you that much."

"Jester, no! Please let me explain. Johnny is my brother—"

He held up a hand, unwilling to listen to another of her lies. "If you think I'd believe anything that came out of your lying mouth now, you're stupid as well as a traitorous bitch." He shrugged. "I suppose it wasn't a total waste of my time. At least I got a few mediocre fucks out of the deal."

The last of the color drained from Emily's face, and Jester felt a millisecond of guilt for causing the look of complete and utter devastation that stared back at him. Then, like a physical slap, an image of Snake's hands on her body popped into his head, and he hoped that she felt at least a fraction of the horror he was feeling.

~ ~ ~ ~

Emily's heart shattered into a million pieces. She'd been trying to prepare herself for this moment for two weeks, but the pain she'd anticipated was nothing compared to the reality of Jester's contempt.

"Jester, I…" The three words died in her throat. She couldn't say it now. He'd never believe her, and probably hate her even more, if that was possible.

"Don't say it. Don't you fucking say it! Get out of my face, Emily." His tone was poisonous.

"Jester," she whispered, trying one more time to get through to him. Tentatively she reached a hand out, and placed it on his chest.

He jerked back as though she'd burned him. "Do you have any idea what I should do to you right now? Do you realize that if you were a man I'd have killed you already?" He charged his six-foot-five frame toward her. "I'd have killed you!"

A sob burst from Emily, and her legs gave out. She

crumbled to the ground. The pain in her heart was so severe, death had to be preferable.

"Get her the fuck out of my face." Jester's boots crunched over the gravel until the sound of a door slamming shook the air.

Striker took charge of the spectators. "Everybody go! That means you too, Lila. Get in the clubhouse."

"But, Striker, maybe I should help you with her."

"Don't push me on this, babe. Get in the clubhouse." He turned and pressed a kiss to his fiancé's lips. "Please."

Lila nodded and walked off.

Emily's sobs had abated and she leaned against the car, her breath coming in choppy gasps. Striker loomed above her, the look on his face only one notch down on the anger scale from Jester's.

"Let's go." He wrapped a surprisingly gentle hand around her arm, and helped her to stand. The touch was so in contrast with his hard voice, it made her head swim.

"What—" She cleared her arid throat. "What are you going to do with me?"

"No questions." He propelled her forward, but she tensed and rooted her feet to the ground.

"If you're going to kill me, I'm not going to go willingly."

Striker rolled his eyes at her and chuckled. The asshole actually laughed at her.

"I'm not going to kill you, Emily. I'm not even going to hurt you. But I can't risk you having any contact with Snake for the next twenty-four hours. We'll sort this out then. Move."

She walked next to him as he steered her toward the garage. Once inside he pointed toward a door at the back of the room. "Go."

She pushed the door open and peered inside the tiny five

by five empty room with a cot in the far corner. One bare light bulb hung from the ceiling and cast a dim light into the room. It could be worse. There wasn't a bed of nails or any other torture devices.

"Make yourself comfortable. A different prospect crashes here each night, so someone's always on the premises."

Emily stepped into the room and turned back to Striker. "Where will they stay tonight?"

He smirked. "Right outside this door, darlin'." He motioned over his shoulder with his thumb.

She supposed she should be grateful he wasn't making someone sleep in here with her.

"One question, and God help you if you lie to me."

She looked him right in the eye. If there was any chance of making him believe her, she had to hold it together. No more falling apart like she did in the parking lot. Johnny still wasn't free. "What's your question?"

"Does Snake know that we will be waiting for him at the mountain pass tomorrow? Truth, Emily."

"No." Her voice sounded strong. That was good. "He knows that you know about his deal tomorrow." She told him word for word what's she'd said to Snake.

One of Striker's eyebrows rose and he looked at her as though she was a puzzle he couldn't decipher.

"That's the truth."

He nodded. "For your sake, I hope so." He turned on his heel and strode toward the door.

"Striker, wait," Emily called after him.

He stopped but didn't turn to look at her.

"Snake has Johnny. He was supposed to let him go today. He lied to me." Fresh tears flowed down her face. "Please, can you—"

"You can't ask me to rescue your lover."

Emily gasped. "He's not my lover. He's—" The door closed, cutting her off. She ran forward and slammed her palm against the metal surface. "He's my brother! Striker, he's my brother!"

Met with silence, Emily sunk to the floor and buried her face in her palms.

Chapter Twenty-Four

Jester stood in the meeting room, his palms down on the table, head bent, bowed between his shoulders. He ignored the sound of the door opening. Striker had ordered him to wait in here when he entered the clubhouse. A strange mix of shock, heartbreak, and betrayal, made him feel somewhat detached from reality.

He rubbed at an unfamiliar ache in his chest that throbbed in time with his head. The only thing he could think of to ease his pain and sorrow would be to lose himself in Emily's sweet softness. It was sick, and made him only one tiny step away from being as much of a traitor as she was.

The door flew open and Striker burst into the room, a dark scowl on his face. "Emily is stashed in the closet in the garage, and my woman is upstairs freaking out. What the fuck happened, brother?"

Jester laughed, a defeated sound of self-disgust. "Snake sent Emily here."

Striker remained silent.

Jester stood and looked Striker in the face. After he'd nearly brought down the club, the least his VP deserved was the straight up truth delivered with respect. "I followed Emily to a house out in Sandy Springs today. She met with Snake. She wasn't there under duress. She walked in and out willingly. Only thing I heard was something about some guy named Johnny. Snake sent her to us to find out what we were planning. She admitted that much to me."

Saying those words out loud was one of the hardest things he'd ever had to do. Admitting his failures and admitting his shame.

Striker rubbed a hand over his face. "Holy fucking shit. I did not see this coming."

Jester grunted. "Glad I'm not the only one."

"Christ, man, I'm sorry. I know she was coming to mean something to you."

He didn't know the half of it, but Jester just shrugged as though it was no big deal, as though the pain in his chest wasn't all consuming. "No matter. I'm done with her now."

Striker folded his arms across his chest and leaned against the closed door. "She claims she threw Snake off our trail. Told him we knew about the drop off, but made up a story about our plans." He filled Jester in on what Emily had relayed to him.

With a heavy sigh, Jester shook his head. "Don't be as stupid as I was, brother. She's good. Knows just how to get you to believe what she needs you to believe. She's probably been fucking Snake this whole time. This Johnny guy too." Nausea rose at the thought of another man's hands on his woman.

"You really believe that, man? She's been with you every fuckin' night. Says Johnny's her brother."

Jester dropped into a chair and banged his forehead against the table. Physical pain was preferable to the emotional anguish. "Christ, she's got my head so fucked up, I don't know what to believe."

Striker pushed off the wall and sat across the table from Jester. "I know you're not going to want to hear this, but it's possible she's telling the truth. You'll get your chance to find out. Snake is bringing Johnny to the mountain pass tomorrow. We snag him, we get some answers."

Jester sat back in his chair, and gripped the edge of the Sergeant at Arms patch on the left side of his cut. With a jerk, he ripped it off in one swipe, and tossed it on the table in front of Striker.

"What the fuck are you doing man?" Striker's voice was full of outrage.

"There's no fuckin' way I deserve that. I brought her here, to the club, to your woman. Christ, Striker, do you know how many of us could be killed tomorrow if Snake is ready for us? And we aren't certain he won't be."

Striker shook his head. "You need to pull your head out of your ass, brother. This is not on you. If she's lying, then we all fell for her act. Every last one of us liked that woman. There was no reason to suspect anything. And like I said, we don't know anything for sure yet."

"What the fuck would Lila do if you'd been killed because of some conniving bitch I brought to the club?" Jester yelled.

"She'd survive, Jester. She knows what the hell our life is, what the risks are. She's a strong woman, and she'd survive. Put that patch back on. We leave in fifteen minutes. I don't want to hear fuck about it again or I'll kick your ass, no matter how much of a giant you are."

Striker held up his hands as though surrendering before he spoke again. "Don't knock me out, but you're not thinking straight right now. All you see is a betrayal from the woman you love. You need to step back and think about it objectively."

"Are you kidding me with this shit? What? You go and get

engaged, now you think you're fuckin' Dr. Phil or something?"

Striker wisely kept his mouth shut.

Jester gripped the edges of the table with enough force to dent the metal, letting out a deafening male growl of frustration. "When I saw Snake walk out of that house, it felt like someone reached in my chest, pulled out my heart and ran over it with a semi. I'd take a bullet over that kind of pain any day." His voice was a croak, thick with suffering.

He shook his head, picked up the patch, and stormed out of the room. He needed to be alone. Well, maybe not totally alone. Jack Daniels was certainly welcome to join him.

Chapter Twenty-Five

Acer slapped Jacko on the back and inclined his head in the direction of the clubhouse. "Take fifteen. I need to ask our guest a few questions."

Jacko nodded and rose from his post. The metal folding chair he sat on, guarding Emily, wouldn't even be comfortable if it came with a free blow job, but such was the life of a prospect.

"Hard to believe, ain't it?" Jacko asked with a shake of his head.

It was. But Acer had learned the hard way that even those you trusted above all others could shove a knife between your shoulder blades without blinking an eye. "Here's your free lesson of the day, prospect. Never take anyone at face value. That way, when they stab you in the back, you won't give a shit."

Jacko raised an eyebrow. "That what you do, man?"

"It is now. Stop asking me stupid questions and take the fuckin' break."

Jacko grunted and jogged out of the garage.

Acer fisted the doorknob. He was a cautious bastard, and never let anyone slip past his defenses anymore. But he liked

Emily. Not the way Jester did, thank God. The ass beating that would accompany any interest shown in her direction was not worth it. But he felt brotherly toward her. She reminded him of someone from his past, someone sweet and kind, someone who life handed a raw deal when she didn't deserve it. Was it the same for Emily?

He tugged the door open and peered inside the closet-sized room. Emily sat on the cot, her back against the wall, knees drawn up to her chest. Her normally gorgeous baby blue eyes were bloodshot and bore the dark rings of the sleep deprived. The combination gave her an appearance of exhausted devastation.

The sound of the metal chair dragging across the concrete floor rivaled nails on a chalkboard, as Acer pulled it into the room. The screeching seemed to pull Emily out of whatever daze she'd been in and she scurried back on the cot until she hit the wall, reminding him of a frightened wild animal cornered by a predator.

He turned the chair around and straddled it, sitting with slow, controlled movements so as not to spook her. "Emily, I'm not gonna hurt you."

Wide, terrified eyes full of suffering and regret stared back at him.

"Wh-what do you want then?"

"The truth. The story, whatever the fuck happened that led you to spy on us for Snake." Shiv trusted his judgment when it came to reading people's bullshit, which was why he'd ordered Acer to feel her out.

She looked down at the cot and rubbed a nonexistent spot. Just when he was going to ask her with a bit more force, she spoke.

"My parents died when I was eighteen." Her voice hitched but she took a breath and continued, not making eye contact with him. "My brother, Johnny, was thirteen at the time." Tears trickled down her cheeks as words poured from her mouth, so fast he almost had trouble keeping up with her.

"Please," she whimpered after telling him about her brother's drug problem and entanglement with the Grimm Brothers. "You have to believe me. I could never do anything to put Jester in harm's way. I lo—"

Acer pursed his lips and waited for her to continue, but she seemed to catch herself and, with a shake of her head, she changed statements.

"Snake will kill my brother. He's all I have left. We'll leave town, immediately." She'd moved to her knees on the cot and folded her hands together in front of her chest. Now she looked him straight in the eye. "Please," she choked out again. "I'm begging you, Acer. I don't expect Jester—or any of you—to forgive me for my part in this, but please help save my brother."

Acer straightened in the chair and replayed her story in his head. Maybe she told the truth. His gut was about eighty percent sure it believed her, but it had failed him before.

"Acer," she pleaded. "You have to help me." Her tears had slowed, but she remained in a kneeling positing on the cot. Nothing about her in this moment indicated deception.

He sighed. "Here's the thing, hon. I have one loyalty here. To my club. And right now my club thinks you sold them out. Even if they believe this story, even if it's completely true, your brother is the reason for this whole clusterfuck. The club won't—and I can't ask them to—put lives at risk to save him."

Her face crumbled before his eyes, and sobs were torn from her throat. He didn't move to comfort her. That wasn't what he was there for, even if a large part of him wanted to. But he waited until she settled before rising from the chair.

"For what it's worth, Emily, I think I believe you and I will pass on everything you shared with me."

She turned her face up and the intense sadness he saw nearly made him promise to save Johnny. It wasn't his decision, and if the club didn't want to take the risk, he'd support that.

"What—" She cleared her throat. "What about Jester? Will you tell him?"

Acer cracked out a sharp laugh. "Jester's passed out, spooned around an empty bottle of Jack."

"What?" Emily gasped and stood. "But he needs to be able to function tomorrow."

She looked sincere. It wasn't easy to fake the panic that crossed her face. No matter the reason she entered Jester's life, Acer believed she loved his brother.

"His hatred for Snake trumps a hangover anyway. He'll be fine. You don't need to worry about Jester."

Emily nodded and sat back down. Defeated was the only word he could think of to describe her.

He lifted the chair to avoid a repeat of the bone jarring screech and opened the door. He hadn't taken two steps out of the garage when he encountered Striker standing in the parking lot, the glow of a cigarette in one hand and a half-full bottle in the other.

"Your woman know what you're out here doing?"

"Nope. And there's only one possible way she could find out, so I'm coming after your ass if she gives me grief."

Acer chuckled. Lila rode them all constantly over their smoking. She might as well try to convince them to sell their bikes while she was at it. The chance of either happening were about the same. Slim and none.

"Talk to me." Striker commanded as he handed off the whisky.

Acer took a drink and told Emily's story, including how he was pretty sure she was in love with Jester.

"Shit." Striker snatched the bottle back and took a long drink. "You believe her?"

Acer nodded. "I think I do."

"Christ, if this is true, that girl's been through hell the last few weeks."

Acer held his hand out for the bottle. The burn of whisky was a welcome distraction from the mess of the day. "Not to mention that she could have sold us out at any time, but she put her ass on the line to protect us. She got on her fucking knees, cried her face off, and begged me to save her brother."

Striker tossed his cigarette down and ground it under the heel of his boot. "Reducing her to begging like that?" He shook his head. "This shit turns out to be true, Jester will kill Snake for that alone."

"You gonna tell him?"

Striker snorted. "Man's dead to the world right now. He's not ready to hear it yet. One more mind fuck and he might not be useful tomorrow. It'll keep until after we hijack the money."

"What about the brother?"

"Shit, I don't know. Goddamn junkies." He sighed and ran a hand over his face.

Being VP of the MC was a position filled with burdens and tough decisions. Acer didn't envy Striker one bit.

"I guess we can snatch him when we take the money. What's one more body in the van?"

Acer stared at his VP in shock. "You do realize all this shit is his doing, right?"

"Yeah, brother, I do. But that's Jester's woman in there, and if he has any chance of fixing this fucked up mess, saving her brother would go a long way toward getting it done."

"Well, look at you, shooting heart shaped arrows. You sprout wings and I'm outta here."

Striker took one last hit of the whisky and held it out to Acer. "Fuck you."

Acer laughed and palmed the bottle.

"I'm heading in. I've wasted enough time with you when my woman is in there, warm and willing. Sorry you gotta make do with your hand tonight, brother." Striker laughed as he walked toward the club house, his form disappearing into the dark of night.

"Good luck getting any from your woman smelling like a tobacco factory."

"Shit," Striker muttered and Acer laughed.

With one last glance at the door that kept Emily at bay, he turned and sauntered toward the clubhouse. He hoped his gut was right about Emily. Last time it failed him, life-altering horrors followed shortly after.

Chapter Twenty-Six

Emily paced the minuscule room, growing dizzy from the frequent changes in direction. The walls seemed to inch closer with each passing minute.

How much time had passed since she'd been locked in here? At least a prospect had brought her some pizza last night. She couldn't stomach it, but it was a mild comfort to know they didn't plan to starve her.

Under normal circumstances she would have found the irony of being the No Prisoners' prisoner amusing. Normal was so far gone she might never experience it again.

Were they at the mountain pass yet? Was Johnny there? Was there a chance they would try to help him? "Please save him." No one was around to hear her, but maybe putting the plea out into the universe could somehow make it come true.

She loved Jester. Despite all the vile hatred he threw at her yesterday, she loved him, and the idea of him believing she betrayed him was almost more than she could stomach.

The door few open and smacked against the wall. "Oh my God," she cried. She backed up to the wall and stared at the colorful face of an unhappy Colt. The bruises weren't as grotesque as they had been immediately after the fight with

Jester, but it was still obvious he'd been in a physical altercation not long ago.

The hairs on the back of her neck rose. He bore the glassy, wide-eyed look of a man who wasn't playing with a full deck. "Um, Colt, what are you doing in here?"

He smirked and stepped into the room. "You've caused me a lot of problems, bitch." He moved closer and was now mere inches away. "But I'm a nice guy. I don't want you to be all alone in here, so I figured I'd stop by and see if maybe I could help."

Emily tensed, her heart pounded, and the space in the room shrunk to the point of suffocating.

"What happened to…um…to the prospect outside the door?"

"Had to take a piss. I got here just in time."

The smell of sweat and booze assaulted her as he stepped close enough to her that a piece of paper would have had a hard time sliding between them. In her effort to remain untouched by him, her shoulder blades and elbows ground into the wall so hard there'd be bruises tomorrow.

If she made it to tomorrow.

Emily counted to ten in her mind, forcing herself to remain still until an opportunity presented itself.

Colt placed his palms on the wall, on each side of her head and pressed toward her. Before he had the chance to make contact, Emily rammed her knee into his groin. The combination of his forward momentum and her upward thrust was powerful. A high-pitched wail flew out of his mouth and he collapsed to the floor clutching his family jewels.

A second of triumph flared in Emily before she shoved his writhing form away, sprang through the door, and slammed it closed. The padlock that had held her captive lay on the floor, so she secured the door, ignoring Colt's screams of pain and hatred. Someone would find him eventually and he'd be their problem to deal with.

She sprinted toward her car, relieved to find her purse sill lying in the dusty gravel. The clock on her phone read eleven fifteen. If she hauled ass, there was a chance she could make it to the mountain pass in time to help Johnny.

~ ~ ~ ~

Everyone was in position, awaiting the Grimm Brothers. Jester's blood hummed with nervous energy and the anticipation of seeing Snake's face when the bastard realized he'd been had. Visions of taking the man apart had been playing in his mind since the moment Jester saw him with Emily. Each man had been briefed on the possibility of increased threat and they were all poised and ready for action.

He forced himself to push Emily out of his thoughts. He needed one hundred percent focus on the task at hand. Glancing around, he scanned all the places No Prisoners were hiding, loaded for bear, waiting to rid Snake of a fuck ton of money.

The day was almost unbearably hot. Directly overhead, the sun beat down, blistering everything in its path. Jester and the other No Prisoners were drenched with a salty sheen. Dust blew with the soft breeze, and mixed with the sweat to form a layer of clay-like muck on any exposed skin.

Jester, Striker, and Acer stood behind the cover of two black panel vans. One of the vans—the one supposed to contain nine hundred and eighty-five thousand dollars of drugs—really held three poor sweltering prospects and their weapons, ready to burst out at the precise time.

"You good, Jester?" Acer asked.

"Fine."

"Sorry about how it all went down with your girl, brother," he continued despite Jester's glare, which would have made a lesser man back down in a heartbeat. "I've been thinking—"

"Shut the fuck up, Acer," Striker said. "I hear pipes."

The rumble of motorcycle pipes grew in the distance. Striker whistled, alerting the men that the Grimms were nearing.

"Fuck, it's hot," Acer complained to no one in particular.

"First time you ever sweat, trust fund baby?" Jester asked, grateful for the normal banter to take the edge off his anxiety.

"Nah man, sweat my ass off when I banged your sister."

Unable to hold it in, Jester laughed. "That was a fail. Don't have a sister."

"Worth a shot."

The noise grew deafening and Jester peeked through the front side windows of the van. Within seconds, ten Grimm Brothers rolled into the mountain pass with their own van in the rear position.

Interesting, they'd expected Snake to arrive with more men. He was a paranoid bastard and should have been traveling with an army.

As soon as the engines cut, Jester gave the signal, and twenty No Prisoners rose from their cover along the mountain, training their assault rifles on all the Grimm Brothers.

Jester, Striker, and Acer slipped from their spots behind the van as the doors opened and the prospects spilled out with their weapons directed at the Grimms.

The Grimms were out manned, and outgunned, but that wouldn't prevent Snake from striking. They stood, weapons readied on each other for a full minute before someone finally spoke.

"Send him out," Snake called back to the van behind him.

Jester exchanged a look with his VP. Neither trusted the slimy creature and both were prepared to shoot if necessary.

A guy who looked like he been to hell and hadn't yet clawed his way out, stumbled from the back of the van. Jesus, he was a kid, looked no older than twenty. He was skin and bones, trade mark of a junkie and bore multiple bruises. His legs wobbled as he staggered forward.

"Jesus Christ," Acer muttered. "Is that—"

Jester shook his head and spoke in an equally low tone. "Shut it." He called, "What the fuck is this, Snake? We don't give two shits about your prisoners."

Snake snarled. "I was supposed to leave this at Emily's house for her. Last part of our deal. You know, since she ratted on you. Told me you'd be waiting to ambush me back at our clubhouse."

Shit. She told the truth?

Despite the fiery heat of the day, Jester's blood froze in his veins. His trigger finger twitched. One more millimeter and Snake's worthless life would be over.

"Hold your shit together, Jester. Bullets start flying and we're just as dead as they are." Striker warned at an almost imperceptible volume.

"Turns out she was a lying bitch. Guess that means I can dispose of him." Snake's jaw was clenched and anger gave his lifeless eyes a spark. He aimed his gun at the bloody man just as a cloud of dust rose up and moved toward the group. Everyone froze as a dark pickup truck rolled to a stop.

"Snake?" A man completely hidden from view called out from the bed of the truck.

Not being able to see him meant they weren't able to shoot him either. What the fuck was Snake up to?

"What you got there, Casper?"

"A little something I think you'd love to have," he called to his president.

A body fell from the tailgate and landed on all fours on the ground. The same voice gave her instructions in a low but still audible tone. "Walk around to the side of the truck. Don't try anything heroic, girlie. I'll put you down before you get two steps away."

Jester watched, not breathing as a filthy and disheveled Emily rounded the truck and came to a stop next to the driver's door. In a knee-jerk reaction, he lunged forward. Striker and Acer both grabbed him, their muscles bulging as they fought to hold him back.

"I told you to hold your shit together. You charge out there you'll be dead in two seconds and that won't do shit for Emily." Striker's voice was hard and authoritative.

Jester locked eyes with Emily. The panic and fear in her gaze refocused him. "I'm cool. I'm not gonna charge." He shook off his brothers' hold but kept his attention on his woman. How the hell had she escaped from the clubhouse?

"Well, well, well. It's a real party now. Welcome, Emily. I was just telling your lover here how much of a lying bitch you are." He stepped closer to Emily and every fiber of Jester's being itched to take him out, but Casper would put a bullet in Emily for sure.

When Snake reached Emily, he slid an arm around her shoulders and tucked her into his side. Body rigid, her gaze pierced Jester's.

Snake leaned in and whispered something to her. She shook her head and struggled against him, but the effort was useless. He towered over her in height and strength, holding her next to him as easily as if she were a small child.

Snake lifted his weapon and pointed it directly at Jester.

225

Despite everything that had happened today, he'd take the bullet if it would spare Emily, but it wouldn't.

"No, no, no, no." Tears streaked down Emily's face as she twisted in vain. "Please don't shoot Jester. I'll do anything you want."

"Well then, in that case..."

In the fraction of a second before it happened, Jester knew what Snake would do. He opened his mouth to scream a warning, but Snake moved so fast, the crack of the bullet was out of the gun and flying toward Johnny before a sound could leave Jester's throat.

"Noo!" The deep cry torn from Emily was so full of tortured anguish that for a moment silence descended upon the mountain pass as each man listened to her weep and fight against Snake.

That sound would play in Jester's nightmares for years to come. Would she have reacted the same if the bullet had struck him? He shook off the shameful thought and tried to block out the sound of her despair so he could focus on getting her to safety.

Then all hell broke loose.

A bullet whizzed by his ear, much too close for comfort. Jester dove for cover behind the van and scrambled until his back was pressed against the heated metal. Pops of gunfire rang out from every direction.

Emily was out in the open. A sitting duck caught in an MC gun battle.

"Hold your fire!" he screamed with as much force as he could muster. "Don't shoot Emily."

"They took her," Striker called from a few feet away, also behind the safety of the van. He reached his arm around the end of the van and shot off ten rounds without looking at his target. "Snake tossed her in the bed of the truck and took

226

off."

Christ, this nightmare grew more horrifying by the second.

"Hear that?" Acer yelled.

Jester didn't have eyes on him but his voice was close. Engines revved and dust filled the mountain pass.

"I hear a bunch of Grimms fleeing like little girls." Striker called back.

"Fuck yeah."

They were safe, and no one was screaming about any fallen brothers, but Jester didn't feel an ounce of that victory. Where the hell would they take his woman?

Chapter Twenty-Seven

All gunfire ceased as the final Grimm brother sprayed gravel and shot out of the mountain pass. Following would be useless. Snake had too much of a lead, and they'd just end up in another firefight if they caught up to the Grimms.

"Three Grimms are down!"

Jester sprang out from behind the van and joined Striker and Acer, jogging toward the fallen bodies. Two Grimm Brothers lie motionless in the dirt, and a third, Johnny, gasped and writhed on the ground.

Blood poured from a wound in the younger man's shoulder. Given the condition he'd been in before he was shot, his chance of survival couldn't be good. Jester tried to care, but it didn't happen. Whoever the hell Johnny was, he was the reason Emily was involved with Snake.

Acer dropped to his knees and yanked his shirt over his head. With steady hands, he balled the fabric up and pressed it to the kid's shoulder using enough force to draw a cry from his bruised lips.

Jester squatted down and pressed the business end of his pistol to the center of the kid's forehead. Johnny looked him square in the eye, earning a tiny fraction of Jester's respect.

"You want me to let him save you?"

The kid nodded.

"Who the fuck are you?"

"Johnny." His voice was raspy, a ragged whisper.

"I know that much. You fucking Emily?"

Despite what had to be excruciating pain and despite the fact that the kid had about three drops of blood left in his body, he let out a bitter laugh followed by a groan. "Don't know what goes on in your freaky family, but no, I'm not fucking my sister."

Familiar pale eyes held his gaze. Not quite as light as Emily's, but bearing a strong resemblance. The weight of his mistake crashed on Jester as heavy as an icy avalanche. His heart cracked wide open and bled far worse than Johnny's shoulder.

One minute.

If he'd given her one minute to explain what happened, she'd be safe and secure, waiting for him and Johnny at the clubhouse.

Instead he chose not to trust her, not to believe that she could love him.

"Fuck!" He paced away from Johnny. Helpless was not something that Jester tolerated. He'd do whatever it took to get Emily back, or die trying. His brothers would take care of her if something happened to him. He had no doubt about that.

If he did rescue her, he'd spend the rest of his life making up for this mistake. And if she told him to fuck off—which she'd have every right to—he'd find some way to make peace with it. As long as Snake didn't harm her, Jester would live with a broken heart if he had to.

He stomped back to Johnny and knelt, returning the pistol to his head. "You're going to agree to three things or Acer here will walk away and let you bleed out."

Acer and Striker exchanged a wary look, but Jester ignored their unease. He would suffer the guilt over his treatment of Emily as long as he lived, but the greatest burden of blame still landed on Johnny.

"Who are you?" Johnny whispered.

"I'm your angel. Whether I'm your angel of death or angel of mercy is up to you. One. Rehab, cold turkey, I don't give a shit, but you're done with whatever your poison is. You will not get another chance. I catch even the slightest whiff that you may be high, and you're done. Say yes."

Johnny turned a bit green but nodded, keeping eye contact with Jester. "Yes." His voice grew weaker by the second.

"Two. You come in contact with any of the Grimm Brothers in any way and you're done."

Johnny nodded again.

"And three." Jester leaned in close, the barrel of his gun steady between Johnny's eyes. He spoke in a low tone his brothers wouldn't overhear. "I see one tear fall down Emily's beautiful face because of something you do to her, and you're done. Your life's not worth a tenth of hers."

"Fair enough." Johnny coughed and groaned when the hacking racked his body.

"Now tell me where the fuck they may have taken her and we'll get you to Striker's woman for some help."

"They got a house." He paused and sucked in a whistled breath. "Shitty neighborhood, last house on the block." Johnny coughed and moaned, trying to hold his hands to his ribs.

Jester resisted the urge to shake him and scream at him to speak faster. He wanted to crawl out of his skin. Every second it took Johnny to get the information out was one more second Emily spent with Snake.

When he calmed, Johnny continued. "Wren Court. Only three other houses, all abandoned."

Jester stood. That's all they needed to find it. He whipped out his phone as he strode toward his bike.

"Whoa. What the fuck you think you're doing, brother?" Striker cut him off, got in his face.

Jester growled at him. "VP, get out of my way."

Striker ignored him. "Jester, you can't hop on your bike and ride out there like a Harley fuckin' cowboy. You got one pistol and you need back up."

He shook his head and tried to shove past Striker. Fuck that. He'd be just fine.

"I'm not askin', brother. We do this smart, go back to the clubhouse and reload. I promise we won't waste time. The Grimms are pissed we got their money and they'll be on the warpath. They're loading Johnny now, and I sent Acer ahead to do whatever the fuck he does with those satellite feeds. We need to be prepared."

Shit. Striker was right. Hard as it was to delay, they needed a solid plan, and more artillery.

"Fine. Let's get the fuck out of here."

He pushed past Striker and mounted his bike. "Wait, VP, did you say we got their money?"

Striker barked out a laugh and pointed across the sand. The Grimm's van was still parked there, four deflated tires rendering it useless.

"Holy shit," Jester muttered. He'd been so consumed with thoughts of Emily he hadn't noticed the van. "How?"

"Hook shot out all four tires. Grimms couldn't drive it out, so they abandoned it."

Jester smiled for the first time in hours. At least one thing went right today. The grin only lasted a fraction of a second as he fired up his bike and shot off toward the clubhouse.

~ ~ ~ ~

Drip. Ninety-seven.

Drip. Ninety-eight.

Drip. Ninety-nine.

Emily huddled in the corner of a dark basement and counted drops of water as they fell from a rusted pipe to a small puddle a foot away from her. The mindless activity was a poor attempt at distracting herself from the unbearable pain deep in her soul.

Every muscle in her body ached from being slammed against the bed of the pickup truck. When the bullets started flying, Snake literally threw her in the truck. She'd fought like a wild animal until he slapped her face hard enough to rattle her brain. Since then it was easier to stare straight ahead, not reacting to anything that happened.

They drove her...somewhere, and tossed her in the basement before they ran off hollering about their stolen money.

A small part of Emily's brain screamed at her to get up. To look for a way out. To be prepared to fight for her life when they returned.

But she didn't move.

What was the point? Johnny was dead. The only person in this world who—despite his many faults—loved her. Not only was he dead, but he died because of her failings. Guilt, remorse, and regret would be her constant companions from here on out.

Then there was Jester. Jester, who'd stood expressionless while she pleaded for his life. Jester, who believed she'd used and betrayed him. Jester, who she loved.

Tears slid down her cheeks, but the energy to lift a hand and swipe them away wasn't there. Everything she cared about had been taken from her. Nothing remained of the life she had before Snake, and nothing of the life she'd come to want since him. Nothing but pain and sorrow.

Nausea rose swift and fierce as an inconceivable thought forced its way into her mind.

Was Jester even alive?

She pitched forward, onto all fours, and retched, painful spasms gripping her stomach. She hadn't eaten since the day before, so there wasn't anything to come up, but that didn't stop her body from trying. When the worst was over she leaned against the wall and closed her eyes.

She didn't deserve to have it answered, but she sent up a prayer anyway, asking for Jester's life to be spared and for some small relief from the pain in her heart.

Chapter Twenty-Eight

Jester hopped off his bike and charged toward the garage. Most of the weapons stock was housed in an underground storage container accessible from the back of the garage.

Acer met him halfway, his arms held out as though prepared to hold Jester back. Over Acer's shoulder Jester could hear a commotion coming from the garage.

"What's with the racket?" he asked Acer.

"Listen, brother," Acer began, his hands still up like he was ready to stop Jester if he charged.

Jester looked over Acer's shoulder. From his vantage point he could see straight into the garage. The door to the room that had held Emily was wide open. Colt sat on the cot with a mulish expression. Shiv paced the small room, obviously yelling.

A sick feeling overtook him. He looked at Acer. "Is he—did that piece of shit—" He didn't bother to finish his question. Jester plowed forward and shoved Acer to the side. No way was there a chance of Acer stopping him at this point.

He burst into the room, and wrapped his hands around Colt's throat despite Shiv's protest. "What the fuck did you do to her? I swear to God if you touched her in any way...."

Colt couldn't answer. His face turned purple and he gagged, grasping and clawing at Jester's forearms, but he was no match for the combination of strength and rage coursing through Jester.

"Jester, let him go." Shiv's voice was calm, but firm.

It would be so easy to squeeze just a little harder, until Colt passed out, then keep squeezing until the life drained from him.

"Jester!" Shiv's voice was sharper this time.

He released one finger at a time, smiling when Colt collapsed on the cot wheezing and gasping.

"Fucking psycho," he managed to choke out amid coughs.

Jester leaned down. "You have no idea. I better not see you when I get back." He stood and turned to Shiv, ignoring Colt's complaint of abuse.

"I'm sorry about how this all played out, Jester," Shiv said. "Weapons are loaded and we got guys ready to go. Acer knows where it is. Not much activity on the street beside the Grimms." He inclined his head toward Colt. "He will be dealt with."

Jester nodded and accepted a brotherly hug from Shiv. He jogged out of the garage, back to his bike.

~ ~ ~ ~

Crushing pain slammed into Emily's side and she jolted awake. With a groan of agony, she tried to clear her head and make sense of her surroundings. She ached and throbbed, the air was surprisingly cold, and she'd apparently been sleeping on the floor.

The day's events flooded back to her and her eyes flew open. She looked up from her spot on the floor.

Casper loomed over her, a giddy smile on his face. Though he was clearly not in charge, he scared her more than Snake.

Something about the look in his eyes. Like an inmate who'd escaped from a prison for the criminally insane.

"I've been hoping for some time alone with you." His nasally voice made her cringe. Nails on a chalkboard would have been preferable.

Emily didn't respond. What did he expect her to say?

He held a pale, skinny arm out to her, palm up, but she just stared at him.

"I'm being nice, girl. I don't have to be nice. Would you rather me haul you up by your hair?"

She stood without his assistance, gritting her teeth as a stabbing pain reached her ribs. Rising to her feet took three times as long to struggle through on her own, but she'd die before voluntarily touching that man.

Casper waited about three feet away from her, a frown on his pasty face. "You must be pretty damn good if you were able to control Jester with your snatch. I can't pass up the chance for a sample." His look of unhappiness with her rejection of his hand morphed into one of lust with the statement.

Oh God. Emily's stomach bottomed. She pressed herself against the wall as though she could disappear through it if she tried hard enough. This, she could not let happen. She refused to die with the memory of Casper's touch on her skin.

He stalked toward her, the outline of an erection visible in against the front of his pants. Bile rose in her throat but she swallowed down. She also fought to keep her face impassive, remembering they got off on her fear. She could not, however, stop the screams in her own head.

When Casper was close enough to touch, Emily spit in his face and enjoyed the look of shock that transformed his bald head for about one second before his fist connected with her face. Pain exploded in her head, blurring her vision and preventing her from being able to protect herself.

Before she had time to recover, his hands were on her. He tore her tank top straight down the center. It had a built in bra, and she was now bare to him from the waist up. He licked his thin lips, and Emily almost vomited.

Tears leaked from her eyes, and while she hated for Casper to see them, she couldn't stop them. She grabbed the edges of her tattered shirt and held them closed. "Don't," she whispered as he stepped closer.

"That's better." He grabbed the torn shirt and pulled. She was no match for his strength and the material was ripped from her fingers and tossed to the ground.

Before she had time to react, he fisted her hair in his hand and yanked her head back. His mouth crashed into her and his opposite hand closed over her breast. Casper's touch was harsh and revolting, and with no thought beyond getting his mouth off of her, Emily bit down on his lip, hard.

With a violent curse, Casper jerked back and released Emily's hair. "That was very foolish." He pinned her to the wall with his upper body, the bony ridges of his chest crushing her breasts. She tried to raise a knee and render him sterile, but his hands had moved to his pants and he swatted her away as though she were a gnat.

The heavy footsteps of a man descending the stairs drowned out the sound of Casper's zipper opening. He froze and stopped his advances as the thudding grew louder with each step.

Emily blew out a breath. What did it say about how terrifying her life had become that she was actually relieved to see Snake?

He stepped off the stairs and strode toward Casper. Emily was still flattened against the wall, her shoulder blades digging so hard into the concrete, she might leave behind an imprint of her body when she finally moved away. Casper's body still crushed hers, but he no longer had a hand on her breast.

Snake's nostrils were flared and his eyes were wild. Anger didn't begin to describe the look on his face.

"Leave us," Snake hissed.

Chapter Twenty-Nine

Jester peered around the front of the rotted out house then turned back toward Acer, who stood on the same side of the house, only at the opposite end. He held up one finger indicating only one guard outside the door.

Acer nodded and inched forward.

The broken down house was poorly guarded. The majority of the Grimms were probably back at the clubhouse losing their shit and trying to come up with a plan to recover their stolen money. Looked like just a few unlucky prospects had been ordered to guard Emily.

If she was even here at all.

Jester shoved that thought away. She had to be here. That was the bottom line.

He wrapped his right hand around the barrel of his gun and, as quietly as possible for a man his size, crept around to the front of the house. If this guard was one of Jester's men, he'd beat the shit out of him for his stupidity.

The prospect stood at the edge of a small concrete patio, facing the opposite side of the house. His jeans were around his knees and he whistled while he pissed in the sand, totally unaware of his surroundings.

Without a sound, Jester slunk closer. When he was two feet away, he lifted his right arm over his head and brought the butt of the gun down with the strength of an elephant. One second before the gun would have connected with the prospect's head, the man sensed his presence and turned, peeing dick and all.

"Shit!" Jester jumped to the side to avoid the spray and still managed to land his gun on the prospect's head, but not with enough force to knock him out.

Frazzled at being caught with his dick in his hands, literally, the prospect scrambled to cover himself. Jester dropped his weapon and plowed a fist into the man's face. He dropped like a stone in a puddle of his own urine.

"Didn't know golden showers were your thing, bro."

Not as aware of his own surroundings as he should have been, Jester jumped. "Shut the fuck up and get in the house."

Hook, Gumby, and Striker joined them at the door. Ten others formed a perimeter around the house. They came prepared, over prepared from the looks of it.

Acer looked over his shoulder at Gumby. "Ready, rubber boy?"

Gumby nodded. "Ready, trust fund baby."

At any other time, Jester would have appreciated their attempt at levity. Now his heart raced with a combination of dread and anticipation. They all needed to shut up and get down to business.

"Shut it and go," ordered Striker.

Acer nodded and rammed his foot against the door knob. This house was so old, and in such poor condition, the entire door collapsed in, hitting a startled Casper.

"What the fu—"

"Got him," Gumby called out. He shoved the door off Casper and secured his hands behind his back with zip ties.

Gumby could have taken him down no problem, but having Casper knocked to the floor by the door just made his job easier.

"Here." Striker tossed Gumby a roll of duct tape.

"Thanks, brother." In seconds Gumby had Casper secured with tape over his mouth and ties on his feet as well as his hands.

Jester and Acer scanned the room, guns drawn, prepared for an attack that never came. A high-pitched shriek rose from behind a door. Jester bolted toward the sound.

~ ~ ~ ~

Any momentary reprieve Emily felt at Snake's arrival vanished like a ghost at his glower.

He grabbed her by the arms and yanked her to him. "Do you have any fucking idea what you cost me today, bitch?"

Spittle landed on her face and she flinched, but didn't speak. Twenty seconds ago, rape was imminent, and she hadn't had a chance to recover from that threat. Would Snake pick up where Casper left off? Would he rape her?

She didn't think so. Snake was too cold, too calculating to lose control in that way.

A wave of fear started at the top of Emily's head and traveled down to the very tips of her toes, making her tremble. Would he just kill her now?

He smiled as though he could sense her fear and reveled in it. "Don't worry, I'm not going to kill you just yet. You see, your boy stole about a million dollars from me today, but I supposed you already know that, since you were in on the plan."

She remained quiet. Even if she had something to say that might help get her out of this situation, fear had paralyzed her vocal cords.

Snake still held her, his face much too close. The stench of stale cigarettes and booze turned her stomach.

"Hmm." He made a dramatic show of contemplating what to do with her. "I think we'll take a little drive into Crystal Rock. I'd really like to deliver you to Jester personally. In fact—" His face transformed from irate to gleeful. "I think I'll let him watch when I kill you."

He released her and she collapsed to the ground, her quivering legs giving out like limp noodles.

Emily took a breath and forced herself back to her feet. She had no choice but to use the wall for support, but at least she was standing. She glared at Snake, ignoring the fact that she was shirtless, and making sure to let her hatred show on her face.

Anger was preferable to the numbing grief and fear, and she had plenty of it. Anger at Johnny for getting her into this mess, anger at Jester for not giving her a chance to explain, anger at Snake for being a sadistic bastard, but mostly anger at herself for the many horrible decisions she'd made over the past two weeks.

She allowed that anger to blossom into fury. Maybe it would do her some good.

She wouldn't go down without a fight. She owed it to Johnny. Someone had to make Snake pay, and if the worst she could do was kick him in the balls and scratch his face, then that's what she'd do.

Rising to her full height, which had to be a good nine inches shorter than Snake, she found her voice. "Fuck you."

The slap to her face came so fast there wasn't any time to prepare. His fist connected with her stomach next, and she bit down on her lip to keep from screaming. The taste of blood filled her mouth as her teeth broke through her lip. She crashed to her knees and gasped for breath, her diaphragm spasming from the blow. While she was down,

Snake kicked her, connecting with the same spot Casper had injured only moments before. She lost the battle to remain stoic and cried out as agony racked her.

He reached under her arm and hauled her to stand. The room spun and her stomach lurched, but she didn't dry heave this time. She blinked her eyes, and tried to focus past the throbbing in her head.

This couldn't be it. This couldn't possibly be the way she was supposed to go out. Beaten and murdered at the hands of a psychopath. She needed to scream, to fight, to do something, but he overpowered her in every possible way. Every way except one.

She was no match for him physically, but no matter what he did to her, she wouldn't let him take her memories of Jester. She closed her eyes and thought of Jester's voice, of his laugh, of his hands on her. She remembered how she felt cherished, protected, and loved.

He wrapped his hands around her throat and squeezed. Her eyes popped open in reflex and her hands shot up in a feeble attempt to remove his from her neck.

"It's fine, Emily. If you'd rather me kill you right here, I have no problem with that. I won't get to enjoy the look on Jester's face as he watches you go down, but dumping your dead body at his doorstep will be almost as satisfying."

The room blurred as she failed to draw in any air.

I'm so sorry, Johnny. I'm so sorry, Jester.

~ ~ ~ ~

Jester flung the door open and bounded down the steps leading to a dank basement, Acer hot on his heels. He skipped the bottom four steps and jumped to the ground.

Greeted by the sight of Snake manhandling Emily, Jester flew into a murderous rage. He charged across the dark basement, intent on ending Snake's life once and for all.

"You think… this makes you…winner?" she croaked when he was halfway across the room, sending a spear through his heart. "It will take a lot more than you to destroy the No Prisoners."

~ ~ ~ ~

Snake let out a cold laugh. "Guess I'll have to settle for what's in front of me, huh? Making you wish you were dead."

Suddenly the pressure around her throat disappeared, and she was on her hands and knees alternating between gasping breaths and hacking coughs. Her body shook like she had hypothermia, and her mind couldn't process what had happened.

The warmth of a soft fabric brushed against her side. A large hand made contact with her bare back and she flinched and tried to scurry away.

"Shh, Emily, it's okay. I'm not going to hurt you. I'm not going to touch you. I'm just trying to cover you up." Acer spoke in a soothing tone, as though she were a wounded animal ready to bolt.

She glanced up at him, holding out a T-shirt to her. He wore a white undershirt and must have removed his top for her. It dawned on her then that she was completely exposed. She reached for the shirt. "Thank you," she said in a small voice, wincing at the gravelly quality of it.

"Can I help you up?"

She shook her head, not sure if she could stand on her own, but knowing she definitely didn't want him to touch her. "Not yet."

"No problem, hon. I'll sit with you until Jester is done."

"He's here? He's alive?" It was then the sound of fists hitting flesh registered with her.

"Just over there." Acer pointed to a spot about twenty feet

across the basement where Jester was beating the hell out of Snake.

~ ~ ~ ~

Jester flung Snake across the room, satisfaction filling him at the asshole's pain-filled grunt when he collided with the wall. He gave Snake no time to recover, rushing him and plowing his fist into his face.

Snake fell to the ground and Jester dropped as well, hurling his body toward the man who dared to terrorize the woman he loved. Again and again his fists collided with Snake's face, his abdomen, his chest. He threw punches without purpose. As long as they connected with Snake's body, they were successful. The rest of the world faded away as he pummeled the slimy bastard until he was barely recognizable.

Never again would he allow someone to scare Emily, to use her and cause her pain. If he had to follow her wherever she went, so be it. He'd use his last breath to ensure her safety and happiness.

"Jester!" Acer's sharp voice cut through the fog of Jester's wrath and he froze. Acer sat on the floor across the room next to a sobbing Emily. After one more crushing blow to Snake's face, Jester left his limp and bloodied form on the ground, and rushed across the room toward his woman.

He crouched next to Emily, unsure of where he could touch her without causing her further pain. "Emily? Baby, how badly are you hurt? Where can I touch you? I promise to be gentle."

She lifted her head, and his heart broke at the sight of her battered face. "I'm sorry," she said, tears streaming from her pretty eyes, which were filled with deep anguish.

"Shhh. No, baby. I'm the one who has to apologize, but we need to get out of here now, before Grimms start showing up. We need to get you to the hospital."

Emily shook her head with surprising vigor. "No hospital, please. I just want to go home."

Jester looked at Acer and had a silent conversation with his brother. With a nod, Acer stood and pulled out his cell phone while he walked to the other side of the basement. Jester overheard him talking to Striker, who was waiting outside. He asked their VP to have Lila meet them at Jester's house as soon as possible, and to bring medical supplies.

"Baby, I'm going to pick you up now. Is that okay? Then we'll take you home."

He waited for her to respond, unsure of how badly she was injured. She was covered in blood, but he didn't see any life-threatening injuries. He'd failed her in so many ways. Seeing the visual evidence of his failure in the form of bruises on her sweet body had a mist forming in his eyes.

"There's no one left."

"What, Em?"

"Snake killed my brother. He's all I had. I can't go home because Snake ruined that too. I was supposed to save him." Her voice was flat, as though reading him a weather report. He didn't know much about medicine, but he knew enough to realize she was going into shock.

Christ.

"Emily!" He put bite into his voice, trying to break through her grief. They didn't have time to waste, but there was no way he could let her continue to believe Johnny was dead. "You need to listen to me, honey, okay?"

She nodded but didn't look at him.

"Johnny's not dead, baby. He was shot in the shoulder. Lila has been working on him."

"Wha-what?"

"He's alive and he's going to stay that way if Lila has any

246

say in the matter."

"Oh my God." She started sobbing again. "Thank you. After what I did to you—"

"Em, we need to leave." He cut her off, unwilling to listen to her berate herself. "Can I pick you up?"

She nodded again. "Yes."

As gently as he could manage, Jester slid his arms under her and lifted her. She gasped in pain and he winced. "Sorry, baby. I'm trying my damnedest not to hurt you."

"It's fine, Jester, I'm just a little banged up." She rested her head against his chest and for the first time since he saw Snake at the house with Emily, he was able to breathe. There was glimmer of hope that maybe what they'd had wasn't completely destroyed.

Moving quickly, he walked with her up the stairs and out into the hot evening air. There wasn't much time to waste. It wouldn't be long before Grimm Brothers came to investigate why none of the men here had checked in.

"Hey, Jester, I'll drive the truck so you can take care of Emily. Kenny and Jacko will ride our bikes back." Striker turned to the two prospects who'd driven out in the truck. "If there is so much as a finger print on either of these bikes that wasn't there before, you'll never fuckin' patch in. Got me?"

"Got it, VP," Kenny answered.

Jester settled into the front seat while Striker barked orders at Acer and the prospects. He held Emily cradled in his lap, resting with her eyes closed. Her face was various shades of purple and blood oozed from her split lower lip.

He closed his eyes, leaned his head against the seat back, and soaked in the sensation of her smaller, softer body in his protective embrace.

The events of the last two days played through his mind, a movie reel of his failings and fuck-ups. Not only had he failed to trust her, to give the woman he loved the benefit of the doubt, he didn't keep her safe from his enemies. Which sin was worse? He'd beat his own ass if the woman in question wasn't counting on him to do something right and get her out of here before trouble arrived.

"You look pissed." Her voice was rough, ravaged from Snake's brutal treatment, but she didn't sound angry. Contempt and blame weren't present in her tone.

They should be. He deserved nothing less.

He stared at her beautiful eyes, filled with sadness and her own self-loathing. "Christ, Em, this is all on me. If I'd only..." He shook his head. "Fuck! I'm so sorry, baby." He bent forward, resting his forehead against the top of her hair. The normally silken strands were matted down with a layer of sweat and dust.

Emily let out a soft gasp that turned into a groan when her ribs protested. "Jester, you are the only one in this situation who is not at fault. I'm not blind to my brother's shortcomings and guilt here. Do you know how many *if onlys* I thought of over the last few weeks? This is not your fault. I could have done so many things differently."

He couldn't listen to another word of her self-blame. Later they would hash it out, after he was convinced none of her injuries were too serious. "Shh, not now. We'll have plenty of time to sort through it all."

Her eyes fluttered closed, and he tightened his arms around her, careful not to squeeze too hard, but he needed her as close as possible. Hell, if he could absorb her into his skin, he would. "You're safe now, Emily," he whispered against her hair. "You can rest. I won't fail you again."

Within seconds her breathing evened out and she was asleep. He was pretty sure she didn't sleep at all in the garage the night before, and the previous night she'd been up as well. Add on the adrenaline of the past two days and it was a wonder her body still functioned. At least she felt safe and comfortable enough with him to let her body get some of the rest it desperately needed.

Chapter Thirty

Jester lifted his head from Emily's as Striker climbed up into the cab of the truck.

"Shit. It's been a while since I drove one of these. She hanging in?" He peeked at Emily before starting the truck.

"I don't have a clue. For now, maybe. I'm sure it's all gonna sink in later. Jesus." He scrubbed a hand over his face before placing it back on Emily's hip.

"That's Acer's shirt she's wearin'." Striker cast a sideways glance in Jester's direction.

Jester swallowed hard and stared at Striker. He didn't need to be reminded of how exposed she was when he found her. "Yeah."

"Do you think...uh...did he, you know?"

Jester's blood ran cold as he recalled Emily in that basement, cold, beaten and afraid, fending off Snake. Jesus, what a fucking nightmare. "No. I think we got her just in time."

Striker nodded. "Gonna be hard enough for her to get over this shit without...that."

Jester could only hope she'd allow him to be around to help her through it. "Did I kill him?"

"I don't think so. Acer said you came close though. He'll be out of commission for a long time. From the look of him, you may have done some permanent damage."

Jester grunted. Too bad. It was better for the club if he let Snake live. It would be an immediately declaration of war if he'd killed him, but, hell, they were one blink away from war anyway. "I couldn't possibly have fucked this up any more."

"Cut yourself some slack, brother." Striker drove fast, exceeding the speed limit by twenty-five miles per hour. They didn't know how badly Emily was injured. The quicker they got her checked out by Lila, the better. "This entire situation was fucked from the beginning. You two will get through it."

Jester hung his head. "You heard the filth I threw at her yesterday. No excuse for that kind of filth."

"Acer told me last night that he thinks Emily loves you. If that's true she'll need to get through this shit."

Jester didn't answer, remaining silent for the rest of the trip. He couldn't imagine Emily would want to be in the same room with him after this, let alone continue their intimate relationship. He held her close and memorized the way her body fit against his, just in case this was the last opportunity he had to hold her in his arms.

As they turned onto his street he made out the outline of a woman sitting on his front porch. Before they pulled into the driveway, Lila jumped to her feet, and ran down the walkway to meet them at the truck. When Jester opened the door and lifted Emily out of the truck, Lila winced at the sight of her bruised face.

"Where do you want her?"

"Put her in your bed so she can be comfortable and sleep after I'm done checking her over." Lila stopped him with a hand on his arm. "She may need a hospital."

He nodded as he turned toward the house. "I know, but I

promised her I'd avoid it, so if it's at all possible I'd like to try to keep at least one promise to her."

Lila frowned as Striker came up behind her. "Come on, babe. I'll carry your med kit."

As the group made their way to the house, Striker murmured to his fiancé. "You doing okay, Lila? Is this too close to home for you?" He was referring to Lila's own terrifying experience only months ago where they had both sustained injuries at the hands of a madman.

"I'm good, Striker, just worried about Emily. Worried about Jester, too."

~ ~ ~ ~

Emily woke with a jolt at the feeling of a hand on her face. For a moment she'd thought she was still in the basement, and startled to struggle against the touch, even though it was light and in no way compared to Snake's.

"Shhh, easy, Emily, it's Lila. You're safe, sweetheart. Your man got you out of there. I'm just examining the bruises on your face. They are spectacular." Lila smiled down at her, immediately putting her at ease.

Her throat was dry and raw but she managed to rasp out a few words. "How's my brother?"

"Stubborn." Lila snorted. "I had no choice but to admit him to the hospital. He'd lost too much blood from the gunshot wound, but he fought me tooth and nail. Kinda amazing for someone who came as close to the end as he did. He's made of tough stuff, like his sister. He'll pull through."

Emily let out a breath. For the first time in fourteen days some of the sick feeling of fear flowed out of her body. Johnny had a long road ahead of him, but he was alive. That was all that mattered.

"Could I get some ice water?" Her throat grew more sore with every passing second, and now that she was talking, she needed something cool to ease the ache. "Snake squeezed it pretty hard and my throat is killing me."

"Fucking hell!"

Emily glanced at the corner of the room where the outburst came from. Jester paced with a homicidal look on his face. "I wish I had five more minutes alone with that fucking scumbag."

She stared at him, unsure what to make of his presence. They hadn't begun to delve into the mess they'd made of their relationship. But one thing she knew for sure was that she loved him, so she chose to see his presence as a positive thing.

"Striker's rummaging around Jester's kitchen looking for a glass. He'll be up with water any second. Jester, why don't you wait out in the den with Striker and I'll call you when I'm through."

"No!" Emily yelled, immediately embarrassed at the needy panic in her voice, but she needed him there. "I mean, he can stay if he'd like."

He seared her with an intense look that in another place and time would have had her nipples hardening and her panties drenching, but now it reassured her that despite her betrayal he didn't despise her.

"I'm not going anywhere, Em."

"Thank you," she whispered as tears flooded her eyes. "I'm sorry. I'm a bit overwhelmed. Do you think…I mean… would you mind…" She trailed off, mortified by her weakness.

"Baby," Jester whispered as he moved to the enormous bed and sat down next to where she lay. "I'll do anything you need me to do."

"Would you hold my hand?" A tear leaked out and she swiped at it grimacing when her hand encountered the bruises on her face.

Jester picked her hand up and held it gently in his, rubbing circles with his thumb over her palm. The simple gesture soothed her taught nerves.

Lila, who had been silent during the exchange spoke up. "Emily, tell me a little about what happened, injury wise, and where you're hurting."

"My face hurts, obviously, they hit me a few times, kicked me in the ribs, choked me."

Jester's hand tightened on hers, which, combined with the ticking of his jaw, was the only indication that her words were affecting him. His face was an unreadable mask.

"Emily?" Lila's voice was soft and comforting. "Were you raped?" She shot Jester a chastising look at his audible intake of breath.

"No," Emily whispered unable to hold the tears back. "Not sure what would have happened if I was there much longer, but no." She cleared her aching throat. "Casper was a little handsy, but that's all."

"Oh, that's all, huh? Fuck! I wish I'd killed them all."

Emily squeezed Jester's hand trying to give back some of the comfort he gave her.

"I'm going to poke around a bit. If anything is too painful let me know."

She tensed at Lila's first touch, but forced herself to relax. After the past few days she wasn't thrilled about the idea of anyone's hands on her, but she trusted Lila.

Jester must have picked up on her distress. "Just look at me," he whispered.

Emily shifted her eyes until they locked with Jester's. He continued to play with her hand, rubbing her palm, stroking her fingers until everything faded away but the feel of his fingertips and the mesmerizing depth of emotion in his eyes.

"I'm all done. You did great, Emily. Seems like mostly bruises. Your face looks bad, swelling wise, but I don't think anything is broken. You'll be uncomfortable for a bit, but should be back to normal in a week or two, at least physically."

Left unspoken was the fact that the emotional trauma of the past four days would take longer than the bruises to fade.

Emily tore her gaze away from Jester to nod at Lila. "Thank you, Lila, for coming out here in the middle of the night. I owe you one."

"No, Emily, I'll owe you until they day I die. You could have sold our guys out to Snake at any time, but you didn't, and you paid an awful price. I'm so sorry, honey." With a gentle squeeze to Emily's shoulder, she turned and departed the room.

Alone with Jester, Emily wasn't sure how to act. She turned her head to find his gaze still intent on her.

"Do you need anything, Em?

"No. I'm just tired. Would you mind staying until I fall asleep? I feel a little out of sorts."

"I'm not going anywhere." He lay down next to her, and, with exquisite care, gathered her close.

"Jester, I need to explain everything that happened. I need to be sure you know the whole truth and why I did what I did."

He placed a finger over her lips. "Shhh. Not tonight Emily. You need to rest and get some sleep."

"Please, I need you to know. I can't live with it anymore. I'm sure you know most of it by now anyway, but I need to tell it all to you." She sounded like she was on the edge, but it was imperative that he didn't spend another moment thinking she played any willing part in Snake's scheme.

Jester lay on his side next to her, and propped his elbow on the bed, holding his head up and looking down at her. "Okay, baby, if it will help, go ahead."

His free hand stroked up and down her leg, under the large T-shirt of his she'd changed into before falling asleep again. It seemed to bother him that she wore Acer's shirt.

Warmth from his body seeped into her and helped her relax for the first time in weeks. She told him everything, starting with her brother and his drug dependence. She surprised herself and held it together well until she spoke about sneaking into the clubhouse.

Her voice quivered and fresh tears left her eyes. He may not be able to forgive this transgression, and now that she knew Johnny was alive and would remain that way, her brain was free to focus on her relationship with Jester. If he cast her away now, she wasn't sure she'd survive it.

"As soon as I snapped a photo of the map, I felt sick. I knew I'd never send it to them. I just couldn't do it. Every time I looked at it I thought of Lila and Marcie, and how devastated they'd be if something happened to Striker or Hook. I didn't have to look at it to think of you. Thoughts of how I could possibly betray you were on my mind every second of every day, and I just couldn't do it." She wanted nothing more than to forget that day, forget the last fourteen days, but that wasn't possible.

"Baby, you can stop if it's too much."

She shook her head. "Jester, I fell in love with you. I know it hasn't been long, and we agreed to just let this burn itself out, but I love you. I tried to find a way to save Johnny without betraying you anymore than I already had."

~ ~ ~ ~

The raw pain in her voice chipped away at his core, one word at a time. She'd been faced with a devastating choice, and that she'd chosen to protect him humbled Jester. Of course, it wasn't acceptable; he didn't need his woman to protect him.

He promised himself then and there he'd work every day to make himself worthy of her decision. "Shhh, baby, please don't cry. I need you to listen to me now, Em. Just for a minute. Really listen to me and really hear me, okay?"

She looked up at him, her light eyes full of self-loathing, but she nodded.

"Johnny signed his death warrant the moment he snorted his sale. There is no chance Snake would have let him live. You could have brought Snake every detail of every aspect of our club, and he would have killed Johnny just the same."

Her eyes widened and a fraction of the guilt cleared. "He would have?"

"I know it without a doubt. This may not be what you want to hear, but it's what our club would have done. It's what happens when you betray the patch. Every one of us knows it, even as a prospect, just as Johnny would have known it. It's just how things are done in the MC life."

"You live in a violent and ruthless world, don't you?"

"It can be, but that's not what it always is. While we aren't the same as the Grimms, we sure as hell aren't boy scouts. We're also a family, and we take that seriously. We didn't know each other two weeks ago, but we do now and I need you to promise me something."

"What? Anything."

"Anyone gives you trouble, about anything, anyone tries to use you to get to me, you tell me. Doesn't matter what it is, what you've done, what I've done. I will not let you be used as a pawn to hurt me. None of my brothers will allow that either."

"You sound as though you want me in your life."

He nodded. That she had to doubt his desire for her

slayed him. "I do. I want you, and more than that, I need you in my life. Every aspect of it."

He held his breath. With just one word she could slice him in two.

"We have some stuff to work out." She drew her bottom lip between her teeth.

"We do." He tapped his finger against her lip and she released it. "Christ, baby," he said resting his forehead against hers. "The hateful things I said to you the other day will haunt me for the rest of my life."

Emily shook her head. "I deserved it, all of it. Snake did send me. I lied to you and your family over and over." Tears filled her eyes again, and he felt her despair deep in his soul.

"You weren't acting of your own free will, Emily. And in the end you stood up for the club. That isn't something we take lightly. The MC demands loyalty above all else. Anyone of us would gladly die for our brothers. The loyalty you've shown to my club family and me before I'd even made you my official ol' lady is amazing. And I nearly destroyed it by not listening to what you were trying to tell me. Jesus, Emily, you were nearly raped and killed because of me."

Her head shook back and forth as she reached a hand up to stroke his face. Her gentle caress on his face after the events of the past few days was a balm to his tattered soul.

"No, Jester." Her voice was strong and sure. "We both want to take on the guilt of this, but we need to lay it at the feet of the man responsible, Snake."

"I'll try if you will," Jester agreed, though he felt a hefty portion of that guilt belonged to Johnny as well. That was a thought he wouldn't be sharing with Emily. "Do you think you can get some rest now?"

"Yes, I feel like I could sleep for a week."

"Go right ahead, Em. I'll be here the whole time. And,

baby?"

"Yes?" she asked, her voice thick with the need for sleep.

"What we do together? Hands down the best fucking of my life. I should be shot for telling you otherwise." He knew the words weren't flowery or romantic. He wasn't really that guy. Hopefully brutal honesty would be enough for her.

She smiled and rested her head against his chest. "I love you Jester."

"I love you too. God, I fuckin' love you. One more thing."

"Hmm?" She sounded half asleep.

"Hope you're good with being my ol' lady because there's no fucking way I'll accept anything else."

She burrowed closer as sleep stole her away.

Chapter Thirty-One

Johnny's eyelids fluttered twice before opening. Emily smiled at him when his attention landed on her. Inside, she was a mess. Her baby brother looked like death, with an IV, oxygen tubing and a catheter all coming off his body. He'd required four units of blood to get his levels to a low, but sustainable number, or so Lila had said.

"Shit, Emily, your face." Johnny sounded as though every bit of saliva had been sucked from his mouth and replaced with cotton balls.

She picked up a Styrofoam cup full of ice chips from a rolling table next to the hospital bed. Two balls of ice slid onto the plastic spoon she dipped in the cup. "My face is fine. I'm fine. You're the one we need to be worried about. Here."

She turned back to him, holding the spoon to his cracked lips. He parted them and the ice cubes slipped into his mouth.

"Thanks," he said, already sounding more human.

"Emily, I'm—"

She shook her head and picked up the hand that didn't have an IV, cradling it between both of hers. "You don't need to say anything."

Johnny's laugh was bitter and filled with disgust. As awful as the past few weeks had been, if this was the catalyst needed for him to finally get his life together, she could make peace with it.

"I'm sorry." His voice was laden with so much anguish it brought tears to Emily's eyes. She didn't want him to suffer for his mistakes, no matter how severe they were.

"It's over. We all made it out alive."

Wetness fell from his eyes and she wanted to crawl into the bed and hold him like she had after their parents died.

"I forgive you," she whispered to her only blood relation.

"You gonna sell the house?" He moved on to an only slightly less uncomfortable topic.

"Yes." She shivered. "I couldn't spend a night there for a million dollars." Heat rose to her face and she bit her lip. "I'm, uh, I'm gonna be staying at Jester's now. Indefinitely."

Johnny's face clouded over and her heart sank. It wasn't as though she expected them to be best buddies, but she harbored hope that sometime in the future they could reach an amicable relationship. Johnny's narrowed-eyed stare and ticking jaw didn't look promising.

"The big guy?" he asked. "Shit, Emily, didn't you learn anything from this horror show? You do not want to hook up with an MC brother."

Emily almost laughed at the fatherly way he scolded her, but the conversation was too serious. "You know nothing about it. And I'm sorry if this sounds mean, but you don't get a say."

Johnny winced. "Fair enough."

"Lila found a rehab for you. It's in Nevada, near Reno. They'll transport you by ambulance as soon as you're stable enough to travel. It's six months. You need to do it. I'm not sure you'll get another chance."

Johnny snorted and closed his eyes, the energy draining out of him. "Your *boyfriend* made that perfectly clear." He said the word as though it left a bad taste in his mouth. "I want to hate him, but the guy does seem to care about you."

Emily frowned. What had Jester said to Johnny? She opened her mouth to ask that very question, but the even rise and fall of his chest stopped her.

~ ~ ~ ~

Jester stood in the hallway, right outside the door, his back against the wall. It was the best he could do. Emily refused to let him in the room with her, wanting a few private moments with her brother, and he'd refused to be more than ten feet away from her since he'd pulled her out of that godforsaken basement.

The compromise was him standing outside the open hospital room door, out of sight, but not out of mind.

Damn straight he'd laid out conditions for Johnny. He didn't trust the kid as far as he could piss, and it would be a long while before he started to.

He sighed. That probably wasn't going to sit too well with Emily. Well, that was just too damned bad. He'd protect her from anything, and if that included her own brother, so be it.

Emily emerged from the hospital room and came to a stop in front of him, hands on her hips and one eyebrow raised in question. "Don't even try to pretend you weren't listening to every word we said."

God, he loved her. Sweet and spicy. She got to him on all levels.

He drew her into an embrace and kissed her deeply before moving his mouth to her ear. "I know he's your brother, your only brother, and I know he's the reason I met you, but he is also the reason I almost lost you. Forever. So give me some time. I can't say he's my favorite person right now, but we've got nothing but time."

She nodded, her nose rubbing up and down along his chest. "Let's go home."

"Sure, baby."

Chapter Thirty-Two

Emily blew out a frustrated breath, as she lay in bed wet, aching, and very unsatisfied. Jester had been by her side for the entire week since he'd rescued her, doting on her and making sure she had everything she needed to heal physically as well as emotionally. It was perfect...except for one thing.

He hadn't touched her.

At all.

Okay, each night he slept spooned around her, but that was the most contact they'd had since the day after he brought her home and Emily was going out of her mind. She craved his touch, his taste, and the feel of him filling her up.

She'd lain awake each night, wanting him with a strength that frightened her, especially since he didn't seem to reciprocate the feeling. Sure, she'd felt his hardness pressing against her a few times, but she was starting to think it was just a consequence of sleeping next to a woman, any woman.

After a full week of this, Emily was beginning to believe Jester only stuck around out of some misplaced sense of guilt. Not what she wanted from him. Not what she needed from him. Jester had introduced her to physical pleasures she hadn't dreamed she'd experience, and now she wanted more. She wasn't secure enough in the current state of their relationship to try and seduce him so she'd endured the frustration.

Well, not tonight. Tonight she was done. She had to make a move. Even rejection had to be better than this state of aroused limbo she'd been living in.

They'd had dinner with Hook and Marcie, and after arriving home Jester tucked her into bed and went to take a shower. Emily waited until she heard the water running for a few minutes before she hopped out of bed.

She felt great, the pain was nearly gone, and while the bruises were still various shades of purple and green, they no longer impeded her function. An x-ray had confirmed that none of her ribs were broken, and they felt almost as good as new. She just had one throbbing ache left, and planned to remedy that in the next few minutes.

She stripped out of her nightshirt and panties, and dashed toward the bathroom door, slipping inside.

Through the fog of the steam filled room, Emily saw Jester standing in the shower. He faced the spray, with his head bent forward, and one arm braced on the wall while the other hand worked up and down his impressive length.

Arousal hit fast and sharp, causing her nipples to tighten and her pussy to clench with almost violent need. The man was sex personified and she wanted him.

Now.

Stepping forward, she reached out and opened the shower door. Jester's fist stilled as his head turned, eyes locking with hers. He stared at her but didn't move.

Well, if she was going to do this, she'd do it all the way. With her gaze fixed on him, Emily placed both hands on her quivering stomach. Moving simultaneously, she slid one hand up to cup a breast, and pinch a sensitive nipple, while the other hand traveled down to her bare mound and below, slipping into her pussy. She gasped at the strong sensation, but wished it was Jester's finger in her channel.

Eyes hooded, his full cock still gripped in his tight fist, Jester watched the show. "Does that feel good, baby?" His voice was deep and wavered a bit, as though he fought a losing battle for control.

Emily added a second finger and moaned before she answered him. "It feels good." She lazily pumped her fingers in and out. Her hips joined the act and thrust in time with her fingers. "But not as good as it would feel if I had what I really need."

Jester began to stroke his cock again with slow, sure movements. He still supported himself against the wall as water ran down his sculpted body. It was hot as hell. Part of her wanted to play this out to the end. To watch him get himself off while he watched her do the same, but that part of her was overshadowed by the intense need to feel his hands on her.

Sweat slicked her body. The heat of his gaze combined with the thick steam of the room overheated her skin, and she slid her hand to the opposite breast with ease. She knew just how to get this man's attention.

"What is it you need, Em?"

"You. I need your hands, your mouth…oh God…your cock." She moaned and increased the speed of her fingers in her sex at the same time she tugged forcefully on her nipple. "I need you to fuck me Jester. I've needed it all week, but you haven't wanted me."

He must have hit his breaking point because he slapped the water off and burst from the shower, stalking toward her. Water flew everywhere but he didn't seem to notice. He moved with purpose, his muscles flexing, streams of moisture running over his skin, and his cock jutting out as though guiding him to her.

When he reached her, he banded one arm around her upper thighs, under her ass, and lifted her as the other hand pulled her fingers out of her pussy and replaced them with two of his own. She held onto his shoulders and gasped as she registered the difference in fullness between his fingers and her own.

"I've wanted you every fuckin' second of every fuckin' day." He practically growled at her as his fingers curled against her sensitive spot, and Emily cried out, arching her back and wrapping her legs around his waist. The action put her breasts fully on display and in the perfect position for his hungry mouth.

Jester didn't waste the opportunity. He dipped his head and latched onto a pointed nipple, sucking like it was vital to his existence.

Emily cried out again as fireworks of sensation shot from her nipple to her clit. "Yes, Jester, finally. More!"

Without much effort, he walked them out of the bathroom toward the bed, leaving a trail of water behind.

Emily pumped her hips, riding his fingers as he carried her. When Jester switched to the other breast, and sucked with the same ferocity, Emily went off like a rocked, bucking and spasming in his arms.

Jester arrived at the bed, and gave her no reprieve as he released her nipple and dropped her to the mattress. She landed with a soft bounce that barely had time to register because Jester grabbed her under her ass and dragged her to the edge of the mattress. He shoved her thighs wide open and stepped between them, at the same time pulling her toward him. Her ass hung off the edge of the bed, and she hooked her ankles behind his back to keep from falling.

A thrill shot through her as she clenched in need, missing the feel of his thick fingers, but eager to have the sensation of his cock deep inside her. She loved him like this, wild and out of control. That she could make this dominant a man mindless with his want for her was exhilarating.

"Fuck. Oh, fuck that's good," he cried out as he plunged his entire shaft into her in one thrust.

"Yesss, so good Jester." Emily moaned. She felt full and stretched to the limit. The sensation bordered on pain, and he held himself still, allowing her to adjust for a second. But she needed him to move. Squeezing him with her internal muscles, she smiled when he bit out a curse.

"You ready, baby?" He groaned above her, hands under her bottom holding her in place. "This isn't going to be easy."

"Please, Jester, fuck me! I don't want easy."

He pulled out to the tip before ramming back into her setting a frenzied pace she could barely keep up with. Fire tore through her body. He plunged to the root again and again. Emily met his thrusts as best she could, working her hips and holding onto the comforter for dear life.

Jester looped one arm under her lower back, lifting her pelvis and angling her so he delved even deeper. His other hand slid under her head, fisting her hair as he leaned over her and brought his mouth to her neck, nipping and sucking. He had complete control over her body and she loved every second of it.

She felt alive and vital. It was exactly what she needed. Too much of the past week had been spent lost in feelings of guilt, worry over Johnny, and uncertainty about her relationship with Jester. The reminder that she'd survived, and her life could still be filled with happiness and pleasure was wonderful.

The orgasm that burst through her was so powerful she screamed his name, and her vision blanked for a second. Her pussy clamped down on him as though her body didn't want him to leave. It sent him over the edge as well, and he came with a roar before collapsing heavily on her sated body.

~ ~ ~ ~

Jester had never come so hard in his life. The feel of her hot, tight pussy gripping him like she never wanted him to leave was enough to make him lose his mind. He'd been out of control, completely taken over by his need to be buried inside his woman. Thankfully she was almost fully recovered—

Shit.

Emily was still injured, and he'd attacked her like an animal, without any thought for the physical or mental ordeal she'd been through. He was a first rate asshole, and wouldn't be surprised if she ran out and never looked at him again.

Jester pushed off of her and searched her face for signs that she was hurting or afraid. With her sprawled on the bed, her upper body heaved with exertion, while her feet dangled, a foot off the floor. He reached a hand out to help her sit on the edge of the bed. "Christ, I'm sorry about that."

"What?" The sated smile on her face flipped into a frown.

"I shouldn't have done you like that. I'm sorry, I don't have any excuses."

"Jester, what the fuck are you talking about?"

Startled by her tone, he looked down at her. She hardly ever swore. "You're still all bruised, and I attacked you like a rabid beast. Not to mention all the psychological trauma you endured."

She laughed at him, actually laughed, as she pushed off the bed and started pacing. "Don't you dare ruin the best orgasm of my life, Jester!"

He wondered if she was aware she was naked, tits bouncing as she walked, her tight ass swaying. Even her angry stomping didn't take away from the seductive nature of her gait. Jester felt his cock stir again, and tried to force his gaze elsewhere.

"I believe I was the one who started this by walking in on you in the shower and fingering myself."

He'd have laughed at her out-of-character, blunt language if he wasn't so pissed at himself.

"What was that nonsense about my mental state?"

"I'm big, Emily, and domineering, and rough." Hopefully, she would get where he was going with this so he wouldn't have to say it outright.

"Yes, you are. And you were all of those things for the first two weeks we spent going at it like bunnies. In case you haven't noticed, Jester, I love all those things about you. I love when you forget to temper yourself and just take what you need. Why would that be any different now?"

He looked at the floor to distract himself from reaching out and caressing her breasts. "You were in that basement with Snake. He touched you, hurt you, and nearly raped you. I don't want to cause you any bad memories. It's only been one week."

Emily stopped pacing and faced him head-on, with her hands on her hips. The position was hot as hell and he lost the battle to remain unaffected. Damn, he loved this woman. Not many would be willing to call him on his bull and go toe to toe with him, naked no less. His cock stiffened and rose from his body. "Christ, Em, you are so fuckin' sexy."

"Are you out of your mind?" She ranted at him, no indication that she'd heard what he said. "Do you honestly think that I could ever associate what you and I do with what

Snake or Casper did, or tried to do?"

"I just don't want you to ever feel forced or afraid of me. And I didn't give you a choice, I attacked you."

She smiled and stepped to him. She wrapped one hand around his hard-on, and gave him a firm squeeze. "I made my choice, Jester. I made my choice when I walked in that bathroom naked and taunted you. I made my choice when I told you I love you. You are raw, and wild and rough, and dominating, and I love all that about you. Please don't treat me differently than you did before. Please attack me and ravage me as often as you want."

She stroked him as she spoke, and it felt so amazing he could barely focus on her words. "Emily," he ground out, placing his hand over hers to still her movement. It didn't work, she cupped his balls with her other hand and lightly massaged them with her soft fingers. "Christ, woman, those hands are lethal. Okay, you win. I give."

"That's exactly what I hoped you'd say." She crawled up on the bed and lay back against the pillows. Sliding her heels up toward her ass, she let her knees drop open. Jester got an eye full of her pussy glistening with the evidence of their recent lovemaking. If he hadn't just conceded the fight to her, the sight of her giving herself to him would have done it.

"You want my cock again, baby?"

Emily nodded, curling her bottom lip between her teeth, she made herself look innocent and wanton at the same time. Damn, his woman knew exactly how to get to him.

Jester scaled the bed and positioned himself over her. There was no point in playing games or making either one of them wait, so he pushed into her, taking his time this go around. She was soft and wet from their previous lovemaking and he sunk in to his balls with no resistance.

Emily pulled his head down to hers. "Jester," she

whispered, her lips right against his ear. "I love you, I need you, and I want you constantly. Please don't treat me like I'm damaged."

He kissed her until he felt his lungs would burst. "I love you so fuckin' much, Emily. And I promise to ravage you like an animal until you're screaming my name as often as possible."

She tightened around him and he saw stars.

"Good. You can start now."

With a grunt Jester quit trying to be gentle, and gave his woman what she demanded.

Epilogue

Jester smiled as Emily's little moan of pleasure reached his ears. It was a sound he was familiar with, but unfortunately, he wasn't the one responsible for the noise this time. He stood in the entrance to a gazebo, and watched her where she stood on the opposite side, gazing out at the lake. In her hand was a small plate with a man-sized, hell a Jester-sized portion, of wedding cake from Striker and Lila's reception.

October was a beautiful month in the desert. The outrageous heat of summer gave way to the milder temperatures that would grace the next few months. Lila and Striker had selected the perfect weekend for their wedding. The golden sun shone across the shimmering lake and added an extra special touch to the day.

The besotted couple had rented a pavilion on the lake for their big day. Emily and Marcie served as Lila's attendants, while Jester and Hook stood up for Striker. When Jester had been off helping load the gifts in a truck, Emily took the opportunity to grab a hunk of cake and sneak away for a quiet moment.

She was probably thinking about her brother. Five months of his six month stay in rehab were complete. When he was released, the plan was for him to stay with them until he was able to support himself financially.

Emily was nervous about it, that much was clear. He couldn't blame her. Johnny's addiction had come close to destroying all the people she cared about. Jester tried not to be an asshole when she talked about her brother, he really did, but it was difficult to think of anything but how Emily looked after he rescued her from that basement.

She'd pointed out that without Johnny's transgressions, they'd never have met. She was right, but he wasn't ready to give the kid credit for much of anything just yet. Letting him live with them was going to be challenge enough, but they'd work it out. Over the past five months he'd found that he could handle just about anything, as long as he had Emily to wake up to and Emily to come home to.

It was quieter over here, the pulsing beat of the music faded into the background. Jester watched her lift a second bite of cake to her sensual mouth. She emitted another moan of appreciation as her lips closed around the fork.

He chuckled, and she turned toward him. Emily looked damn pretty today in the simple but elegant strapless turquoise dress Lila had chosen. It hugged her body on top and flared a bit past her hips, flowing when she walked or danced. With her hair swept up in a pile on top of her head, she appeared classy and sophisticated. He couldn't wait to muss her up.

"What's so funny?"

"Nothing, baby, just enjoying your moans, although I'd rather hear them with something besides cake in your mouth."

She rolled her eyes and giggled. "This cake is delicious. Want to try some?" She held out the fork with the chocolaty, white icing covered treat.

Jester sauntered toward her. When he reached her, he bent down and kissed her, long and deep. When she was distracted enough by the kiss, he took advantage of the moment and slid the zipper of her dress down her back.

Emily broke away and gasped in surprise. "Jester! We're out in the open, and there are tons of people just over there." She gestured with the fork down at the pavilion on the beach.

"No one can see us, gorgeous. We're plenty far from the party." While he spoke he lowered the front of the dress, and grew painfully aroused at the sight of Emily's bare breasts and pointed nipples. "You're not wearing a bra." He rasped out the statement.

Emily laughed. "Surprise! There's one built into the dress." She lowered her voice to a seductive pitch. "That's not the only thing I'm not wearing."

"There's no way you're getting out of this now." He groaned, and swiped his finger through the frosting of the cake Emily still held."

"Hey!" she protested around a laugh. "I do have a fork, you know."

He ignored her and rubbed his finger in circles around a hardened nipple, covering it in the sweet confection. His mouth followed his finger and he sucked the sugary-coated nipple between his lips, dragging a moan from both of them.

"Mmmm," he said around her nipple before he lifted his head. "You're right. That's delicious. I want some more." He treated the other nipple to the same behavior, noting the hitch in Emily's breathing, as she grew more aroused.

"Jester, that feels really good."

He smiled. "I know what my baby likes."

"Yes you do." She let the plate fall to the floor of the gazebo with a clatter. She arched back and pushed her breast farther into his mouth. Her hands fisted in his hair as she grew more desperate. Her grip was her tell, like in poker, and it betrayed her need every time.

"Greedy, baby."

She moaned a response and pulled on the strands trapped between her fingers just as Jester became aware of another presence. Damnit! He pulled off her nipple with a pop.

"Motherfucker," he muttered under his breath. Whoever it was better have a damn good reason for interrupting him with his woman like this. Jester placed a tender kiss to the reddened bud before pulling her dress up and reaching around to zip it back up.

"Sorry, babe," he whispered in her ear before he turned to confront their intruder. He'd reserve judgment on whether he'd let the bastard live.

"What? What's happening?" Emily asked, a flushed and bewildered expression on her lovely face.

"We have a visitor."

She inhaled sharply as Acer stepped into the gazebo.

"This better be fucking good, dipshit. And if you saw one inch of what's hiding under this dress, you better start running."

Emily giggled, and slapped his arm. "Play nice, Jester."

A slow smile spread across Acer's face. "Yeah, brother, play nice. I'm a gentlemen and I didn't see a thing. Heard a lot though. Sounds like you were enjoying the cake. I'll be sure and tell the happy couple you approve."

~ ~ ~ ~

Emily flushed and rolled her eyes at Acer. After months of being with Jester, she'd gotten used to the guys' brash and overly sexual way of doing just about anything, including their humor. Besides, she couldn't deny it. The cake was delicious, as was the feeling of Jester's mouth licking it off her skin.

Jester scowled at Acer. "Is there a point to this little convention?"

Acer smiled again and nodded, his eyes on Emily. He looked unbelievably sexy in his suit. This was the first time she'd seen any of the guys in something other than jeans and T-shirts. Of course, they wore their cuts instead of jackets, but somehow it only made them sexier. A combination of elegant and badass, all in one.

Without saying anything Acer took a step toward Emily. Ever protective, Jester pulled her slightly behind his back.

Acer raised a brow at him. "Seriously, brother?"

Without a word, Jester stared at him. Emily rolled her eyes again, and slipped her arm from Jester's hold. There wasn't a chance Acer would try to harm her. She stepped around Jester's big body, and looked directly at Acer. "What's up?"

"I'm heading out, and I hadn't had a chance to catch you away from the fray. Just wanted to let you know that Johnny's doing well. Really well. So well, they offered to let him out a few weeks early, but he elected to stay the full six months."

She hadn't realized how much she needed to hear that until her knees buckled with relief. Jester wrapped a supportive arm around her middle and prevented her from collapsing to the ground. "How do you know?"

"I read his chart."

"What? How? Lila called multiple times for me and they wouldn't even tell her anything. How did you—"

The combination of Jester's light squeeze at her waist and firm set of Acer's mouth ended her inquiry. "Right. Don't ask, don't tell."

Both men laughed.

"Well, however you did it, thank you. I've been worried."

Acer nodded. "I know." He winked at her and rolled his eyes when Jester cleared his throat in an overly dramatic fashion.

"Hey, sorry about a few minutes ago," Jester said, his voice gruff. "I've been a little overly protective since…you know."

"No worries. It's how you should be." With a nod to Emily, Acer turned and left them alone in the gazebo.

Jester spun Emily in his arms until she could look up and see his concerned face.

"Is something going on with him?" she asked.

He shrugged and slid his hands down her back and over her bottom, drawing her to his body. "Not sure what it is. He was in L.A. last weekend and he's been all broody and weird in the eyes since he came back. Don't worry, babe. He'll snap out of it."

"Hope so. We need to get him a girl."

He grunted. "Good luck there. He's one closed up bastard. A woman would need some serious explosives to bust down his walls."

Emily wasn't convinced.

Jester pressed a tender kiss to her lips. "Love you so fuckin' much, Em. You own every part of me."

Emily stood on her toes and fused her mouth with his. The men in her life were safe, and she was free to allow herself to revel in the ecstasy she found with Jester.

Thank you so much for spending some time in the No Prisoners' world. If you enjoyed the book please feel free to leave a review on Goodreads or your favorite retailer.

Join Lilly's mailing list for **FREE** No Prisoners Bonus Content.
www.lillyatlas.com

Keep reading for a preview of Acer, No Prisoners MC Book 3
On Sale January 31, 2017

Acer Chapter One

Fia stepped into the ballroom and ran a trembling hand down the front of her dress. She plastered what was probably an overly syrupy smile on her face and nodded at the son of a California State Senator who raised a hand in greeting. It wouldn't serve her well to wear her anger on the outside, so she put years of practice and grooming to good use and played the rich socialite.

The senator's son abandoned his conversation and strode toward her, a smug, women-love-me-for-my-money-and-looks smile on his face. Fia resisted the urge to roll her eyes. Gordon had been pursuing her for a while now, and she had less than no interest in the man who thought he was God's gift to women everywhere.

"Good evening, Serafina. I must say, you look lovely tonight."

She winced. Strike one.

"Hello, Gordon. You're looking very handsome yourself, and please call me Fia."

He wrinkled his perfect nose. "I don't know why you insist on people calling you by that foolish nickname. Serafina is a lovely name, and you should be proud to have it." He took her hand and drew her out on the dance floor.

It took every ounce of strength she possessed to avoid ripping her hand from his weak hold. Arrogant jerk didn't even have the decency to ask if she'd like to dance with him. No, he just assumed any woman would be honored to have the privilege of being led around the floor by him.

Sure, his five-hundred-dollar haircut had each dark strand lying in a perfect arrangement, and his manicured nails were impeccable, but the soft hands they adorned did nothing for her as a woman. Neither did the metaphorically turned up nose and literal lack of work ethic. There are some things a thousand-watt smile and gorgeous deep green eyes just can't overcome.

She hated these events. If rich people actually donated as much money to charities as they spent on balls and banquets, the unfortunate would be much more fortunate. But, tonight's event was for a cause she believed in, so she was here. And with no desire to embarrass herself or her family, she'd behave, even if that meant enduring a dance with a man who viewed himself as an angle sent to earth for the sake of women everywhere.

Fia preferred her angels with a bit of a crooked halo.

Her own was pretty off kilter.

She allowed Gordon to draw her into his embrace and swayed with him to the music, careful to keep a bit of distance between their bodies. Too bad he couldn't take a hint.

He leaned down and brushed his nose along the curve of her neck. "You smell lovely, Serafina."

Did the man know any compliments besides lovely?"

"Fia," she ground out.

He chuckled against her ear as though she were a child

who'd said something cute, and she pulled her head back, narrowing her eyes at him. He really was handsome. He was tall and wore a suite well. Unfortunately, she'd seen him at the country club, and what was under the suit could only be described as soft. He was a man who spent his time indoors, behind a desk.

Not her type.

"Okay, fine, *Fia*."

"Thank you."

Gordon rambled on about his ambitions to take over his father's seat in the senate, and she tuned him out, instead letting her gaze drift around the room. Her focus landed on a man, standing in the corner with a scowl on his face as he listened to another, older gentleman speak.

She couldn't quite put her finger on what it was about the man that captured her attention. At first glance, he looked like any other male in the room, expensive tuxedo, expertly styled dark blond hair, flawless facial features. But the energy he gave off was almost palpable, like a caged tiger seconds away from escape. She shivered. If all that power was unleashed, the effects could be devastating.

Gordon turned them and Fia lost sight of the intriguing guy.

With a laugh, Gordon let out a surprising and unrefined curse. "Shit, there he is. And I wagered this would be the year he finally quit showing up here and upsetting his family."

Fia pulled back and looked up at him. "Who are you talking about?"

He spun her a second time so they both faced the very man she'd been staring at, only he wasn't in the same spot he'd been in seconds before. She watched the back of his head as he trailed after the man he'd been speaking with.

"See the blond guy, the one walking out of the room?"

"Yes, I see him, who is he?"

"That's Adam Wellington."

Her jaw dropped and Gordon laughed at her. Adam was a bit of an urban society legend. He was the only son of corporate developer Reginald Wellington. Story was, he'd dropped out of society to join a gang after a friend of his went to prison for assault.

Fia wasn't stupid enough to believe the story was that simple, but it was intriguing.

"He comes to this one charity event every year. No one knows why. Some say he's planning something. Biding his time until he can get back at everyone he blames for his low status in life now."

Fia rolled her eyes. "That's the stupidest thing I've ever heard."

The man in question turned, meeting her gaze as though he heard her from fifty feet away. His eyes smoldered with a mixture of anger, frustration and…could that be desire?

Unnerved by the intensity, she tore her gaze away and stepped back from Gordon as the song ended. "Thank you for the dance, Gordon. Please excuse me, I'm going to get some air."

He nodded. "Would you like me to join you, Serafina?" His tone suggested she'd be getting more than air.

Striker three.

"No, Gordon, I'd like a moment alone. And if I have to tell you to call me Fia again, I'll be doing so while you're doubled over with my knee against your balls."

She turned and walked away from a slack-jawed Gordon.

Whoops. So much for acting like a lady.

Relief was instantaneous as she stepped outside onto a balcony and into the warm night air. It wasn't fresh air, as it was L.A., but at least she was no longer surrounded by hundreds of society's most elite and pretentious.

Today had been long day full of frustrations and failures. What she really wanted was peace, quiet and a warm bath full of bubbles. And wine, lots of wine. But she believed in the cause and wanted to show her support.

Once a year, at a different one of his hotels, Reginald Wellington held a large gala to raise money for state penitentiaries in whichever state the ball was held in. The money was used to provide counseling services to inmates.

Fia had a friend in college who ran into some trouble with the law, and spent a year in jail. When he got out, he remained on a straight path, and was now a successful defense attorney, but his time in prison had taken a large psychological toll, and she'd watched her friend struggle for years with depression.

This event meant something to her, and with her own career in jeopardy, it gave her something to focus on besides her own battles. She grasped the railing of the balcony and stared at the glittering lights of L.A. She had some significant decisions to make, and no clue which direction she should take.

About the Author

Lilly Atlas is a contemporary romance author, proud Navy wife, and mother of two spunky girls. By day, she works as a Physical Therapist at a hospital in Virginia. For years, Lilly has been daydreaming and plotting characters in her head while driving, showering, and sometimes when she was supposed to be paying attention to something else. She finally decided to get the ideas out of her head and into books.

Every time Lilly downloads a new ebook she expects her Kindle App to tell her it's exhausted and overworked. She's been waiting for the pop up asking to please give it some rest. Thankfully that hasn't happened yet, so she can often be found absorbed in a new book.

Made in the USA
San Bernardino, CA
01 May 2019